Ghosts of Waikīkī

Ghosts of Waikīkī

A Novel

JENNIFER K. MORITA

NEW YORK

This is a work of fiction. All of the names, characters, organizations, places, and events portrayed in this novel are either products of the author's imagination or are used fictitiously. Any resemblance to real or actual events, locales, or persons, living or dead, is entirely coincidental.

Published in the United States by Crooked Lane Books, an imprint of The Quick Brown Fox & Company LLC.

Crooked Lane Books and its logo are trademarks of The Quick Brown Fox & Company LLC.

Library of Congress Catalog-in-Publication data available upon request.

ISBN (hardcover): 978-1-63910-939-5
ISBN (ebook): 978-1-63910-940-1

Cover design by Jerry Todd

Printed in the United States.

www.crookedlanebooks.com

Crooked Lane Books
34 West 27th St., 10th Floor
New York, NY 10001

First Edition: November 2024

10 9 8 7 6 5 4 3 2 1

To Brandon, Emi & Miya

Prologue

Lani once called me the ghost of Waikīkī as a joke, a dig for years of avoiding home.

"You're here," she'd said, her gold bangle bracelets clinking a familiar tune. "But you're not."

Wrinkling her nose at the black knit dress in my hand, a workplace staple back in California, she added it to the pile of rejects. Another questionable life choice for my growing list.

"You going to a funeral or what?" she asked in the singsong lilt most Islanders have. She studied a rack of clothes at her Kaimukī boutique before thrusting a dress with a purple abstract print at me.

"It's sleeveless," I protested. "This is a work thing."

"You've been on the mainland too long, Maya." Lani huffed, as if I'd proved her point. "See? Like a ghost."

But for once, my best friend was wrong.

The ghost wasn't me.

Chapter One

The woman who answered the door introduced herself simply as Mrs. Goto. Age was a tough call, but streaks of gray in the wiry dark hair twisted into a knot on her head and barely mottled hands put her somewhere in her seventies.

"Mr. Hamilton sends his apologies. He had a last-minute meeting with the mayor," she said, leading me into a sunlit living room, her purple muʻumuʻu sweeping over polished koa wood floors. I followed her through French doors onto the porch, and we descended the stairs onto a flagstone path leading to a terraced patio.

A trellis crawling with jasmine protected the cushioned patio furniture from the Hawaiian sun. Platters of pastries and fresh fruit were laid out on a low table along with a pitcher of iced tea.

"You can wait for Mr. Hamilton on the lanai. His overseas call should be pau soon."

Earlier she'd said it was a meeting with the mayor. Who was ghosting who?

I'd taken the scenic route to shake the first-day jitters. Hotels and restaurants had given way to gated mansions barely visible through the foliage. Glimpses of turquoise lifted my mood as I drove along the base of Diamond Head. I'd pulled up to an imposing wrought iron gate and punched in the security code, following the private road until it curved into a circular driveway. I'd eased my ancient Civic between a Tesla and Porsche, their gleaming red and chrome exteriors making the Honda's sun-weathered green paint seem duller.

Looking up at the century-old Craftsman mansion *Architectural Digest* once touted as the prettiest home in Hawaiʻi, I'd felt the nagging doubts return. *What had I gotten myself into?*

A half hour later and my host had yet to show up for the meeting it'd taken weeks to set up.

"Try go for a walk, ya?" Mrs. Goto said when she saw me checking my watch again. "Mr. Hamilton's great-grandfather, Charles Hamilton I, designed the house and gardens himself in 1927. It's on the National Register of Historic Places, but not many people are lucky enough to see it."

Her eyes narrowed suddenly. Kicking off a worn, leather zori, Mrs. Goto took aim at the B-52 crawling across the lanai, squashing the cockroach. A kill shot.

There's no place like home. And if home is a tropical island paradise, there's bound to be big bugs. Even historic mansions overlooking the Pacific Ocean.

"Go wander around," she said, sliding her foot back into the slipper. "Someone will find you when it's time." Paving stones gave way to pebbles, and I followed the meandering trail to a garden shaded by a large, old banyan tree, where ʻawapuhi and plumeria perfumed the air. Waves crashed on the shore from somewhere nearby, but overgrown trees and bushes obscured the ocean. The outline of a traditional Japanese garden—usually quiet, serene, every branch in its place—was visible, but pebbles were scattered across the walkway, and red maples left a lacy stain on the stone pagoda spotted with lichen. Golden koi writhed in a pond, mouths gaping perpetually in search of food.

It was easy to see why the Hamilton estate was the envy of the Islands. But something seemed off.

"Who're you?"

I jumped at the male voice. The sudden movement sent the koi diving below the pond's surface. I could've sworn I was alone, but now a man stood under the banyan as if appearing out of nowhere.

He was around my age, maybe a few years older, his skin browned by the sun. Dirt and leaves clung to his cargo shorts, the gray tank top exposing well-muscled arms. Sunlight glinted off the silver diver's watch on his left wrist.

I recovered from the initial surprise and took a step forward, stumbling on a loose paving. The stranger caught me before I could fall onto the stone path.

"You okay?" he asked, genuine concern in his voice.

"Yeah, I'm fine. Thanks," I said, righting myself. "Just a little embarrassed." Our eyes met, and his kind smile put me at ease. I held out my hand. "I'm Maya Wong. Mr. Hamilton's . . . new research assistant."

I'd almost forgotten the cover story concocted by the attorney who'd hired me.

"What are you researching?"

"Hamilton family history. He's writing a book."

I waited expectantly for a name, but the man didn't offer one. The silence grew awkward. He glanced around, nervous. "Uh, I was just checking the hibiscus."

A high-pitched hum filled the air, and I turned, half-expecting to see a UFO, or at the very least a drone, flying over the Hamilton estate. But the sky was clear.

"What was—?" I turned back to discover I was talking to myself.

The man had vanished.

Alone in the garden, I could hear the fading slap of his flip-flops.

Chapter Two

"Care for a malasada? They're fresh from Leonard's."

I looked up from my notes. My host brushed sugar off his aloha shirt, a casual mosaic of palm fronds and maile leaves that probably cost a hundred bucks or more. He held out a pink pastry box with familiar blue lettering. "No, thank you. I had papaya earlier," I said. "About your book . . ."

Parker chuckled. "You ladies—always watching your waistline." He bit into the sugar-coated pastry, haupia cream filling oozing out as he chewed.

I smiled politely.

I'd missed a lot about Hawai'i in the dozen or so years I'd been away. The scent of plumerias drifting on cool trade winds. Backyard parties and freshly picked mangoes. Portuguese doughnuts hot from Leonard's Bakery were also high on the list.

But this was no vacation, and I'd already spent half the day waiting for him.

Parker Hamilton was the biggest developer on the Islands, heir to a vast fortune and scion to one of the wealthiest, most influential families in Hawai'i—and my new boss.

Two months ago, I'd been huddled in my damp basement studio in San Francisco, eating Thanksgiving leftovers while bundled in fleece, when a phone call changed my life.

My journalism career had peaked while newspapers across the country tanked. The large California daily I worked for limped along for years—shrinking in size and depth until barely a handful of disgruntled souls wandered the empty newsroom. When the paper folded for good, bulldozers demolished its headquarters to make way for a luxury high-rise dubbed the Press.

It didn't take long to discover freelance work barely covered rent, let alone food and utilities. This ghostwriting gig—a first for me—came days after my landlord announced he was raising my rent. So I packed my bags and bid aloha to the Golden State, promising myself it was only for a year, until I finished the book.

Light footsteps descending the porch stairs signaled a new arrival. Parker hoisted his six-foot frame from the cushioned patio chair, the sprinkling of gray on his close-cropped chestnut hair the only hint at his sixty-plus years, and greeted the newcomer.

I recognized the cool blonde from society page photos. No one would mistake Elizabeth Hamilton for a local. From the strand of pearls around her neck to the pebbled leather ballet flats, she gave off blue-blooded East Coast vibes but exuded Island hospitality.

"Welcome to Hawai'i," she said, smiling warmly as she clasped my hand in both of hers. "I'm so sorry for leaving you alone all morning. I hope you at least had the chance to explore the grounds."

She sat, crossing her legs at the ankles, and signaled the maid. "Please have Mrs. Goto send down sandwiches. The fruit platter could use refreshing as well."

A glance at my watch told me it was nearly noon. I closed my notebook, resigned.

"Our son Stephen had a meeting, but he'll be joining us in a minute," Elizabeth said. "Parker's always wanted to write a book about the Hamiltons. We're all very excited to get started on this project."

But their son didn't look enthused when he made an appearance a few minutes later.

Stephen Hamilton was a younger, blonder, more serious version of Parker. He was thirty-four, single and apparently had spent his life being groomed to take over Hamilton, Inc., along with his father. His button-down shirt and tie, tucked neatly into pressed tan slacks, was out of place for an alfresco brunch in Hawai'i, where most people lived in shorts and flip-flops.

"Sorry I'm late, but I can't stay long," he said, bending to kiss his mother's cheek. A quick nod was his only acknowledgement of Parker.

"You're looking at our next state senator," Elizabeth said. She patted his hand as he sat beside her and gazed at him affectionately. "And from there, Washington."

Parker made a sound that could have been a scoff.

Stephen cleared his throat and reached for a sandwich. "Tell us about yourself, Maya. I don't know much about you other than you're a little old school," he said, jutting his chin at the narrow spiral notebook in my lap. "The only writer I know who used one of those retired years ago."

Most reporters my age had ditched pen and paper for digital recording devices, using apps to transcribe their interviews. But I preferred to take notes, recording on my phone only as backup.

I shrugged and smiled sheepishly. "I'm a throwback, I guess. My college mentor was a dyed-in-the-wool newspaperman, and I can't shake the habit. But I do all my writing on the computer. My life's on my laptop."

"Where'd you go to school? I thought Dad wanted to hire a local ghostwriter, but I understand you're from California?"

I'd left Hawai'i for grad school, but I'd stayed away for personal reasons. Now I wondered if coming back to write a rich, white guy's biography was a good thing.

"I got my master's at Cal," I said. "I grew up here. My dad is originally from the mainland, but my mom is from Hawai'i."

I'd had misgivings about the job. Ghostwriting a self-published biography for a man whose family colonized Hawai'i wasn't exactly prize-winning journalism. But, as Mom was quick to point out, beggars can't be choosers.

"It's fate telling you to come home," my grandmother had said.

More likely an algorithmic glitch in the online marketplace I used to find writing jobs. I hadn't even known there was a ghostwriting box to check until the posting appeared in my inbox. I'd applied on a whim, never thinking I'd beat out writers with actual ghosting experience.

But I didn't see this job as a rainbow on the horizon.

For starters, the hiring process had been very hush-hush, a series of Zoom interviews with men in suits who wouldn't tell me who I'd be ghosting until they offered me the job.

Once I'd made it through a third round, first with an attorney then an entire marketing team, I turned to the online writing community for advice.

"You have to shadow him," someone on a ghostwriting chat site had said. "Get inside your subject's head."

So far I'd done more waiting than shadowing.

It was well after lunch before Parker and I were left alone to work. I took out my phone and opened a recording app.

"So I can check my notes later," I said, as he waved his assent. I glanced at the time—already past one thirty. "Tell me about this book. What are you trying to get across to readers?"

His lawyer had pitched Parker's book as an autobiography and a history of his illustrious family's role in the formation of the fiftieth state. But I wanted Parker's take.

He leaned back and crossed his legs, staring at me thoughtfully. "I'm entrusting you with my legacy," he said. "My family made Hawai'i, and I need you to write our story. It will be our gift to the people of this beautiful state."

This was the literary equivalent of the hideous Chinese porcelain elephant PoPo always threatened to leave me and my sister in her will.

In school, we learned that undersea volcanoes spewing tons of molten lava over thousands of years made the Islands. Native Hawaiian legends say the fire goddess Pele created them while fighting with her ex, Kamapuaʻa, the pig god.

But those lessons had nothing to do with the resorts lining Waikīkī Beach or the valleys and mountains dotted with homes—all built by the Hamiltons.

"You went to Punahou, right?" I'd read somewhere his father had been one of the private school's major donors. "Isn't there a math wing named after one of your ancestors?" Not to mention a bridge over Kalanianaʻole Highway and my own alma mater—a public high school in the suburbs of Honolulu.

Parker waved it off, as if having one's family name emblazoned on major landmarks was commonplace. For him, I guess it was.

We'd been working steadily for a couple hours by then, but I still didn't have a good feel for Parker Hamilton beyond what I'd read on his company's website and I'd been able to dig up online.

"Tell me about Elizabeth. How'd you two meet?" People were suckers for a good love story.

"She shot me."

My pen stopped at this, and Parker emitted a deep chuckle. "It was the annual Yale charity dinner hosted by the university president. I was reeling in a millionaire's widow for a big, fat check, when a blinding white light hit me in the face. I opened my eyes, and there was Lizzie and her camera. It was love at first sight."

Parker could spin a yarn, I'd give him that, even if it wasn't as funny as he assumed. I scrawled a heart beside my notes, reminding myself to get Elizabeth's version of their meet-cute. Stories tended to take on lives of their own, especially after years of retelling. Tapping my phone screen, I checked to make sure it was still recording, noting the time.

I had more questions, but Parker rambled on.

"You know, Lizzie's family goes way back to the Mayflower days. Her father was an entrepreneur . . . knew everyone in town." He snapped his fingers. "That reminds me, I've got something for you."

He stood and disappeared inside the house, handing me a bulging file folder when he returned.

"I gathered some notes and ideas I had. There's a copy of the manuscript I started years ago, before I realized I'm a terrible writer," he said, reaching for the iced tea pitcher. Finding it empty, he sipped what was left in his glass. "Who knows? It might be helpful. I threw in a few photos too."

Curious, I unfastened the overstretched elastic on the file folder and peeked inside. Several legal tablets, covered in a narrow, slanted script, filled the folder along with photographs yellowed with age.

I was too absorbed in sifting through the papers to register the crunch of footsteps on the pebbled path until Mrs. Goto appeared at his side.

"Sorry to disturb you, but the mayor is on the phone," she said to her employer. "You can take his call in your office."

He rose and glanced at his watch, large, gold, and presumably Rolex. "It's already three thirty? My sincerest apologies, Maya. The day got away from me. I hope you can stick around to meet Dad. This won't take long."

Parker hurried up the porch steps, leaving me to wait. I hauled myself to my feet and stretched. Elizabeth was on the porch holding a glass of iced tea. She nodded and smiled at me before disappearing back inside the house.

I went for another walk, wishing I had my running shoes. I'd skipped my morning jog.

I was circling back to the lanai when I heard dishes clattering. A man with a full head of wavy white hair rounded the tall hedge of hibiscus. He was barefoot and wore only turquoise swim trunks and a towel draped around his neck.

". . . and don't forget my shake. I haven't had it yet today. Just this blasted sweet tea," he said, the drink in his hand sloshing with every step. Turning, his eyes widened when he noticed me.

"Cat, where've you been? I was looking for you all morning." The Hamilton family patriarch stopped and frowned. "You're not Cat."

Charles Hamilton II was tall and fit, like his son, with faded blue eyes and only a slight stoop despite being well into his eighties. I'd read he was semiretired and had left the family corporation to his only child.

"You must be the ghostwriter," he said.

I introduced myself. Charles grasped my extended hand, something hard and cold biting into my flesh. I looked down to see a gold signet ring etched with a stick-figure design glinting from his pinky.

"Let's talk. Walk with me."

He had a surprisingly brisk pace, and I found myself rushing to match his long strides as we took a lap around the house, eventually ending up back on the lanai.

"This book is long overdue." He sat in Parker's abandoned chair and took a long sip of his drink, grimacing. "Hawai'i wouldn't be what it is today if it hadn't been for my great-grandfather. When our book is done, it will be in every high school in the state, not to mention required reading for history classes at UH."

I bit back a groan. Technically, he wasn't wrong about the impact his family had on the Islands. It also wasn't my job to start a debate. This would be Parker's book, told from the perspective of a Hamilton.

"Do an old man a favor, Cat," he said, handing me his nearly full glass. "Go in the house and sneak me a little bourbon for this god-awful tea."

"I don't—"

Parker and Elizabeth's arrival saved me.

"Charles, you know you're supposed to lay off the alcohol. Doctor's orders. Don't make Maya your accomplice."

His back straightened as he bristled from Elizabeth's gentle scolding. She took the glass from me and handed it to her husband.

A crash broke the awkward tension, and all eyes turned to Parker. Iced tea dripped down his bare legs, forming a puddle under the shattered fragments at his feet.

"Oh, Parker, you're such a klutz." Elizabeth tsked as she handed a cloth napkin to her husband.

I automatically bent to pick up the shards of glass, tiny clumps of sweetener and bits of tea leaves still clinging to the larger pieces.

"Stop." Elizabeth's sharp command startled everyone. "You'll cut yourself. Let the housekeeper do that." She summoned help with a flick of her fingers.

Mrs. Goto quickly restored order. She was sweeping the last bit of glass when a muffled beep sounded from where I'd been sitting. I dug between the cushions where my phone had slipped. The screen lit up with a low-battery warning. I tapped the stop button on the recording app, hoping I'd managed to get the last bit of my interview with Parker.

I turned to Charles. "I'm sure you have some great stories we can use. Can we set up an interview?"

Charles winked at me and grinned. "You have good instincts. How about a late lunch tomorrow at the O'ahu Country Club? You'll love the Caesar salad." Snapping his fingers, he summoned his daughter-in-law. "Lizzie, what's my schedule look like? Book us a reservation after my golf round, will you? And don't forget to reorder the protein supplement for my morning shake."

Her lips tightened for a moment before stretching into a gracious smile. "I'll speak with your secretary."

Charles slapped his thigh and stood. "Time to hit the water."

We watched as he strolled down to the pool, tossing his towel onto a nearby chaise before diving in.

"My dad is strong as a horse. He's been swimming fifty laps a day for as long as I can remember," Parker said.

We spent the next hour drafting a chapter outline for Parker's book before calling it a day. I was about to confirm tomorrow's meeting time when a long piercing scream pealed through the estate.

I blinked, confused, as Mrs. Goto ran outside onto the mansion's wraparound porch.

"Call 911," she shouted, kicking off her slippers. Lifting her muʻumuʻu, she raced down the porch steps, the long skirt flapping in her wake.

I grabbed my phone and hit the emergency numbers. Mrs. Goto was sprinting across the sloped lawn toward the pool several hundred yards away.

Something was floating in the water.

"Send an ambulance," I said when the dispatcher answered, unable to keep the quaver out of my voice. "There's a body in the pool."

* * *

The sun was setting by the time I left the Hamilton estate.

Elizabeth had been the one to spot Charles Hamilton floating face down in the pool from her balcony, but it was Mrs. Goto who'd pulled him from the water and performed CPR. Driving back to Waikīkī, I couldn't shake the image of his lithe, powerful body stepping up to the edge of the pool, knees bent, before he dove gracefully into the still waters with barely a splash.

A niggling thought worked its way into my head.

How does a man who swam fifty laps a day drown in his own pool?

Chapter Three

"How'd your meeting go?" Lani asked.

I drained what was left of my fizzy liliko'i cocktail and ordered another. I'd already eaten half the poke appetizer waiting for my friends at the brew pub in Kaimukī, an old Honolulu neighborhood in the midst of a renaissance. I'd thought about bailing on our girls' night, but I'd already flaked twice before.

Lani arched her brows, large lash-fringed eyes widening as she and Willa surveyed the table. My friends knew me well enough to know I was stress eating.

"That bad? What happened? You tell him what you really think of his lame book or what?"

I glared at Lani, scooping a chunk of fresh ahi with a fried wonton chip. When I finished chewing, I told them the whole tragic tale.

"Charles Hamilton died? Was it a heart attack?" Willa said.

"He's still alive, at least when the ambulance took him away. I heard Elizabeth tell the paramedics he's on heart meds. She thinks he must've had a stroke while he was swimming, but I was talking to him minutes before, and he was fine." I paused, reaching for another chip. "On the upside, you were right about the dress, Lani."

She smirked. "Tell me something I don't know. Like why you took this job."

Gorgeous, brilliant, and highly opinionated, Lani had been my best friend since we were kids. But two and a half thousand miles of ocean can be hard on friendships, and for the last several years we'd exchanged more Instagram hearts than phone calls.

She glanced around the crowded restaurant, dark hair rippling over her shoulders as she jabbed a fry at me, voice lowered. "He's public enemy number one here in Kaimukī, and you're not even getting a—what's it called—byline? I mean, you're a writer. Not some rich guy's research assistant."

Maybe this debriefing/girls' night out wasn't such a great idea after all. I sipped my drink and looked up to find Lani studying me closely.

"Why is he public enemy number one?" I asked cautiously.

Fry forgotten, she leaned in, fixing black eyes on me. "He didn't say anything about Kaimukī?"

Lani was well aware she was treading in dangerous waters since her own boyfriend, Luke, had helped me negotiate the nondisclosure agreement I signed with the Hamiltons.

"If he had, I couldn't talk about it," I said, trying not to think about Parker's mysterious overseas call and last-minute meetings with the mayor.

"So he didn't." She sat back. "I figured as much. There's no way you'd be able to keep it secret. It's just a rumor, anyways."

"What is?"

Glancing around again, she leaned forward and said, "Over the years, there's been talk about developers building a fancy shopping center here. Nothing's ever come of it, ya? But now, a couple property owners have been approached by a real estate agent about selling their buildings. The agent won't say who he represents, but something's up and some of us have already started organizing to fight it."

I knew she was talking about Luke Yamada, her longtime boyfriend, a land-use attorney who went toe-to-toe with developers—and occasionally the U.S. military—to protect what was left of Hawai'i's natural habitats and sacred landmarks. From the sound of things, he'd also become the unofficial leader of the Kaimukī merchants group.

It was the same old story, one I'd written about plenty of times on the mainland. Fancy new shopping centers attracted big national retailers who eventually drove away the mom-and-pop stores. But surrounded by water in Hawai'i, local business owners had nowhere to go.

I hated the thought of Kaimukī turning into another generic suburban mall like the ones up and down California's I-5.

"So, what's that got to do with the Hamiltons? They usually only deal with undeveloped land," I said. Bulldozing Hawaiian heiaus to put up cookie-cutter homes was their usual M.O.

Lani's half-raised glass came down with a bang, the dark Maui stout sloshing dangerously close to the rim. The trio of gold Hawaiian bangle bracelets she always wore clanked angrily.

"Who else would it be?" she asked.

Not for the first time, I was relieved my name wouldn't be on the cover of Parker's biography.

"So? Why did you take this job?" Lani repeated.

Desperation. And I'd mistakenly believed ghostwriting could save my career.

"I need the work, and it pays well," I said.

Willa patted my arm sympathetically. "Whatever the reason, we're glad you're home now."

The three of us had been friends since we roamed the neighborhood on our bikes, our tight-knit trio eventually giving way to include Luke and his cousin Koa. Willa was the first to marry, and Lani and Luke—together since our freshman year at UH—were as good as hitched. A few of us still got together whenever I was in town.

"You haven't been back in five years. Didn't you miss being home?" Lani asked.

I'd been living on the mainland for more than a decade, nearly my entire adult life. But when my plane had banked left on its final descent, I'd glimpsed Kaneohe Bay and the Koʻolaus, recognizable even from the aisle seat. A sudden longing hit me full force, and I'd spent several moments swiping away inexplicable tears.

"I've been busy—"

"Working. We know," Lani said.

"Anyways," Willa said, giving our friend a pointed look. "I worry about you living by yourself in Waikīkī. Have you heard about the recent crime spree? It's been all over the news. Tourists are getting robbed in broad daylight."

Waikīkī had always been a hotspot for thieves, with its herds of visitors ripe for the picking, but recently the area had seen an uptick in muggings and thefts, according to the local press.

"I'm not a tourist. Besides, my neighborhood in San Francisco was a lot tougher than Waikīkī. I'll be fine."

The waiter interrupted with a second round of drinks, ube cheesecake, and spoons for sharing. I was digging into the macadamia graham cracker crust when Lani broke the silence.

"You should call Koa," she said.

Even Willa nodded in agreement. "Luke's party is next week. We'll all be there. You're coming, ya?"

I drained my cocktail glass. "Yeah, sounds fun. I'll think about it."

No amount of time or distance would make Lani and Willa fall for my white lie.

"You know, he asks about you," Willa said.

The television above the bar caught my attention as a familiar face flashed on the screen.

"Hey, turn that up will you, brah?" Lani asked the bartender, who pointed the remote at the flatscreen TV.

"In breaking news, Charles Hamilton II, whose family helped develop much of Waikīkī and Honolulu, making Hawai'i the center of a global marketplace, died today in an apparent accidental drowning. He was 83."

Lani let out a low whistle. She sat back and reached for her beer. "Looks like your book just got a helluva lot more interesting, ya?"

Chapter Four

It was still dark when I hauled myself out of bed for a run the morning after Charles Hamilton died. My overdue catchup with the girls had gone late into the night, and I was still bleary-eyed and yawning as I shoved my feet into sneakers. By the time I trudged past my building's automatic glass doors, waving to the manager, it was six thirty.

Back in California, the cold morning damp usually shocked me awake. But here on O'ahu, where temperatures rolled gently between the low 70s and 80s all year long, I had no need for the long-sleeved shirts or thermal leggings packed away in a storage unit off Interstate 80.

Hawai'i isn't any cheaper than the Bay Area, and my parents' suburban home on the eastern edge of Honolulu had been a soft place to land.

Temporarily.

There's only so much Asian mothering a thirty-three-year-old single gal can take, even if it is rent-free and comes with steaming bowls of saimin and homemade chashu. *(Yes, Mom, I ate jook for breakfast. No, PoPo, I haven't met any nice, single, American-born Chinese doctors. Yes, my underwear is clean.)*

My old newspaper editor's "condotel"—a five-hundred-square-foot glorified hotel room with a kitchenette and balcony overlooking Waikīkī—became my salvation, and I'd moved in just in time to start my new job.

There were definite perks to living in a hotel/condo. In addition to a large, well-lit lobby, the newly renovated Seventies-era hotel had a front desk staffed 24/7, a pool, and a fitness center. Plus, tourists aren't typically chatty, which I considered a bonus.

My new, temporary home was in a pocket of Waikīkī bordered by the two main drags, Ala Moana Boulevard and Kalākaua Avenue, and the Ala Wai Canal, a stone's throw from where the last princess of Hawai'i lived and died over a hundred years ago. The Ainahau was named after her beloved estate, which was torn down in the 1950s to build hotels and apartments.

Developers must love irony.

I warmed my muscles with a brisk walk down Kalākaua, past kitschy souvenir shops, overpriced restaurants, and luxury brand storefronts, their gleaming window displays enticing shoppers even after hours. Waikīkī's signature musk of salt air, sunscreen, and coconut oil grew stronger the closer I got to Kūhīo Beach. A shortcut through the surfboard racks opened onto a near empty beach.

Paradise.

My feet hit sand, and I broke into a jog. The coral horizon on my left was brightening into blue, and behind me a rainbow arced over Diamond Head. My old Brooks running shoes tread across the beach following the water line until I hit the Pink Palace, where I picked up my pace on a narrow walkway.

The tide was still high. Occasionally, a wave crashed onto the concrete path, hitting me with its salty spray. The paved route ended, and I was back on the sand, dodging swells as I ran along Kahanamoku Beach.

I slowed after rounding the lagoon, letting my heart rate return to normal before treating myself to an iced pour-over coffee from a hotel cafe. I never truly felt awake until that first cup, so I savored the deep, rich Kona brew—doctored with cream and sugar—as I walked back to my apartment.

I'd tossed and turned most of the night. Even in the clear light of day, I couldn't get yesterday's events out of my mind. The TV news outlets were sketchy on details, and a quick perusal of the local newspaper's website hadn't offered anything I didn't already know.

When paramedics arrived at the estate, they'd found an unresponsive Charles Hamilton by the side of the pool. All attempts to revive him had been unsuccessful, and he'd been transported to the hospital, where doctors pronounced him dead. Nothing about a stroke or heart failure.

I was dying to get a look at the police report, but my press credentials had long since expired.

I took my time walking home. Waikīkī was waking up. Shopkeepers were sweeping sand from the sidewalk as they prepared to open for the day. Hotel gardening crews were hard at work picking up fallen plumeria petals and leafy fronds from the pathways, while groundskeepers raked uniform lines in the sand.

My phone emitted a series of beeps, and I glanced at the screen. Google letting me know my meetings with Parker had been canceled, leaving my schedule wide open for the next week—at least.

At this rate, it would take longer than a year for me to finish Parker's book.

My phone tweeted again when I reached my building, and this text made my heart flutter.

My flight got pushed back. Free for breakfast?

I'd met Mark Nichols my first week back on the Islands at the opening of a new exhibit of artifacts once belonging to ancient Hawaiian leaders known as ali'i. The Hamiltons, who were major contributors to the Bishop Museum, sent me an invitation. I'd gone, excited to finally meet my new employer, but no one from the family made an appearance.

Instead, I'd been seated next to an attorney with hazel eyes and a laid-back, easygoing charm.

In between his bids on a week's stay at a private Waikoloa villa, we'd hit it off over lomi lomi and chicken long rice at the luau in front of the museum's impressive Romanesque-stye building. He was from Sacramento, a Stanford grad working in the Honolulu office of a law firm based in L.A.

After exchanging numbers, he'd apologetically explained he traveled frequently to the Big Island and Asia for business, which suited me fine. I liked my independence and had no desire for anything serious.

He called a week later, and we'd gone to an up-and-coming new restaurant, where the food was delicious and the company even better.

It had been a long time since a man inspired butterflies in me, and I was enjoying the heady anticipation of a new romance before the sparks inevitably fizzled. I tapped a quick reply and arranged to meet him at the Wailana, a few blocks from my building, then hurried upstairs to shower and change.

Mark was already seated at a booth when I walked into the diner. He slid out when he saw me and bent over to give me a quick peck on the cheek.

"I'm glad you could make it," he said, when we'd settled into the booth. "I have a last-minute trip to the Big Island, and I'm not sure when I'll be free again. I had a lot of fun the other night."

He flashed a disarming grin, and my stomach did a little flip.

"Me too," I replied with an answering smile.

We ordered breakfast—Portuguese sausage and eggs for me, pancakes for him—chatting about his upcoming trip until the food arrived. I nodded approvingly to myself as he reached past the maple syrup and drizzled a mix of liliko'i and coconut syrups over his pancakes.

When in Hawai'i, eat like a local.

I broke into my eggs, letting the yolk color the rice yellow before scooping a forkful along with an orangey red bite of garlicky, slightly spicy sausage.

The perfect Hawaiian breakfast.

"This is the only place in Waikīkī where you can still get good food at a decent price," I mumbled between bites.

"So why *do* you live here?" Mark asked, echoing a sentiment already voiced several times by my family and friends.

Waikīkī—with its fake culture, pedicabs, and tourists in thongs—was an unusual choice for a local girl to call home. But somehow, it suited me. Coming back after so many years on the mainland, I was straddling two worlds, and Hawai'i's version of Tinseltown embodied how I felt.

"It's convenient—close to downtown, restaurants, and the beach. I can walk to a lot of places," I said. "Plus, I got a deal on the rent."

Mark, who lived in a swanky condo with a view of Kewalo Harbor in one of Honolulu's trendiest neighborhoods, didn't seem convinced. He wiped syrup from his mouth with a napkin.

"I hear you met Steve," he said, pushing his plate away.

At first I drew a blank. *Steve?* "You mean Stephen Hamilton? How did you—?"

"He's a college buddy of mine. We pledged the same fraternity. He called to tell me about his grandfather. When Steve said his dad had been meeting with a writer named Maya, I realized he was talking about you."

"Oh." Half a dozen questions popped into my head, but there was no time to organize them. "I had no idea you knew him. Wait . . . I thought he went to Yale, like his dad."

"He did. I was there as an undergrad, but I couldn't stand the idea of another winter back East, so I came home for law school."

My brows arched involuntarily at the information overload. Yale and Stanford? I suddenly wondered what I was getting into with Mark. I was feeling a little out of my league.

But I was more curious about the Hamiltons. "Are you close?"

"We kept in touch. I stayed with his family once or twice during breaks. One year I spent Thanksgiving at their ranch on the Big Island, and Charlie was there. He certainly is . . . was . . . a character." He smiled at the memory. "A few years back, I needed a change of scenery, so when my firm had an opening here, I went for it."

He cleared his throat. "I can't believe Charlie's gone. He was . . . larger than life, you know?"

"I'm so sorry." Then I remembered something. "When we met, he thought I was someone named Cat."

He let out a breath of air. "There were signs of dementia."

My ears pricked at this bit of information. Nothing I'd read about Charles Hamilton or Hamilton, Inc., had any mention of health problems. All reports seemed to indicate the businessman had been as robust as ever. I'd been surprised when he'd called me by the wrong name after I'd introduced myself.

"Do you know who Cat is?" I asked.

Mark shook his head. "One of the household staff, maybe? He'd forget his assistant's name too. Misplace documents, that sort of thing. He was once a no-show for an important meeting and turned up all the way in Nuʻuanu. The family thought he was in the early stages, but he refused to see a doctor. He still ran the Hamilton company with an iron fist, though. He knew the tiniest detail of every single project they had going. Parker hated it."

"Was it about the mall project? The important meeting, I mean." The question was automatic. The part of me I couldn't shut off wanted to know more about the Kaimukī rumor, even though it had nothing to do with my job.

Mark sipped his coffee and shrugged. "I have no idea. Charlie never mentioned anything about Kaimukī, and Hamilton, Inc., isn't one of my firm's clients. I hadn't seen him in weeks. I've been busy with this Big Island deal, in meetings all day. Didn't even hear about Charlie until this morning."

He paused.

Silence often encourages people to say more, so I said nothing. It worked.

"I do know there was a dustup with protestors," he said.

I resisted the urge to lean forward. "What happened?"

"You can take the reporter out of the newspaper, but—"

I matched his grin with a smile. "Pretty much."

He chuckled and put down his coffee mug. "It's par for the course in this business. There's a new housing project making its way through approvals, and some of the neighbors are up in arms about it because of traffic concerns. There's also a Native Hawaiian group upset about the destruction of ancient sites. Lately, the opposition has gotten more vocal, and protestors have been picketing the Hamiltons' home."

"I saw some of their reels on TikTok," I said. "They seemed peaceful enough."

"They were, for the most part. But a few weeks back there were picketers outside the front gate. One of them managed to sneak onto the estate, probably from the beach. Parker chased him off but not before Charlie got ahold of a rifle."

I couldn't keep the shock off my face. *This was Hawai'i. Not the Wild West.*

Seeing my expression, Mark added, "I know how it sounds, but it's not like they have an arsenal. It's just the one gun, a keepsake from their ranch. They locked it away and took every precaution to make sure Charlie no longer had access to it."

He tilted his head and looked at me. "Am I off the hot seat? I feel like I'm doing all the talking. I know you grew up here, but how'd you end up in California?"

I gave him the edited version: how my dad escaped the Sacramento heat one summer by taking an ethnic studies class at the

University of Hawaiʻi, met my mom, and never left. "Other than summers with Dad's side of the family, I spent most of my life here. Until grad school."

"You didn't try to get a job at any of the local papers?"

I lifted a shoulder, deflecting. Date No. 2 was too soon for the personal history lesson.

"Better opportunities on the mainland."

He peered at me over his coffee. "I get the feeling there's more to the story, but there's time for all that later. So, what have you got going on today?"

"Not much." I should've been having lunch with Charles, and I sobered as I thought of what his family must be feeling. "I might head into town to do some research. I need to go to the library, maybe check something at city hall."

I'd thought about this while jogging, but Mark's story about the protestors had convinced me to do a little digging into the rumored Kaimukī project.

"What about you? I know you're off to the Big Island again. Is that where you were yesterday?" I asked.

Mark glanced at his watch, apologizing as he threw down two twenty-dollar bills between our empty plates.

"Sorry to cut this short, but I gotta run if I'm going to catch my plane," he said, sliding out of the booth.

We said goodbye in front of the Wailana, where Mark kissed me as cars, scooters, and buses whizzed past on the busy Ala Moana Boulevard. I barely noticed. He turned out to be a very good kisser, and I smiled all the way back to the Ainahau, already anticipating our next date.

I was back in my condotel before I realized Mark never answered my question.

Chapter Five

My day went downhill from there.

Back at my place, I settled onto the lanai and opened my laptop, pleased to see a message from Deidre, a magazine editor I worked with from time to time, with a potential freelance job. She lived in L.A., and every now and then we'd meet up for drinks when she was in San Francisco. Rather than exchanging a volley of emails, I decided to call her.

"I totally thought of you when I pitched this," Deidre said. "We want a first-person piece—eight hundred words or so—with advice and tips on how to get men to swipe right."

I knew enough about dating apps to get her gist, but I'd never used one myself, something she found shocking when I told her.

"What? I thought you were single," she said.

"I am. I just prefer meeting people IRL."

"Not really working for you, is it?"

Trying not to sound defensive, I said, "I do okay."

"How old are you? Never mind, forget I asked. Asians always read a little younger . . . you have great skin. What moisturizer do you use?"

Experience told me it was better to let her ramble. She'd circle back eventually. I used the time to mentally calculate how much an eight-hundred-word piece could add to my bank account.

". . . even better. 'Tales of a Tinder Virgin.' You'll need to update your profile pic. Know any good photographers? The magazine will pay—"

"Wait. What?" I asked, my alarm growing as she outlined a hare-brained scheme. Dinner and drinks with Deidre never failed to entertain—she always had great stories. But now I was hellbent on not becoming one of them. "I'm not creating a fake profile just to score a date for a story."

"It won't be fake. It'll still be you—just airbrushed."

I groaned inwardly. "Not the photo. The whole thing. I'm not that desperate," I said.

"Oh, Maya," she tsked, oozing sympathy. "When was the last time you went on a date?"

"I meant, I'm not that desperate for work." *Not this month, any-way.* "I'm actually working on a new writing project, so unless you have something quick and dirty . . ."

"We can make it work. Everyone loved that last piece you did for us. Send me some ideas."

I hesitated. But only for a few seconds. I refused to parade my love life online—I had some standards after all—but I couldn't afford to turn down jobs, and Deidre's magazine paid well. Enough to upgrade my running shoes, maybe even buy another Island-appropriate outfit from Lani. I might need the extra cash. I had no idea if Charles Hamilton's death would change this ghostwriting gig.

"I'll have something to you by the end of the week," I said.

"Oh, and Maya? Update your socials. We want to play this big, so you'll need an online presence."

I thought of my treadless shoes and sighed. "Sure, Deidre."

We hung up after settling on a tentative deadline, and I reluctantly opened my Facebook page. It took me down a rabbit hole of friends' engagement posts, vacation photo dumps, and endless foodie pics. Judging by the ads for Hawaiian jewelry, resort wear, and flip-flops, the social networking platform knew I was back on the Islands even if all my IRL friends didn't.

I clicked on my profile and winced. Deidre had a point. It'd been a while since I'd checked my feed, let alone posted anything. And my profile photo was practically ancient by digital content standards.

I peered at the closely cropped headshot of a brown-skinned girl with dark hair pulled back into a loose braid. I'd lopped it off my first year in California. Sometimes I could still feel its weight tapping against the small of my back.

I browsed through the photos on my phone, rejecting the paler versions of myself. Maybe I'd get Lani to help me snap a better selfie. Right now, I had some research to do.

I packed up my laptop and headed for the library. It was another perfect day in paradise. The sun was out, and a lovely breeze made the air smell sweet and kept the temperatures low.

It was an easy bike ride over the Ala Wai Canal and through the streets of Honolulu. Hawai'i drivers are mellow and never in a hurry. Here *minimum* speed signs are needed to keep traffic moving along some highways.

Twenty minutes later, I rode up to the classical revival building on South King Street, locking my bike before strolling inside through the wide, white columns.

Ensconced at a computer terminal, I searched the database for articles about the Hamiltons, quickly discovering the archives went back over a hundred years. The database provided the name of the periodical, date of publication, headline, and first two paragraphs of each article. I selected several pieces and headed to the reference desk to request microfiche spools before settling down to read.

Like most locals, I'd grown up with the basics. When Parker's attorney revealed his client's identity, I'd spent hours researching the man who'd been a household name in Hawai'i. But I'd totally missed the Kaimukī project. Now my reporter's instincts were on overdrive.

Horatio Alger could've written the book on Charles Hamilton I, who arrived on the Islands as a stowaway from England in the late 1800s and years later built one of the first resorts in Waikīkī. Decades later, his descendants pushed east, developing Hawai'i Kai, where my parents bought their first home.

Parker took up the mantle after earning his degree at Yale and returning to the Islands with his bride in 1983. He joined the family business while the new Mrs. Elizabeth Hamilton, née Bradford, quickly joined the MOBS, becoming a patron of Honolulu's museum, opera, ballet, and symphony. The young couple had moved into the Hamilton estate with Charles, who had been widowed years earlier when Parker's mom died of cancer.

But aside from a brief wedding announcement, I found very little information on Elizabeth prior to her marriage. I scrolled past several pages of articles, skipping over more recent society page and business stories, expecting to find references to her family. Hadn't Parker said Elizabeth's father was an entrepreneur? I paused briefly at a small item buried deep in the *Boston Globe*'s metro section about a house fire, but realized it was a photo credit for a woman with a similar name.

I had plenty to read, dutifully tapping out notes on my laptop. Over the years, while the family hosted charity balls for cancer research, paid for the construction of a new children's wing at Kapi'olani Medical Center and became a patron of the arts, they also courted controversy. There were numerous lawsuits alleging breach of contract—at least one a year—and they seemed perpetually at loggerheads with Native Hawaiian leaders over land rights, eliciting even more legal action.

No surprise there. Like Mark said, it was pretty standard stuff for a company the size of Hamilton, Inc.

Not a whiff on the Kaimukī shopping center project Lani and Willa had mentioned. I had to remind myself I wasn't a reporter anymore—just nosy. I should know about my client's projects, if for no other reason than to head off any potential controversies, right?

Hitting the print button, I gathered the articles and my notes before returning the spools to the reference desk. A check of my watch showed I had enough time for a quick stop at the city's planning department.

Ten minutes later, I was standing in line at the public counter, wondering if I should have called instead. But sometimes the personal touch pays off.

I pulled out my phone and checked for messages before slipping it back into my bag. The glass door to the planning office opened, and a man in a Rainbow Warriors baseball cap entered, standing in line behind me.

"Next. How can I help you?"

I stepped up to the counter, where a friendly, middle-aged clerk smiled warmly.

"Aloha. I was wondering if there were any permit applications on file for the 800 block of Wai'alae Avenue in Kaimukī? Maybe under Hamilton, Inc.?"

"Let me check, ya?" She turned to the computer screen and began tapping on the keyboard. She shook her head slowly. "There's nothing on file for that address or anywhere else in Kaimukī."

"Can you check Hamilton, Inc.? I'm looking for a redevelopment project."

The only one she could find was a shopping center in Hawai'i Kai, but it had already been approved and construction was well underway. *Maybe the rumors were wrong.*

"Could be it's too soon for the developer to file an application," the clerk told me. "Check back next week, ya?"

I thanked the clerk and left, absently noting the man behind me was gone. I adjusted my bag and made my way to the bike rack. Three marked police cars were parked next to the row of bicycles, and several officers were milling around nearby.

I secured my helmet, tossed my bag into the basket, and rode out onto the street.

The easy ride was uneventful until my front tire started feeling sluggish when I reached Kalākaua Avenue. I knew I had a flat. With a sigh, I hopped off and bent to examine the tire. Sure enough, I could see the round head of a small, silver nail.

My building was only a few blocks away. I retrieved my bag to start the walk home when I felt a hard yank on the strap as I started to drape it across my shoulder.

Instinctively, I gripped the strap harder and found myself in a tug of war with a man in a baseball cap.

"Hey!" I shouted, frantically looking around for help or a weapon to go on the offense.

Letting go would've been the smart thing to do. A bag of papers and a six-year-old laptop wasn't worth getting hurt or dying for.

But it was mine, and I wasn't going to give any of it up without a fight.

Planting my sneakers in a wide stance, I let my arms go slack long enough to make my attacker shift his weight. Then I tightened my grip on the strap and pulled as hard as I could, catching him off guard and throwing him off balance.

He let go, stumbling over his flip-flops. The momentum sent me crashing back onto the concrete sidewalk. He took off down Kalākaua, leaving something behind before he disappeared into a swarm of tourists. I limped over, pleased when I saw what he'd dropped. Backed by knowledge gleaned from eighteen seasons of *Law & Order*, I used a pen to pick up the 'Bows hat and let it fall into my bag.

"Are you okay?"

I jumped at the voice approaching from behind, relaxing the grip on my bag when I turned and recognized the woman pedaling toward me. She was about my age, and I'd seen her locking down her bike and in the lobby at my building, but we'd never spoken.

The brakes on her bike squeaked as she skidded to a stop beside me.

"You want me to call 911? I saw what happened, but it went down so fast I couldn't even get my phone out. You need an ambulance or what?" she said, breathless.

I shook my head. The would-be thief was long gone. What could the police do now, except take a report? "Thanks, but I just want to get home. I'll file a report online."

By the time I wheeled my bike behind the apartment building, locking it in the chain link enclosure, I was already feeling the aches and stings from my one-woman battle. In addition to a scraped-up palm that had begun to bleed, I was sweaty and dusty. Damp hair clung to my face.

I wanted nothing more than to take a refreshing shower and relax on my balcony with takeout and a glass of wine.

Pushing open the glass door of my building, I welcomed the blast of frigid lobby air, dimly registering the man and woman talking to the manager's son at the front desk. I headed for the elevator.

My heart stopped when I heard a deep, all-too familiar voice from the past behind me brusquely calling my name.

Crap.

Swearing under my breath, I started a mental check of my appearance but gave up in despair. I took a deep breath and turned around.

"Hello, Maya," Koa Yamada said.

He'd transformed from the gangly college kid I'd known to a lean, muscular man. He got his perpetual tan and wavy black hair from his Native Hawaiian mother. His warm, serious eyes—dark chocolate framed by long lashes—were near replicas of his Japanese father's.

His good looks had not dimmed over the years, which somehow added to the day's irritations.

"Hi." My voice cracked. I'd gone for nonchalant surprise but came off sounding like a high-strung canary. Hastily, I reached up to take off my helmet, self-consciously tucking my hair behind my ears. I rebounded with an artificially bright smile that faded as I took in Koa's attire.

He wore a navy-blue polo shirt tucked neatly into khaki slacks with a pair of sturdy brown leather loafers, a casual ensemble on the mainland but akin to a three-piece suit here in Hawai'i. The Honolulu Police Department logo embroidered below the lapel was no surprise nor the gold detective shield clipped to his belt.

But the holstered gun triggered an inner alarm.

Belatedly, I noticed the petite woman beside him. Black hair coiled in a tight bun at the nape of her neck. Clothes, badge, and pistol a match to his.

"How've you been?" he asked.

But I wasn't fooled.

This wasn't an old friend stopping by to talk story. Fake smile gone, I faced Koa, locking eyes with my ex for the first time since he'd broken my heart over a decade ago. "What the hell is going on?"

Chapter Six

O'ahu is only the third largest island in the Hawaiian chain geographically, but its nickname is "The Gathering Place," and it's home to nearly one million people, living in the middle of the Pacific Ocean on a volcanic rock roughly half the size of Rhode Island.

Koa and I were bound to run into each other eventually. In my fantasy, though, I was decked out in a fancy designer gown. Not streaked in bicycle grease, flushed and sweating in clothes I'd gotten off a discount outlet clearance rack.

I should've listened to Lani and Willa.

Koa coughed. "Can we go up to your place? We need to talk."

The official tone and presence of his partner sent my thoughts reeling. I reached for my phone, cursing when I couldn't find it in the front pocket of my bag. Mom and Dad never kept their devices close by, but Kiyomi would know where our parents were.

Koa rushed to reassure me. "Everyone's fine, Maya. This is about the Hamiltons."

"The Hamiltons . . .?" Realization dawned. "*You're* investigating Charlie Hamilton's death?"

The female detective's brow raised, but she flashed a polite smile. "It would be better if we could talk in private."

One uncomfortable elevator ride later, I was leading two of HPD's finest into my humble studio.

"What happened to your hand?" Koa asked when I reached into my bag for keys.

"Nothing," I said, throwing open the door and standing aside to let them in. "I . . . fell."

His eyes narrowed, and I looked away, startled to realize, like Lani and Willa, he wouldn't buy the white lie. We'd known each other our whole lives—with the exception of the last dozen or so years. It was the classic friends to lovers story. But instead of happily ever after, I'd ended up in California alone.

The last thing I wanted was to prolong our reunion by telling him about the mugging.

I dropped my bag and helmet by the door next to a small pile of shoes. Thinking back to my unmade bed and the running clothes I'd tossed on the duvet, I hurried to close the pocket door. Koa left the loveseat to his partner, who I learned was Detective Amy Reyes, standing with his arms crossed as he surveyed the room. I did my best to freshen up, washing off blood, dust, and grease at the kitchenette sink.

I shook water from my hands, wishing I could cast off memories so easily.

Playing the dutiful host, I foraged in the cabinet for some cookies and dumped them on a plate before turning to face my unexpected visitors.

Koa tilted his head, studying me as I perched on a bistro chair, his brows furrowed. "You cut your hair."

I faltered, remembering the sudden decision to chop five inches from my thick mane the night before I left home for good. I'd been wearing the unruly waves in the same no-fuss, no-muss style the hairdresser called a "jagged bob" ever since.

"Yeah, about twelve years ago," I replied in a clipped voice.

Detective Reyes cleared her throat. "Ms. Wong, this is a routine investigation into the incident at the Hamilton home yesterday. We're interviewing everyone who was present at the time."

"Is the coroner's report in already?" I asked. "Did he have a stroke?"

Koa's jaw tightened as he and his partner exchanged glances. Again, she smiled politely. "Actually, Ms. Wong, we prefer to ask the questions."

"Sorry, force of habit," I apologized, not really meaning it. I sat back. "Please, call me Maya. Fire away."

She nodded and placed a tape recorder on the coffee table. "Do you mind if we record this?"

I hesitated, suddenly remembering the recording on my phone. I hadn't replayed it since the interview. I debated whether to mention it. But there couldn't be anything relevant to their investigation, and if I told them about it, they could confiscate my phone.

"What is it?" Koa asked.

"Nothing." I lied smoothly this time, meeting his gaze before turning to Detective Reyes. "Go ahead."

She took the lead, asking basic questions and jotting down my date of birth and contact information before asking me the purpose of my visit to the Hamilton estate.

I had to tread carefully. It wasn't common knowledge I was ghost-writing Parker Hamilton's biography, and I'd signed a nondisclosure agreement preventing me from revealing confidential information about him and his family. But I'd made sure there were some exceptions.

Turning to the detective, I explained my ghostwriting deal and took her through the events of the previous day, without getting into the content of my discussions with the Hamiltons. I also summarized my brief conversation with Parker's father.

"We made plans to meet for lunch at his club. He went for a swim and—" I raised my hands helplessly.

"When did Parker Hamilton arrive?" Reyes asked.

Shaking my head, I shrugged again. "The only people I saw until about noon were household staff. Parker had some last-minute business meeting. I assumed the family was there. There were cars in the driveway when I arrived around eight. A Porsche and a Tesla," I added, anticipating her question.

"Plaid?"

I frowned. "Was what plaid?"

"The Tesla."

"It was just red," I replied, mystified. Koa's mouth twisted in amusement.

Reyes looked up from her leather notebook. "I meant, the model. An S Plaid or maybe a Three?"

"What's the difference?'"

"About eighty grand," Koa said.

"It was one of the smaller ones."

Koa switched tack. "Other than the family, who else was there that day?"

"Just Mrs. Goto . . . Oh. Wait. A gardener was there too."

Two pairs of eyes looked at me sharply.

"Gardener?" Koa asked.

"Yeah, he was digging up the hibiscus or something."

"Can you describe him?"

I thought back to my encounter with the stranger in the garden. "Local. Dark hair, dark eyes. About your age and height, but broader . . . more muscular," I clarified. I pictured the man's face, remembering a long, narrow nose and angular cheekbones.

"He could be hapa," I added, using the Hawaiian term for someone of mixed Asian Pacific Islander and Caucasian ancestry.

"What was he wearing?" Reyes jumped in.

"Khaki cargo shorts and a gray Local Motion tank top." Something bothered me, but I couldn't put my finger on it.

"Anything unusual happen?" Koa asked.

"Other than my boss's dad drowning in the pool? No."

Detective Reyes shifted, adjusting the weapon on her belt, and I remembered what Mark had told me. I hesitated before adding, "Have you checked social media? You might find some interesting reels of the estate."

"Why? What've you heard?" Koa asked, studying me closely.

"Just take a look, and then ask the family about protestors."

Detective Reyes clicked her pen and started to close her notebook. Looking up, she said, casually, "Why'd you call him Charlie?"

Her question caught me off guard. "I did?"

"Earlier. Down in the lobby."

I shrugged. "My friend Mark calls him that. It just slipped out, I guess."

Again, they exchanged glances.

"Would that be Mark Nichols?" she asked.

"Uh, yeah. You know him?"

Both detectives stared at me, a frown creasing Koa's brow. He was silent as his partner continued her questioning.

"What exactly is the nature of your relationship?"

I wouldn't fill out my Facebook profile, and now two police detectives expected me to declare my relationship status with a guy I'd just met.

"He's a . . . friend. He knows the Hamiltons, and we were talking about them at breakfast—"

"I see." Detective Reyes threw a pointed glance at Koa, then turned back to me. "You have breakfast with him a lot?"

My cheeks flushed at the intrusion into my private life, not to mention her implication. "We've gone out twice. We met for breakfast at the Wailana Cafe because he had a plane to catch. I don't see how it's relevant to your investigation."

It was unfair of me, but I glared at Koa. He'd sat there, not saying a word the whole time his partner grilled me. As flustered as I was, I couldn't help wondering what knowing Mark had to do with their so-called "routine" inquiry.

"Why are homicide cops investigating an 'accidental drowning'?" I asked.

Reyes pulled her lips into another tight smile. "We never said we're homicide detectives."

"I have my sources," I said, maybe with a trace of smugness. This earned a disapproving glance from Koa.

He turned to his partner. "Lani and Maya are friends."

"Lani—your cousin's girlfriend?" Reyes's brows arched as she studied me. "Small world."

"Small island," I said. "So why'd HPD send you two, when any patrol officer could've taken my statement?"

Like peas in a pod, they assumed identical stoic expressions. I stood, signaling I was done.

"I'll meet you at the car, Amy," Koa said to his partner. His tone brooked no argument, and she reluctantly left. Turning to me, he started to say something but dug into his pocket and extended a clean tissue instead.

"What's this for?" I asked, puzzled.

Koa swiped the tip of his nose with his index finger. "You've got some dirt . . ."

Temper flared, I snatched the tissue from his hand. Koa was pushing all my buttons.

"Maybe if I'd had a little warning, I could've made myself more presentable," I snapped. "You could've called, you know."

He threw me a look that said I was being unreasonable. "Like you would've answered. I'm a homicide detective. We don't call suspects to say we're dropping by to talk story. Kinda defeats the purpose, ya?"

I stopped rubbing my nose with the tissue and glared at him. "So I'm one of your suspects now?"

He faltered. "No, course not." Sighing, he took out a business card, scribbling something on the back before handing it to me. "Look, if you think of anything else, call me. Anytime."

He turned to leave, then stopped and looked back at me. "It was good seeing you again, Maya."

Sure it was. "Yeah, you too."

I went in search of my phone as soon as he was gone, curious to see how much of my conversation with Charles had been recorded—if any. I retrieved the bag I'd dropped by the door and slipped my hand in the front pocket. My fingers touched my leather wallet and a stack of business cards, but no phone. I searched the other pocket, then the main compartment, until I resorted to emptying all its contents on the dining table. Finally, I had to face the truth.

Like any modern woman, my phone was my lifeline—and it was gone.

I hadn't thought to check if anything was missing after my showdown with the man in the baseball cap. I groaned thinking of all the information I had on my phone, notes, contacts, messages—not to mention the recording of my meeting with Parker.

I'd managed to hold on to my laptop, but I might've been better off saving my phone. I went online to order a new one, paying an exorbitant fee for overnight delivery and noted grumpily it cost about the same as a new computer. Tired and sore, I went to take a long overdue shower. By the time I emerged, clean and feeling slightly revived, I was starving. Grabbing my bag, I headed to Kaimukī for culinary comfort à la Korean BBQ.

Chapter Seven

Hawai'i never changes—or so I thought.

I could close my eyes and picture the drive into downtown Honolulu—the ocean on my left and Koko Head behind me. There was the bus stop on Kalaniana'ole Highway a few blocks from my junior high, the old drive-in movie theater with the haunted bathroom, and the rattan furniture store with the white wicker sofa that never seemed to sell.

It stayed that way for years after I'd left home.

Until someone finally bought the sofa—and the store.

Then the music shop where all the kids on O'ahu went for instrument rentals, sheet music, and ukulele strings fell victim to cheaper online retailers and shuttered its doors after nearly seventy years.

The corner candy store was next to go, taking with it the salty-sweet, mouth-puckering preserved plums we had bought by the bagful.

I headed to the one place I knew was still there.

Turning onto 12th Avenue, I quickly found an off-street spot in the rear lot for stores fronting Wai'alae. The smell of grilled meat and spices hit me the moment I opened my car door and spurred me across black asphalt, where a white Toyota pulling in barely missed me. The man behind the wheel put up a hand in apology. I hurried by and strode into the beloved mom-and-pop restaurant through its back door.

From the mint-green Naugahyde booths to the faux marble Formica, Kim Chee 2 hadn't changed in all the years my family had been eating there. Even the beady-eyed stuffed mongoose still bared its teeth from behind its plexiglass display.

Soy, garlic, gochujang chili paste, and charcoal blended into a heady fragrance, triggering a rush of warm, comforting memories. I breathed in happily—it was starting to feel like I'd come home.

I was too hungry for takeout and chose to dine alone at a corner booth. I ordered and started reading the articles I'd printed at the library. As I read I nibbled from several small plates of kim chee—cabbage, daikon, cucumbers, spinach, and bean sprouts, pickled and fermented in a variety of savory, sweet, or spicy brines.

I was reading the only interesting article I'd found on Parker's wife—a *Honolulu* magazine piece on the foundation she'd created to provide food, shelter, and books to the poorest children in Hawai'i—when a shadow fell over the table.

Koa slid onto the bench in front of me. "Why'd you turn off your phone?" he asked, not bothering with a hello.

Glancing around, I leaned forward. "Are you tailing me?" I hissed.

"Didn't have to. It's Friday. I played the odds."

Dumbfounded, I remembered my family's Friday night tradition had been our weekly date.

"Still dodging my calls after all these years?"

The waiter's appearance spared me from answering. "What can I get you, brah?" he asked Koa.

"He's not stay—"

"She got the short ribs, ya? I'll take chicken," he said, after the waiter nodded confirmation.

When he disappeared back behind the Formica counter, Koa turned to me expectantly, still waiting for an answer to his question. I considered hedging, but I'd have to file a police report anyway.

"My phone was stolen. I haven't had a chance to replace it yet."

A single brow arched, and I knew what he was thinking before he said it. "You sure you didn't lose it?"

"A man took it from my bag this afternoon in Waikīkī."

Koa frowned. "Why didn't you tell me before?"

"Because," I answered testily, "I didn't realize it was missing until after you left. How'd you get my number anyway? From Lani?"

He sidestepped my question and reached into his back pocket for a notebook, a small, black pad like the ones I'd seen countless other cops use.

"What happened?"

I pursed my lips, weighing my options.

"You can either tell me now, or . . ."

I rolled my eyes. "Are you trying to play 'bad cop'? With me? Seriously, Koa. The things I could tell your partner . . ."

But he wasn't taking the bait. Wishing I'd filed an online report, I reluctantly told him everything. He didn't interrupt, withholding any questions or comments until I finished, but his grim face and tight lips gave him away.

"Jesus, Maya. Do you have any idea how lucky you were? He could've had a knife or a gun. You could've been—"

"I know. It was stupid. I should've let him have my bag."

Koa rubbed his face in frustration, then took a calming breath. "Is that how you hurt your hand and why you were limping? Did you get checked out by a doctor?"

"Just a few scrapes and bruises. I'll be fine," I said.

"Did you at least get a good look at the guy?"

I shook my head. "He was wearing a baseball hat. I couldn't see his face, and everything happened so fast, I didn't really take in any details. I'm not even sure what he was wearing."

Then I remembered. "Any chance you can get DNA off a hat?"

"Why?"

I told him, and he started to laugh, but stopped abruptly. "You watch too much TV. HPD doesn't pay to run DNA tests for muggings."

"But—"

His mouth twisted. "There's been a rash of property crimes in Waikīkī. The city council has been on the chief's ass to crack down."

"Bad for tourism?"

He nodded, eyeing me thoughtfully. "Leave the hat with me. You never know."

The waiter brought our drinks—Coke for me and a bottle of Hite for him.

"What was so urgent, anyway?" I asked, chasing a bite of spicy cucumber with a sip of Coke.

"We spoke to Mrs. Goto again. The Hamiltons fired their gardener two months ago, and he's a fifty-five-year-old haole. So whoever you saw, it wasn't the gardener," Koa said. "We need you to come by the station tomorrow to do a composite sketch."

I suddenly remembered the sound of the man's hurried footsteps, and I realized what was bugging me earlier. Even in Hawai'i, gardeners wore closed-toe shoes.

"He wore slippers," I murmured. I turned to Koa and held his gaze. "It wasn't an accident or stroke, was it?"

Koa's only response was the same stern, impassive expression I'd seen on other cops trying to block reporters. But I didn't need him to confirm what I'd known since seeing Charles Hamilton's body floating in the pool. He took a long pull on his beer.

"So if it wasn't an accident or natural causes, what killed him?" I asked. By the time I'd reached him Mrs. Goto was already performing CPR, but I hadn't noticed any obvious signs of violence. "Poison? Rare, but—"

"Stop." The thunk of Koa's bottle hitting Formica punctuated his one-word sentence. "I'm only gonna say this once: Butt. Out."

"Relax, I was just thinking out loud."

"That's what scares me. I know you. Some random idea pops in your head, and you don't let go." He let out a breath and glanced around the crowded restaurant. "What time can you be at the station tomorrow? The earlier the better."

My day was wide open, but my reluctance must have shown on my face. "I don't like this any more than you do," Koa said. "I spent an hour in the chief's office explaining how my ex-girlfriend got mixed up in my case. But you're our only eyewitness, and we need you to cooperate. You can deal with Amy, if that's what you want."

I shrugged. "Whatever. I can be there in the morning."

Our food arrived, and my stomach growled. The waiter rearranged kim chee plates and deposited a cast-iron platter heaped with beef short ribs slightly blackened and still sizzling from the grill in the center of the table. Next came the spicy BBQ chicken, accompanied by fat mandoo dumplings, and two bowls of rice.

Piling beef, chicken, and kim chee on a mound of rice in one of the bowls, Koa handed it to me. "I heard you were freelancing."

I looked at him in surprise. "You read my work?"

But he shook his head. "Lani sent me one of your pieces—something about tights."

Registering the faint disapproval in his voice, I felt heat crawl up my neck. "Leggings."

"What?"

"It was about leggings. Not tights."

"What's the difference?"

"Read the story."

As usual, when it came to fashion, I'd enlisted Lani's help. But why'd she send it to Koa? Eyeing the jeans and faded shirt he'd changed into, it was clear his sartorial interests hadn't evolved much over the years—or at all.

Using chopsticks, I tweezed a bite of cold spinach and beef with a scoop of rice.

"That's the kind of stuff you're writing now?" he said.

I used to say a good story was like good mochi—a nice chew with a hint of sweetness. It had been a long time since I'd had either. But I didn't need him to point out how far I'd fallen. Koa was the last person I wanted to discuss my career trajectory with.

"I write the kind of stuff that pays the rent," I said, longing for the solitude and peace of my little basement apartment. I focused my attention on a wayward beansprout and changed the subject. "How're Matt and your dad?"

He shot me a knowing look over a mandoo suspended between chopsticks.

"They're good. They ask about you." He dunked the dumpling into a bowl of soy and aromatics. "It was funny."

I waited, but he didn't elaborate. "What was?"

"The thing about tights—leggings. It was funny. I could hear your voice."

I suddenly remembered Koa's sweet side. Exhaling, I felt the tension leave my shoulders.

Over satisfying bites of meat, rice, and spicy pickles, we chatted, filling in the missing years of an otherwise lifelong friendship. Koa's brusque exterior chipped a little, and I saw a glimpse of the boy I remembered. Even with a few awkward pauses, it was surprisingly easy to slip back into old rhythms. It had been the same with Lani. A long time ago, they were the people who'd known me best.

And Koa had a good memory.

"You wanna tell me what you lied about earlier?"

I blinked, momentarily confused. "Is this some weird new interrogation technique?" I hedged.

"Quit stalling, ya? I know a perp's lying when he answers a question with a question."

"Is that what they taught you in detective school?"

He sat back, folded his arms, and waited. Resigned, I told him about recording my interview with Parker.

Koa rubbed his brow. "You really know how to step in it, don't you? You should've said something. It's evidence."

"Evidence in what? You're investigating an 'accidental drowning.'"

Koa's eyes narrowed, his index finger tapping twice on the table. I knew he was reconsidering.

"I'm only telling you this because I know you're not going to let it go, and I don't want you messing up my investigation. But you can't breathe a word to anyone, and you have to *swear* you won't go around asking a bunch of questions. I mean it, Maya."

I held up my right hand. "Scout's honor."

"Since when were you a Boy Scout?"

"Boy Scout, Girl Scout. Same thing."

"You were never a Girl Scout."

I rolled my eyes. "Look, I promise I won't ask questions about your 'accidental drowning' case, but I still have a book to write and, like it or not, Parker Hamilton and his family are my subjects. I need this job. So get used to it, because you're stuck with me until I finish the job or you solve the case."

His exhaled breath sounded like a groan. "The medical examiner found faint bruising on the body that's not consistent with efforts to revive him. There's no official ruling yet, but something's hinky. We need to track down everyone who was there that day."

"You think someone held him underwater? There were at least half a dozen people on the estate at any given time. Anyone could've passed by and seen what was happening."

Koa leaned forward, fixing me with his stare. "I know how stubborn you are, Maya. But there's a killer out there, so don't go poking your nose where it doesn't belong, ya?"

"Fine."

I was eager to go, but Koa took his time, nursing the last bit of his beer while the waiter returned with our check and takeout boxes.

"How'd you get the job with Hamilton?" he asked, as we scraped beef and chicken into compostable containers.

"Online job site." I told him about the listing that appeared in my inbox. "It was all very clandestine at first. One of his lawyers handled everything. I didn't know who I'd be ghosting until shortly before I had to sign the contract."

He stilled, then closed the lid and turned to me. "Don't take this the wrong way, but you don't think it's strange, someone like Hamilton, with all his wealth and connections, used a website to find a ghostwriter? I'd think he'd have his pick."

"Yeah, that's what I thought too. But he's not prominent enough nationally to get a big publisher to commission a ghostwriter. He said he wanted someone local. Plus, I'm cheap, and I have the feeling they're not as flush as they seem."

I reached for my wallet, but Koa threw some bills on the table and stood.

"I got this," he said. "Old time's sake, ya?"

He held out his hand, but I slid out of the booth without it. He handed me the takeout box, and we left the restaurant.

A car engine started as we made our way across the parking lot, and I caught a glimpse of a white sedan. Beside me, Koa tensed, his back straightening. I glanced up to see his eyes tracking the car as it sped away.

"What's wrong?" I asked.

We stopped at my Honda, Koa still scanning the lot. "Thought I saw that car earlier. It's probably nothing. I'll follow you home and get that hat from you."

"I can drop it off when I do the sketch thing—"

"—or I'll get it tonight."

It was useless arguing. I sighed and rummaged through my tote for my keys as Koa let out a surprised chuckle.

"You still drive this old thing?" he said, giving the green Civic a pat.

"Just while I'm here," I said, defensively. "My real car is in storage back home in California, but it costs a fortune to ship, so this is my ride for now."

He raised his eyebrows and studied me. "Back home? You're not staying?"

I reached past him to open my door. "You sound like my mom."

Chapter Eight

My unofficial police escort insisted on a thorough security sweep.

It didn't take long. I watched from the kitchen while Koa checked the bathroom door, examined the windows and locks and then slid open the pocket door to the sleeping area.

"All clear?" I asked, gesturing to the empty space. He ignored my sarcasm, and I brushed past him to retrieve the Ziploc bag where I'd put the baseball cap.

I turned around to find him securing the sliding glass door to the balcony.

"You notice anyone strange hanging around? Or following you?" he asked.

"Besides you?"

He gestured to the windows. "You should shut those when you're out," he said in a no-nonsense tone I was already beginning to recognize as his cop voice.

"I use the security bar," I said, pointing to the metal rod that prevented anyone from sliding the window open any wider than a few inches. "Besides, I'm twelve floors up—who do you think's gonna break in? A gang of geckos?"

Ignoring me, he pointed to the front door. "Your lock sticks. You need to get your building manager to fix it."

"Sure. I'll get on it right away." I held out my makeshift evidence bag. "Looks like your Waikīkī bandit is a 'Bows fan."

"That'll narrow the suspects," he said, taking the Rainbow Warriors hat. He turned and looked at the dining table where I'd left my open laptop and a growing stack of articles and files for work. "What about the recording—you've got it on tape?"

I was confused for a moment. "You mean, my interview with Parker? What decade are you living in? There's an app for that. It was on my—"

"Let me guess—your phone. So the file's gone? Or are you finally backing up to the cloud?"

I paused, suddenly realizing all might not be lost. For now, I'd keep that to myself. "You'd need a warrant, anyway. The Hamiltons made me sign a nondisclosure agreement."

"You're one of those reporters, huh?" Koa said.

"You mean ethical? I can't hand over my confidential notes just because we're . . . friends."

A frown flickered across his face before it smoothed back into its usual stony, impassive position. "Not even vital evidence in a murder investigation because it's the right thing to do?"

I snorted. "Nice try, detective. But the medical examiner hasn't ruled Charles's death a homicide yet, and you'd need probable cause to seize my phone. Find the guy who stole it and it's yours to use as evidence."

"You sound like a lawyer."

"If I find anything, I'll talk to Luke and work something out. It's the best I can do."

Mollified, he turned to leave. "Where'd you meet that guy anyway?"

"What guy? Oh, you mean Mark?" I followed him to the door. "Are you asking as a friend or a homicide detective?"

Koa shrugged. "Both. More as a friend."

I told him about the museum fundraiser. His brows arched.

"Charity event, huh? You've come a long way from those parties in the backyard, ya?"

Disapproval lingered long after the door shut behind him. I told myself I didn't care. Eager to play a hunch, I hurried to the small round dining table that doubled as my desk. I woke the laptop with a few quick taps and opened the cloud account where my files were stored. I let out a soft cry of victory.

A red flag above one of the folders alerted me to a new audio file—Parker's interview. Thrown by the mugging and Koa's unexpected appearance, I'd completely forgotten my phone automatically backed up certain files to the cloud.

I opened the free app I sometimes used to transcribe long interviews. By the time I'd brewed a cup of decaf brown rice tea, I was skimming through pages of text, trying to decipher the garbled sentences and mangled Hawaiian words. It was past midnight when I finally closed my laptop, satisfied nothing on the file would help Koa's investigation. The recording had been over three hours long, far more than I'd realized because I'd forgotten to pause the app when Parker left to take a call. But it was mostly inaudible.

I yawned, stretching muscles cramped from sitting so long at the computer. I carried my empty tea cup into the kitchen and was about to go to bed when I had a sudden thought.

Rooting around in a zippered cloth bag made from kimono fragments, I found a thumb drive and slipped it into one of the USB ports. I clicked "copy files" and watched the progress bar slowly turn blue.

Never hurts to be careful, I thought as I dropped the thumb drive back into the bag and went to bed. I had grand plans of waking at dawn, a long run on the beach, and coffee on the lanai.

* * *

I forgot I didn't have a phone. No phone meant no alarm, and I slept until I was startled into consciousness by a loud banging at the door.

Street noise drifting through the open windows in my room told me I'd overshot my usual wakeup time by hours, not minutes. I scrambled out of bed and hurried to the door.

"Ms. Wong, you have a delivery. I tried calling, but—" The building manager's twentysomething son—a premed student at UH and the apple of his mother's eye—shrugged and held out a box marked with a mobile carrier's logo. "I guess this explains why your phone was shut off."

"Thanks, Brent. Sorry to drag you up here."

I shut the door and went to wash up, trying to recalibrate my plans for the day. It was overcast, which worked in my favor. I could get in a morning run, and if I kept it short, I could set up my new phone first. I followed the prompts on the screen, and text alerts confirmed I'd been successful. Two new messages were waiting to be read.

First I opened Mark's.

Flying back for Charlie's service. See you there?

I clicked the second text, an invitation from the family to attend Charles Hamilton II's memorial on Friday at Kawaiahaʻo Church. Relieved to have a friendly face to buffer me from the Honolulu muckety-mucks bound to be in attendance, I arranged to meet Mark at the church, then headed out for my run.

I was hitting my stride, my sneakers churning over wet sand at an even pace, when Siri's voice broke into my audiobook, mispronouncing Lani's name—in an Australian accent.

Lani said: ?! 😁😉

Mystified, I decided Lani could wait until after my run. But moments later, another alert interrupted the audiobook's big reveal.

Kiyomi Wong said: How was dinner? 😉

I stumbled on a palm frond. How did my sister know about Koa? I hadn't noticed any familiar faces in the restaurant—even the waiter was new to me. But if Lani and Kiyomi had the scoop, then by now so did half the island.

I picked up the pace, planning a containment strategy before my mom got wind of it, when—

Mom said: Invite Koa to Sunday dinner.

I never made it to the hotel with the good coffee. I tried to push through, but as I neared the halfway point, Lani abandoned her pictogram-filled texts and went old school and called.

"We need to talk. I'm at your place. Where are you?" Lani asked when I answered on the fourth ring.

"Run." I wheezed, sucking in air as I struggled to talk and run. "Why?"

"You know why. Try running home, ya?"

A beep, followed by silence told me she'd hung up. I skidded to a halt and bent over, willing the stitch in my side to subside. When my heart rate slowed and I could breathe again, I trekked across Ala Moana back to the Ainahau.

"How come you didn't tell me you called Koa?" Lani pounced the moment I walked through the glass doors, softening her demand with a large jasmine boba tea.

I accepted, sucking in the milky, sweet, floral hit of caffeine. Careful not to choke on tapioca pearls, I eyed my friend as she crossed her arms, sun-browned skin contrasting with the white cotton shirt she wore half-tucked into denim shorts. Only Lani could make a T-shirt and cutoffs look elegant.

By then, the first wave of tourists had landed, and the line of guests waiting to check into their rooms wound through the lobby. Children, antsy from hours cooped in a plane, screamed as they zigzagged between the potted monstera, while their parents haggled with the concierge over their ocean view. A man in a blazing orange Hawaiian shirt nearly mowed us down with his rolling suitcase racing for the elevator doors.

"So?" she asked, as we picked our way through the hotel guests.

I chewed a boba and pressed the cup to my face, letting the condensation cool my heated cheeks. "You came all the way over here just to ask about dinner?"

"I had a meeting downtown."

"With who?"

She waved her hand, gold bangles jangling on her wrist. "Nobody you know. It was just business. Quit avoiding the subject. Why didn't you tell me you were seeing Koa?"

"Because I wasn't," I said. "He and his police partner showed up unannounced. They had to take my statement about—"

"The dead guy? It's Koa's case?"

I nodded. "How'd you find out, anyways? Was it Kiyomi?"

"Jimmy."

"Who's—"

"Never mind," Lani said.

We waited for the next elevator car beside a Japanese couple in matching floral prints, their pale arms and legs colored bright pink from too much time in the sun. Lani threw side-eye at two women with New York accents who were complaining loudly about the room service.

When both elevators arrived simultaneously, we followed the sunburnt tourists.

"I don't understand—Koa and Amy questioned you, and then the three of you went to dinner?"

Amy? I couldn't help wondering how friendly Lani and Detective Reyes were . . . and why. I told myself the twinge of jealousy was more about my best friend than my ex.

I shook my head.

"Just Koa." I waited until we were alone before spilling the whole story, starting with my ill-fated bike ride downtown.

"You should've called him, like I said." As I led Lani down the hall, I could hear the suppressed laughter in her voice. "You've been living in California too long. Why were you riding a bike anyways? I swear, if you start eating avocado toast, I'm gonna stage an intervention."

We stopped at my door. I unlocked it and stepped inside, Lani at my heels. We collided trying to take off our shoes, and in the few steps it took us to reach the kitchenette, her large lauhala bag kept bumping into my arm.

Lani turned, surveying her surroundings. "You said you got an apartment."

"I think the word I used was 'studio.'"

"This is a hotel room, Maya. You live in a hotel."

"They're called 'condotels,'" I said, again rummaging through a cupboard for cookies or rice crackers. At this rate, I'd need a Costco membership just for snacks to serve surprise guests. "I hear they're the latest thing in real estate."

Lani rolled her eyes, dropping her bag on the bistro table I used as a desk. "It's like you don't even live here."

"It's only temporary."

"Well, that's a relief." She smiled, relaxing visibly as she sat at the table. "Where are you looking? I know the manager of an apartment building in Kaimukī. You want his number?"

"Uh . . ."

But she was already scrolling through her contacts. A moment later, I heard my phone ding.

"Anyways, what are you doing Friday? I was thinking we could all hang out—"

I cut her off, knowing where this conversation was headed. "I'm going to a funeral," I said, offering some leftover kakimochi cookies my mom had given me.

"Sure you are."

"No, really. Charles Hamilton's service is on Friday. I'm meeting Mark—"

Lani nearly choked on her cookie. "Are you telling me, your next hot date with this new guy is at a funeral? How romantic."

"It's not a date. It's work. I'm supposed to be shadowing the Hamiltons, remember?"

"Right. How much you wanna bet we're never meeting this guy?"

* * *

After Lani left, I hit the shower. I was toweling off when my phone beeped. I never got this much activity back in California.

Meet me at the station in 15.—K

How did he know I had a new phone? I texted back, negotiating for more time, and went back into the bedroom to get dressed, not waiting for a response. For reasons I didn't care to explore, I took the time to apply makeup and even scrunched styling product into my hair.

It was closer to forty minutes by the time I climbed the steps to HPD's downtown headquarters. Koa was leaning against one of the columns, arms akimbo, waiting for me.

I checked my watch, reading his face. "I said I'd stop by in the morning. It's eleven thirty. Where's Detective Reyes?"

"On her way." Koa led me into the building, squiring me through security and into a windowless office crammed with metal file cabinets secured by padlocks. A computer with a large-screen monitor stood on a desk.

"Have a seat," he said, motioning to a metal chair beside the desk. "Thanks for the tip about the protestors."

"Sure."

"We want to show the composite to the Hamiltons, see if they recognize the man you saw, before we go to the media," Koa added.

A beep sounded, and he dug into his pocket. Frowning as he studied his screen, he said, "Wait here. Amy'll be with you in a few minutes."

The door clicked shut, and he was gone, leaving me to bide my time. I grumpily wondered why I'd bothered hurrying down to the station.

I fished out my earbuds and put on an audiobook, which I listened to while scrolling through dozens of messages I'd missed being offline nearly twenty-four hours. I was all caught up—and four more chapters into my book—when the door opened and Detective Reyes's serious face appeared.

After a perfunctory greeting, she sat at the desk and opened a leather portfolio embossed with the HPD logo. Taking out a file, she slid it over to me. "I typed up your statement. Read it over carefully and sign it," she said.

While I read, she opened the laptop and began tapping the keys.

"There's a couple misspellings, but otherwise accurate," I said.

Wordlessly, she handed me a pen, and I signed and dated my formal statement.

"How do you know Detective Yamada?"

So he was doing the tight-lipped, enigmatic thing with his partner too. Typical.

"We grew up together. There was a bunch of us. Koa, Luke, Lani, Willa—we've known each other since we were kids," I said.

"Them, I know. He's never mentioned you."

Studying the detective's sharp, pointed face—pretty even when scowling—I wondered if jealousy was behind her animosity toward me. My throat tightened. Was something going on between her and Koa? I was sure HPD frowned on partners hooking up, but it was bound to happen. I lifted a shoulder nonchalantly. "We lost touch a long time ago."

"'Lost touch.' For a kama'aina, you sound a lot like a haole."

Inwardly I bristled, but I had no desire to get into a discussion about race and local linguistics with this woman. I wasn't a Native Hawaiian, but I was born and raised on the Islands. I was a local no matter who I sounded like.

"Koa said something about a sketch artist?" I said.

"Facial composite. This isn't Frisco. We don't have a full-time artist just hanging around the station."

She angled the monitor so we both had a clear view of the screen. With a few clicks of the mouse, she switched to a window and opened what looked like some type of graphic art program. A blank canvas dominated the screen, but after a few more taps a faceless head appeared along with a catalog of facial features to drag and drop.

The choices were endless. Starting with the suspect's head shape, I had to pick hair, the shape and color of his eyes, and whether he had thick or thin eyebrows. Was his nose Roman or snub? Did he have facial hair? Distinguishing features such as a tattoo or mole? The more I struggled to remember, the more the noses and ear shapes looked the same. Two grueling hours later, the detective and I studied the facial collage I'd come up with.

"That him?" she asked.

"Um, yeah. I guess."

"You guess?"

"It's . . . maybe."

Her lips tightened for the umpteenth time. I cringed. "Look, I've never done this before, and I only saw him for a minute or two."

A quick rap on the door spared me further humiliation. For once I was relieved to see Koa. He acknowledged me with a nod, then turned to his partner. "How'd it go?" he asked.

She didn't answer. Looking over her shoulder at the computer screen, he said, "Better than nothing."

Detective Reyes arched thinly shaped brows at him. She nodded slowly. "But not much."

Chapter Nine

The ombre button dared me to click.

I let my cursor hover, wondering if it was too late to back out of the dating app story. Deidre wasn't excited about any of the ideas I'd pitched, and my deadline loomed. I steeled myself, tapping the touchpad only to be prompted to create an account using a phone number, Google, or Facebook login.

I hit the back button. Too soon to commit.

My phone twittered. It was a number I didn't recognize, but I answered, thankful for any excuse to procrastinate. If I didn't find a new angle for this story soon, I'd be forced to join the world of online dating.

"Maya? Are you busy this afternoon? I thought we could have tea at the Moana."

It took a moment to place the feminine voice and its faint, vaguely Bostonian accent, as Elizabeth Hamilton's.

"I apologize for the late notice," she went on. "But I had to get out of the house, and it occurred to me this might be the perfect opportunity to get to know you better. What do you say?"

"Sure," I said, mentally reviewing my minimal wardrobe. I had no clue what one wears to tea. "What time?"

An hour later I hurried down Kalākaua Avenue, wishing I'd sprung for an Uber instead of walking a mile from one end of Waikīkī to the other. Blisters were already forming on my heels from my cute new strappy leather sandals, and I could feel sweat seeping through my pink T-shirt dress.

By the time I passed through the white columns of the 118-year-old hotel, I was rethinking the wisdom of bangs on a tropical island.

Unlike her husband, Elizabeth didn't keep me waiting. I followed the restaurant hostess onto the lanai, where I spotted her flaxen knot and signature pearls, milky white against a navy blue linen dress. Last minute or not, Elizabeth had managed to score the table with the best view of Waikīkī Beach.

"The entire household has been in an uproar ever since poor Charles." She removed dark tortoiseshell glasses, revealing reddened eyes. "Between the police crawling all over the estate and planning a memorial service, I was about to lose my mind. I had to escape for a few hours."

I could imagine.

A waitress appeared with the menu—an assortment of finger sandwiches, miniature desserts, and a selection of fine teas. Elizabeth gave it a fleeting glance before tossing it aside.

"Screw tea. I'll have champagne. Maya, how about you?"

I ordered the same. It was easy to like Elizabeth Hamilton.

Our drinks arrived along with tiered tea trays of ginger chicken salad, haupia rolls, and strawberry guava macarons—a British tradition with local flair.

"When will we see a draft of the book?" Elizabeth asked. "I know it's early, but it's imperative to release our book as soon as Stephen announces his bid to run for office."

This was the first I'd heard about an upcoming election.

Elizabeth went on. "The state senator for our district is retiring at the end of his term, and we're planning to announce Stephen's candidacy any time now. Parker did tell you about Stephen running for office, didn't he?" She stopped and looked at me, then exhaled in a small sigh. "No, of course he didn't."

"I'll do my best to meet the time line you want, but it's been hard to get enough alone time with Parker," I said. "So far, I have a loose outline, and I typed up a chapter about how you two met. It would be great to get your perspective." I took out my notebook, and she let out a twinkly laugh.

"Parker told you I shot him, did he? My husband loves to tell that story. But between you and me, that's not how we met."

"It wasn't at the president's dinner?"

"Oh, that part's true. But I wasn't shooting the event. I was serving the food. My father ran a restaurant near campus. I was a townie." She paused to sip her tea-infused champagne, while I absorbed the shock and shame for having jumped to conclusions about her. This tidbit explained why I hadn't been able to find any mention of the Bradfords prior to her marriage.

"We . . . had a moment. Isn't that what you young people say? We didn't start dating until six months later. By then I'd gotten a scholarship and was working for the Yale paper."

So much for the sweet love story I'd drafted on my laptop the other night.

I remembered the photo credit I'd seen when I was researching the Hamiltons at the library. "Wait. Did you work for the *Globe*?" I asked.

Elizabeth raised her glass at me in a mock toast. "You've done your research. No one's asked me about my photography in years, but yes . . . once upon a time, I interned there. I wanted to be a photojournalist. But it was a long time ago."

Back when newspapers still thrived, it was a coup to score an internship at a paper like the *Boston Globe*. I'd worked at the *Honolulu Star Bulletin* every summer until I left for the mainland. Elizabeth was more impressive by the minute.

"So, what happened?" I thought I knew but wanted to hear it from her.

Her smile wavered the tiniest fraction, then snapped back into place. "I fell in love," she said. "Parker was . . . intoxicating. When he proposed, I had to choose between his world and mine."

So she'd traded her ambitions for his and crafted a whole new identity as a philanthropist and community leader. I should've been writing her biography, I thought, not Parker's.

"Do you ever wonder what might've been?" The question slipped out before I could edit myself.

"I believe in staying the course," she said, after weighing her answer. "And now our son will continue the family legacy, taking the Hamiltons further than his father or grandfather ever did."

A server refilled our water glasses, and Elizabeth ordered more champagne. Wishing I'd recorded our interview, I underlined the words I'd scrawled down verbatim. I was dying to ask about Charles's death but hadn't found a way to ease into it.

Elizabeth saved me the trouble.

"Like I said, we want to announce Stephen's candidacy as soon as possible. But we've had to put everything on hold—including his engagement, and after everything we went through."

Nothing in my research had linked Stephen romantically with anyone. I waited for her to elaborate.

"There was a brief dalliance last year. Totally inappropriate—they had nothing in common. But he's been seeing a lovely young woman from California. The governor's daughter, actually. We're expecting him to pop the question any moment."

Elizabeth paused to let the waitress set down her drink, then continued in a hushed voice.

"I know the police are trying to be thorough, but they dragged Stephen and Mark in for questioning and want us to account for every moment of the day. Now we have this cloud of suspicion hanging over us."

She eyed me over the rim of her glass. "I understand you know one of the officers. What is his name . . . Yamura?"

Suddenly I understood the reason for her invitation to tea. She wanted to pump me for information, and I could hardly fault her.

"Forgive me," she said. "O'ahu is a small island."

And the Hamiltons were big fish.

"It's Yamada. Detective Koa Yamada," I managed to say. "We grew up together, but lost touch a long time ago. From what I hear, he's good at his job."

She sat back with a sigh. "Well, they've been very tight-lipped. Charles was a very successful businessman. He had his share of enemies, particularly the local activist groups. We've had protesters picketing the beach on numerous occasions. The estate is wide open for anyone to wander onto. I've been arguing for years to beef up security."

"Did anyone recognize the man in the police sketch?" I hesitated. "Was he the intruder Charles shot at?"

If Elizabeth was surprised I knew about the gun incident, her face didn't show it. "He looked like any other local on the street, but who else could it have been?" She checked the slender, diamond-encrusted watch on her wrist, signaling the end of our tea.

* * *

Waikīkī night music usually soothed me.

The strains of a Hawaiian lullaby drifting across the lagoon from one of the resorts would accompany my tapping keys as I worked on the balcony. The trade winds betrayed me that night. Even from my perch high above the lights, there was no escaping the false twang of bad ukulele music and whiffs of aloe vera and coconut oil. I wanted to hurl a burning tiki torch at the tourists below.

It wasn't their fault the word count on this book was spinning backward.

I'd been writing and rewriting the Hamiltons' love story with nothing but a blank screen to show for it, and the problem wasn't writer's block.

What did the other ghostwriter say? *Get inside your subject's head.* From my meeting with Parker, he seemed exactly like the profile pieces I'd read in the glossy magazines lying around the estate. Even at home, he kept up the public facade. Or at least he had around me. I'd given the family space after Charles's death, but once the funeral was over, things would have to change if I had a prayer of getting this book done before the November election.

My phone beeped, and a photo of an infinity pool stretching into the Pacific Ocean popped onto my screen.

Mark Nichols: Looks like I won the museum's silent auction after all. A long weekend in a private villa. Care to join me?

My lips curved as I pictured the light sprinkling of freckles on the bridge of his nose. I didn't care what Lani said—Mark was great. The whole package. But was I ready to go on a tropical island getaway with him?

My phone twittered again.

Mark Nichols: Too soon?

I squelched my instinct to hit the back button and tapped a reply.

Sounds fun. I'll check my calendar.

Chapter Ten

It rained the morning of the funeral. The light tropical mist dampened my skin as I waited for Mark in front of Kawaiahaʻo Church, and by the time he arrived a rainbow arced over downtown Honolulu.

Mark got out of a white Lexus Uber, his handsome face breaking into a smile as he spotted me.

"You have no idea how happy I am to see you," he said, giving me a light, sweet peck on the lips. My pulse quickened.

Mark mingled easily among the crowd gathered outside the church, introducing me to a who's who of Honolulu, including the mayor and a pro golfer even I recognized. It dawned on me Mark was on a first-name basis with people I'd only read about in the news.

"You get around for someone who's only been on the island a few years," I said, after exchanging cards with the mayor, who was eager to chat about Parker's book.

He shrugged. "Charlie knows . . . knew a lot of people, and he kind of took me under his wing."

A man in a black and gray aloha shirt strode toward us, and Stephen Hamilton clapped Mark on the back. "Thanks for coming. I know you had to move your schedule around to make it, but Pops would've loved it."

"It was no problem. I'd do anything for Charlie. You know that."

Stephen's smile was wistful, and I murmured my own, more formal, condolences. I glanced around, looking for signs of the fiancée. But he seemed to be flying solo.

"Thank you." His eyes roved the crowd as he gave the occasional nod or wave at a guest. "Mom asked me to get in touch with you to put something on the calendar, but it's been crazy."

I jumped at the opening. "How about Monday? What's on your schedule?"

"Monday doesn't work." Stephen scrolled the calendar on his phone. "Dad and I have a meeting with an investor."

"That's okay. I can shadow you. You won't even know I'm there."

"I don't think . . ."

Stephen's voice faded as he spotted something in the distance and frowned. I followed his gaze to a man under a banyan tree standing apart from the other people.

It was Koa, looking every inch the cop, his scowl visible even from across the churchyard. He'd traded his usual polo and jeans for an aloha shirt and pressed slacks, but his stiff posture and occasional scan of the crowd from behind dark sunglasses were dead giveaways.

"Actually, I know—"

The arrival of a black limousine pulling up to the stone gate interrupted me. The crowd quieted as it made its way up the drive and stopped in front of the church steps. Stephen, his mouth set in a grim line, excused himself to open the passenger door.

Parker stepped out of the limo, smoothing his navy blue aloha shirt and embracing his son before wading into the gathering of well-wishers. Stephen held out a hand for Elizabeth, who emerged in an immaculately tailored black sheath dress with pearls at her throat and earlobes. Anywhere else, she would've fit right in with a crowd of mourners. But in Hawai'i, where mu'umu'us and aloha shirts were perfectly acceptable funeral attire—especially when the invitation specified it—she stood out.

Stephen bent to kiss Elizabeth's cheek, and when he straightened, offered his elbow. The mother and son climbed the steps of the church arm in arm, taking their places behind Parker, who was glad-handing community and civic leaders from all over Hawai'i. Camera shutters clicked furiously from across the churchyard, where the press stood post on the other side of the stone wall.

Ten minutes later, Mark and the chamber of commerce president were embroiled in a discussion about streamlining the city's building permit process, so I slipped away in search of a restroom. On my way back, I took the time to explore the grounds. I followed the paved walkway behind the church, and a flash of color against the gray stone building several yards ahead caught my eye.

A woman with dark curls in a teal dress was whispering to someone hidden by foliage, an expensive designer handbag dangling from the crook of her arm. Oversized sunglasses obscured much of her face.

"Meet me tonight." Something in the man's intimate tone brought me to a halt. I knew that voice.

Parker Hamilton.

I didn't stick around for visual confirmation. I didn't need it. Moments after I rejoined Mark, I spotted Parker strolling down the path I'd just come from. He sidled up to his family, and my stomach clenched as I watched Elizabeth loop her arm through his, her expression adoring.

"You okay?" Mark asked.

I plastered on a smile. "Fine."

But I wasn't. There was nothing innocent about the rendezvous I'd witnessed. Parker's body language and the furtive meeting revealed a side he wouldn't want in his book.

Maybe I'd scratched too deep below the surface.

Church bells tolled, ending further discussion. The Hamiltons made their way up the stairs into the church, the crowd filing behind them. Mark steered me to the front, his hand resting on the small of my back, into a pew directly behind Parker.

I looked away, still inwardly fuming at Parker's behavior.

Halfway down the aisle, Mrs. Goto chatted politely with a man. She was the only member of the household staff at the funeral and was apparently there alone.

I caught sight of Koa in the last pew next to his partner. Minus the dark glasses, his cop stare softened when our eyes met. I returned his nod with a quick smile.

"You know him?"

A flush crept up my neck at Mark's hushed question. I started to repeat the same vague explanation I'd given Elizabeth and Detective Reyes, but decided he deserved better. "We dated in college. I hadn't seen him in years until he showed up asking questions about Charles."

Mark's face registered surprise, and he looked back over his shoulder at Koa.

"He and Detective Reyes have been questioning all of us," he said. "I think they're looking at everyone close to the family."

"But you weren't even there."

Mark's mumbled response was lost in a mass shuffling of bodies as everyone rose to sing a hymn. The pastor ascended the pulpit for a prayer then launched into his eulogy—a list of Charles Hamilton II's contributions to Hawai'i—nothing I hadn't read about in his press clippings.

Until Stephen took center stage. Reserved and serious, he looked vaguely uncomfortable in the casual Hawaiian shirt, as if he preferred a suit and tie. But his words were sentimental, his voice full of warmth for the grandfather he clearly loved.

"Thank you, Reverend, for the glowing remarks about my grandfather. He was certainly all those things, but to me he was just Pops." He cleared his throat. "I was never the most athletic kid. I preferred books to baseball, and that was okay with him. But he was determined to get me on a horse."

He went on to say that his summer vacations and school breaks were spent on the family ranch with a trainer until he became as enamored of the animals as his grandfather. Together they'd started a horse breeding business.

"My grandfather accomplished many things in his life, but to me, he'll always be the cowboy who taught me to ride."

A screen lowered, and a video montage of Charles Hamilton, accompanied by Hawaiian music, began to play.

Mark bowed his head. Without thinking, I reached out to give his hand a comforting squeeze. He turned, flashing a quick smile. The warm glow faded as questions crept into my head.

Mark had called Stephen a frat buddy, who'd invited him to visit the Islands a few times during college. Now I realized he was much more than a casual friend of the family. So why hadn't he mentioned knowing them sooner? There'd been plenty of chances: the museum fundraiser when I was sure I'd told him I was in Hawai'i to work for the Hamiltons, not to mention our first date.

The choir drowned out my thoughts, and when the service ended a few minutes later, we filed out of the church. While Mark spoke with Stephen, I found myself standing next to the man who'd been talking to Mrs. Goto earlier.

"I knew Parker, of course. We were at Punahou together. And I knew Mrs. Goto's daughter," he said.

"Oh, is her daughter here too?" I hadn't seen any woman with Mrs. Goto.

He gave a quick shake of his head. "She died. Years ago," he said. "So, I hear you're his new research assistant for this book of his. I'm guessing that's a euphemism for ghostwriter, ya? Back in school, he always got girls to write his papers for him."

This book could not get done fast enough. "I thought he was valedictorian."

"Parker? Nah . . . no way. He skated by on charm and family connections."

I distinctly remembered academic accolades being part of the file Parker had given me along with official-looking transcripts, but I didn't think I'd have to authenticate them. Who'd go through the trouble of falsifying a high school report card when a few simple keystrokes could expose the truth?

Parker Hamilton, apparently.

Misgivings turned to full-blown regret. I'd let the promise of a fat paycheck lure me back to Hawai'i against my better judgment, and now I was stuck. Even if Luke could get me out of my contract, there weren't enough online dating stories in the publication universe to pay back what I'd already spent of my advance. Scanning the courtyard, I saw the woman in the teal dress again. On impulse, I took out my phone and snapped a few photos before she rounded the corner out of sight.

"What are you doing?"

Koa had come up behind me, but I knew him too well to be intimidated by the sharp demand.

"Nothing," I said, slipping my phone back in the tiny purse Lani had loaned me. "Just admiring the church."

Koa's narrowed eyes told me he wasn't buying it. "Why are you here, Maya?"

For a split second, I didn't know if he meant Charles's funeral or Hawai'i. I took a gamble. "I could ask you the same thing," I said.

"I'm working."

"So am I."

Koa cursed softly under his breath. "I thought we agreed you wouldn't go poking around. I'm trying to catch a killer—probably someone here—and you keep turning up. If you don't quit butting in,

Amy is gonna arrest you for interfering with an investigation or withholding evidence. Take your pick."

"Too chicken to do it yourself?"

"Yes," he said, without missing a beat. "Lani would kill me."

I tried to stifle the unexpected chuckle bubbling in my throat but snorted anyway. Even Koa cracked a smile. It faded as he did another visual sweep.

I glanced over my shoulder. Honolulu's balding, redheaded chief of police was pumping hands with Parker.

"Aren't they chummy," I commented.

Koa's eyes darted back to me, and he straightened. "These are powerful people. I'm in the chief's office every morning briefing him. You need to—"

"I know. I promise, I won't do anything to screw up your case. I've been cooperative, haven't I?"

My computerized sketch had made the six o'clock news, but despite a social media blitz by HPD, the only tips it had generated turned out to be false leads by well-meaning citizens and vengeful exes. I'd flexed atrophied reporting skills to wrangle that info out of Koa in a text exchange.

He frowned at me. "Do me a favor, ya? Before you start 'thinking out loud,' be careful who's listening."

A hush fell over the churchyard, and we watched as pallbearers carried the casket containing Charles Hamilton's earthly remains down the church steps. Mark's face was solemn as he helped load gleaming mahogany and brass into the waiting hearse.

"Fancy crowd you're hanging with these days," Koa said, and again I couldn't help noting his faint disapproval.

I stiffened, pursing my lips. "It's just work."

"Yeah, sure." He expelled a breath, glancing over his shoulder. When he reached up to tug on his ear—an unconscious tic I remembered all too well—I knew something was wrong.

"I shouldn't be telling you this," he began, lowering his voice. "Did you know Nichols is Stephen Hamilton's alibi?"

I frowned in confusion. "No, Mark said he was working. He doesn't work for the Hamiltons. He wasn't there . . ." I stopped as I realized Mark had never said where he was. A prick of doubt crept into my heart.

Koa studied me, his brow furrowed. "He was there—they both were. And we don't have a clear handle on the timeline yet."

He took my elbow in a firm but gentle grip, locking eyes with me. "I'm worried about you, Maya. You need to stay away from this."

"Wait." I couldn't keep a tinge of anger out of my voice. "Are you telling me to stop seeing Mark?"

He glanced over to where the family had been, and I followed his gaze. The man in question was strolling toward us.

"No," he said after a lengthy pause. "But ask yourself how well you know this guy. And watch your back."

Chapter Eleven

My past and present were about to collide in the churchyard.

"Don't you have someone to interrogate?" I asked Koa when Mark was halfway across the lawn.

"No."

I gritted my teeth, anxiety mounting the closer Mark got. But my forced smile eased when he casually slipped his arm around my waist.

"Good to see you again, detective," he said to Koa.

Koa nodded and extended his hand along with condolences. I let out a quiet breath of relief.

"I assume, since you're here, whoever killed Charlie is still on the loose," Mark asked Koa. "Has anyone come forward with a name yet? Should Maya be worried? She's the only one who can ID the guy—"

"I'm perfectly safe. He doesn't know who I am, let alone where I live." I didn't like where the conversation was headed.

"He's a person of interest. We haven't ruled out anyone yet." Koa's noncommittal reply was classic cop speak. "It would help us if you and your friend could come in and clarify a few things."

Mark countered with legalese. "Steve and his father sought the advice of counsel. Their attorney will be in touch."

"I thought you were his lawyer."

"I specialize in real estate. This is not my area of expertise."

Did Mark just admit to working for the Hamiltons? It seemed Koa had wanted to question someone after all.

Raised male voices broke the awkward silence. Father and son were too far away to make out any words, but Stephen's rigid posture spoke volumes. He turned his back on Parker and stalked to the curb, where he got into his car and sped off. *Wonder what that was about*, I thought.

Mark turned to me and asked, "I had to bump up my flight. Any chance you could give me a lift to the airport?"

I thought for a moment, but it was time to leave anyway. "Sure."

We left Koa to say goodbye to Elizabeth and Parker. A few minutes later, I led Mark across the street to my car. We were getting inside when a horn blared, a rarity in Hawai'i, and we turned to see a red Tesla zip away from the church.

* * *

"What were you and that detective talking about?" Mark asked as I checked the side mirror.

I'd hastily tossed files and books into the back seat to make room for Mark and his long legs. Now, as my Civic rattled down South King Street, I wondered if he regretted not using Uber Lux.

"Just catching up." Waiting a beat, I said, "I didn't know you were at the Hamilton estate the day Charles died."

Friday traffic was heavy, so I couldn't turn to see his reaction. I got enough from the corner of my eye to know he'd grown still.

"Who told you—never mind. You'd think discussing a case with civilians would be off limits even in Hawai'i."

"What's that supposed to mean?"

"Nothing. Sorry, it's been a tough day." He let out a long breath. "Look, I'm in a difficult spot. I'll tell you what I told the cops. I can vouch for Steve—I was with him most of the day because he's hired me to work on something for him. But now that Parker's attorney is involved, I've been advised not to say anything more."

"The Hamiltons hired a lawyer?"

"People like the Hamiltons have a team of lawyers at their beck and call, 24/7, 365 days of the year."

A criminal lawyer?

"Are you one of them? I thought you said you didn't work for the Hamiltons."

"I don't. Not the family, anyway." Mark shifted in his seat and rubbed his brow. When he spoke again, his voice was hushed. "I'm helping Steve out with a project he wants to keep under wraps. He doesn't want Parker getting wind of it, which is why I haven't been entirely forthcoming."

The awkward tension eased. It explained a lot—including the argument we'd seen between father and son after the funeral.

"They don't get along?" I asked.

"They put up a good front in public, but no. Parker was a crap father and an even worse husband. Steve adores his mom so he's very protective of her. It didn't help that Charlie cultivated a rivalry between father and son."

"What do you mean?"

"Well, Parker didn't exactly inherit Charlie's knack for business, and Steve did. Parker's better at schmoozing investors than putting together a solid project. He's had a few bad investments, and Charlie was making noise about putting Steve in control."

I realized Stephen hadn't arrived at the church in the limousine with his parents, and he'd been the only family member to eulogize Charles. I thought about the woman in the teal dress.

"Did you happen to notice a woman at the service?" I said, describing her clothes. "Asian. Mid-thirties. Attractive. She and Parker seemed . . . friendly. Any idea who she is?"

Mark gave a mirthless laugh. "Could've been the social coordinator at their club, or the barista at his favorite café. I hear he even had a thing with a city councilwoman—" He stopped. "Sorry, that's probably more than you want to know. But he's known for having a wandering eye."

I turned onto Dillingham. From there, it was a straight shot to the airport.

"Can I ask a personal question?" Mark said. "Was it serious with you and Detective Yamada?"

I veered to the right to make my exit, cutting off a minivan. I waved an apology before answering Mark.

"I thought so at the time. But I wanted to go to grad school on the mainland, and he didn't, so we broke up."

It was the watered-down version, but it would take too long to explain something I didn't fully understand myself.

"It worked out for the best." I continued. "Uncle David had a heart attack a few months after I left. Koa's mom was long gone by then, so he was there to take care of his dad and make sure his little brother finished school."

Mark's brow furrowed, a strange look flickering over his face. "I assume you're using the word 'uncle' honorifically? Koa's dad isn't actually a blood relative?"

"We're not related," I said, smiling at his confusion. "Just family friends."

I hadn't thought of Koa's mom in years, and now I wondered again about Mrs. Goto's absent spouse.

"Come to think of it, no one's ever mentioned a husband," Mark said when I asked him about it. "I never met the daughter. I think she was a nanny or something for them, until she got hooked on drugs."

"I'm still fuzzy on Mrs. Goto's role in the family," I said. "I get the sense she's more than a housekeeper."

"She's been with the Hamiltons since Parker was a kid, but she works for the company, not the family. She has her hands in everything—appointments, finances, investors. The business would probably fall apart without her. I know Parker would." Mark turned to me. "I can see why you're a journalist. You're good at getting people to talk . . . and you're a very talented writer."

"You've read my work?" I asked, smiling.

"I may have Googled you the night we met at the museum," he confessed with a grin.

Naturally, I'd done the same. Cyber research on a prospective date is a must for any modern-day woman. Remembering the easy way he'd mingled with the upper crust of Honolulu, I wondered if I'd dug deep enough.

Chapter Twelve

But a deep dive on Mark would have to wait.

When I told my parents I was moving into my former editor's condotel, my mom said she'd let me go on one condition: Friday night dinners. It wouldn't have been wise to remind her I was an adult who didn't need her permission to move out. So I negotiated semiregular family meals instead.

After I dropped Mark at the airport, I had enough time to eat lunch, change, and pick up dessert from Liliha Bakery before heading over to my parents' place. I pulled up to my old house at the same time as my sister.

Our parents, both longtime UH bureaucrats, and maternal grandmother PoPo still lived in the house we grew up in—An Eighties era suburban home at the end of Lunalilo Home Road. It was a standard, cookie-cutter, middle-class house. But situated high up in the valley, I had an almost panoramic view of Koko Head Crater from my bedroom window.

My sister, Kiyomi, still wore a flour-coated apron from the downtown café she'd opened a year ago. She'd moved back home so she could start her own business, but it had also helped ease Mom's duties in caring for PoPo.

"How was the funeral? Or was it a date? I forget which," she said, grinning.

I made a face. "You've been talking to Lani."

"And Koa. He stops by the café every now and then."

Being Asian in Hawai'i meant living in a fishbowl, something both annoying and comforting.

We let ourselves in, slipping off our shoes and leaving them at the door next to neat rows of zoris, sandals, and sneakers. PoPo was pouring herself a cup of tea from the ancient metal thermos that always stood in the middle of the dining table.

"Have you girls eaten?" she asked, getting up and shuffling into the kitchen in her house slippers.

"No, thanks, PoPo," I said, when she held up a bag of wafer cookies. "I just had lunch."

"What did you have?"

"A salad."

She scoffed and opened a cupboard, reaching for a plate with one hand and pointing to a pink bakery box on the counter with another. "Salad's not food. Have the leftover dim sum."

Like trying to pay for dinner at a restaurant, it's impossible to win an argument about food with a Chinese grandma. Dutifully, Kiyomi and I took our places at the table.

"Mom and Dad aren't home yet?" I asked, dipping har gow into a tiny bowl of soy and chili oil. Dark sauce coated the dumpling's white skin, translucent enough to see the pink shrimp filling inside.

"No," PoPo said, slurping her steaming tea. "So, who is this boy Kiyo says you're seeing?"

I looked at Kiyomi, who popped shu mai into her mouth and shrugged.

"He's a lawyer," said my sister, the spin doctor of the family.

Although they rank below doctors, lawyers are still a pretty hot commodity among Chinese grandmothers the world over. Sure enough, PoPo gave a grudging sniff of approval.

"Where'd he go to school?"

"Yale and Stanford."

I waited for the inevitable question.

"Chinese?" she asked.

"Haole."

PoPo shook her head and sighed into her tea cup. "Aiya, why can't you meet a nice Chinese boy?"

I wanted to protest for many reasons, but it would've been futile. And deep down I knew matchmaking and dim sum were the purest expressions of PoPo's love. I leaned over and kissed a cheek kept supple by a concoction of special creams.

"I'll try," I said as she patted my hand.

The rice cooker belted an out-of-tune rendition of "Twinkle, Twinkle, Little Star." As if on cue, Mom and Dad walked in.

"Oh, good, you're here," Mom said. Her smile flickered as she scanned the room. "Where's Koa? We haven't seen him in a while."

Kiyomi grinned at me from behind Mom's back before escaping to help Dad grill chicken in the backyard.

"I didn't ask him," I said, busying myself with putting away the last of the dim sum.

"Why not? I thought you two were talking again."

"We are. Kind of."

A dog barked in the distance, and I wondered idly when our neighbor had replaced her beloved Boston terrier, Mushu. Mom put an apron over her work clothes and opened the fridge, taking out covered blue-and-white Japanese ceramic bowls of tsukemono, mac salad, and cold marinated spinach.

Together we set the table and several minutes later Dad and Kiyomi added a platter of yakitori.

"Turn off your phones," Mom said, as we sat down. I didn't bother—it was buried in my tote in the den.

The thing about coming back home is you quickly discover you never really grow up.

"I was hoping Koa would be here," Dad said, his tone unusually serious. "I wanted to talk to him about this Hamilton thing. I don't like you working for them when there's a killer loose."

"It's an ongoing investigation. He can't tell you anything more than what you've read in the paper," I said.

"Maybe we should call David," Mom suggested.

I ignored Kiyomi's snicker. "I can't believe I have to say this, but you can't call Koa's dad. First of all, I'm not in high school anymore. And secondly, he wouldn't know anything, anyways."

"Have you talked to him much?" Dad asked.

"Uncle David? No—"

"Not Uncle David," Kiyomi interjected. "*Koa.*"

"Oh." I weighed my answer. I wasn't sure how much I wanted my parents to know about my involvement in the case, and I definitely didn't want to fuel any speculation about me and Koa. "He and his partner interviewed me the day after it happened."

"Is that all?" Mom asked.

"Pretty much."

"You two were so close."

I avoided a reply by stabbing my knife into a chicken thigh.

"He was so naughty when he was a little kid. Do you remember when he put a gecko in your backpack?" Mom grinned at the memory.

"Well, that kid is a highly decorated law enforcement officer now," Dad reminded us. "Youngest HPD officer to make the homicide squad. He was in the news a while back when he cracked some cold case. David's real proud."

He looked at me, a stern expression on his face. "Does Koa think it's safe for you to be working with the Hamiltons?"

Highly decorated or not, it didn't matter what Koa thought. But saying so probably wouldn't help.

"Of course," I lied.

* * *

Everyone scattered after dinner—Mom and Kiyo plated dessert and made coffee while Dad cleaned up the barbecue, and PoPo rested in her room. It was just me and the geckos. From my side of the dining room window, I was content watching them snack on bugs, sipping my soda as they clicked to each other in lizard Morse code.

A neighbor's dog barked. Several seconds passed before I realized the yelps were too constant to be a living, breathing canine. I suddenly remembered the childish delight I'd taken in assigning a special ringtone for Koa when I grudgingly added his number to my new phone.

I hurried into the den and located my purse, rummaging around until I found my phone. "Guess Mrs. Matsunaga didn't get a new dog after all," I murmured under my breath. I could hear my family's voices in the other room, so I hit the ignore button. Better to talk to Koa from the privacy of my own apartment.

Sinking into the old twill sofa, I looked at the photos of the woman I'd seen Parker talking to at the funeral. I pinched the screen, zooming in on her face. A shadow fell over my screen as Kiyomi perched on the sofa's armrest, looking over my shoulder.

"Why do you have a picture of Ms. Gluten-Free Bran Muffin?" she asked.

"What?" I said, surprised. "You know her? Who is she?"

"Don't know her name. She comes into the bakery once or twice a week, always orders the same thing. I think the real question is, why are you spying on my customer?" She reached for my phone, scrolling through the photos. "What's going on, Maya? Wait. I know—you're working for Koa, ya?"

"No." I snatched my phone back. "I saw her at the funeral today. I was just . . . curious. What do you know about her, other than what she eats for breakfast?"

Kiyomi tapped her lips thoughtfully. "Works downtown, obvs. Always pays cash. I'm pretty sure she's with the state or county. You can always tell. We get a lot of cops, and lawyers 'cause of the courthouse but there's a lot of municipal offices too." She paused. "But I think she's come into some money recently."

I sat up straighter. "How could you possibly know that?" I asked, skeptical. I should've known better—my sister is nothing if not observant.

"'Cause she used to carry a J.Crew tote, and then one day she's sporting the Louis Vuitton Speedy 30, iconic monogram. Plus new designer clothes, manicures, an expensive new 'do. She's still wearing her wedding ring, though, so it's not like a postdivorce thing."

I turned to stare at my sister. "You've really thought this through."

"I like to know my customers," Kiyo said with a shrug. "Helps to pass the time. Come to think of it, your girl works with architects or contractors. She met a guy one time, and they sat outside looking at blueprints for like an hour."

Blueprints. Kiyo's café was in the heart of downtown Honolulu, easy walking distance to plenty of city offices like the planning department. I wondered if Parker's surreptitious meeting with the mystery woman had anything to do with the Kaimukī project. On one hand, it was only natural that Parker would be acquainted with the people in charge of approving his company's building permits. Then again, it came down to how well they knew each other.

"You have any photos of the guy you're seeing? Or is that pau already?" Kiyomi swiped a finger across her throat and waggled her brows at me. "I hear Koa's been hanging around Waikīkī a lot lately."

It was pointless to ask how, or even why, she knew where Koa spent his time. "I'm seeing Mark, so don't give Mom and Dad any ideas."

"Okay, fine. What's he like? Where's he from?"

I sighed. It was a lot easier maintaining a private life back home in California. "He's nice. He's from Sacramento."

Kiyomi's eyes widened, and she reached into her back pocket to take out her own phone. "That's it? Did you Google him? Forget being a reporter—that's just Dating 101."

Two years my junior, she tweets, Toks, and slays the 'Gram with baking tutorials and a blog.

"Of course I Googled him," I said, defensively. But with a name like Mark Nichols, there'd been several pages of hits, and I'd zeroed in on the first few—a bio and headshot on his firm's website as well as a short article about changing land development and environmental mitigation regulations in a law journal. It confirmed what he'd told me when we met, and I hadn't looked further. Nothing about him had set off any alarms.

Kiyomi was already swiping her phone. Her eyes widened, and she emitted a low whistle before showing me the screen.

"Marry this guy, Maya. Talk about a catch."

A quick look revealed Mark was the oldest grandson of a former Sacramento mayor, whose family had also produced a state legislator and U.S. senator. His law firm's website hadn't mentioned any of that.

It seemed Mark's family had gotten their start in land development with holdings up and down California, before branching into politics. There was even a photo of his dad shaking hands with Ted Kennedy. Reading between the lines, it appeared Mark was being groomed to follow in his father's footsteps.

What had Mark said? *People like the Hamiltons* . . . as if he wasn't one of them. Dinner roiled in my stomach.

My mom liked to say we were descended from a long line of very noble peasants, and it was a running joke in our house while my sister and I were growing up.

The more I had learned about our country's history—including the anti-Asian laws prohibiting our ancestors from entering America or owning property simply because of the shape of their eyes, the government's land grab and overthrow of the Hawaiian monarchy, and its incarceration of a hundred thousand Japanese American citizens behind barbed wire during World War II—the more I started to think my mom was right all along.

After all, those people were the ones who braved the long journey overseas to a strange new world. They overcame adversity and faced down hostility and danger to make better lives for themselves and their families. Along the way, they created rich, vibrant communities. Our country was built on the backs of those early peasant immigrants—what could be more noble?

But still I was skeptical that a middle-class girl like me would have anything in common with someone who grew up rubbing shoulders with the Kennedys.

Mom came into the living room carrying a platter of her homemade macadamia nut shortbread cookies. She eyed us and clucked her tongue. "Off with the phones, girls. It's family time."

Dutifully, we both shut off our phones.

PoPo wanted me to marry a nice Chinese doctor, but I'd settle for someone I didn't have to decipher. Mark hadn't lied per se, but he wasn't exactly upfront either. Resolving to do extensive background checks on every guy I dated in the future, I wondered why Mark would be evasive about his pedigree. Could there possibly be any truth to Koa's suspicions?

Kiyomi eyed me curiously and said in a hushed voice, "This isn't just about some date, is it?"

I didn't reply, and that was all the answer my sister needed.

She narrowed her eyes, studying me. "This is about the Hamilton case. Man, you'd better hope Mom and Dad don't find out."

Chapter Thirteen

I obsessed about Mark on the drive back to Waikīkī. I tried to remember what he'd said about his cases and the work he did on the Big Island, but realized he hadn't spilled any details. It wasn't surprising. Lawyers are supposed to be tight-lipped about their cases, right?

But then again, there's a fine line between discreet and shady.

My inner alarm was ringing, which usually made me cut and run. But I liked Mark, and I wasn't ready to ditch him for not telling me his life story after only two dates. There could be plenty of reasons for keeping some things private, and we barely knew each other. Besides, I wanted to know more about his connection to the Hamiltons. It could help me finish the book, I rationalized. But deep down, I knew I was more interested in who killed Charles. Was Kiyomi right? Did I care more about the case than Mark? Fleetingly I wondered what that said about me.

I was so preoccupied, I didn't notice the commotion in front of the Ainahau until I was nearly on top of it. Several police patrol cars were parked haphazardly, partially blocking the street, lights flashing. I thought I caught a glimpse of yellow caution tape as I slowed the Honda. I didn't give it much thought. It wouldn't be a night in Waikīkī without at least one bar fight or stolen purse.

Checking my blind spot, I steered around the black-and-whites. I had to circle the area a few times before finding a parking spot on a small side street three blocks away. I turned off the ignition and grabbed my tote, hitching it over my shoulder. I was locking my car when I remembered to turn my phone on, then dropped it back in my bag.

The street turned out to be more like an alley—dimly lit, narrow, and deserted. I could see lights from the busy Ala Moana Boulevard a block ahead. I heard rustling behind me and turned my head, nervously checking my surroundings. I caught sight of a figure in the shadows, head bowed and face covered by the brim of a baseball hat.

My pulse quickened and I walked faster, glad I'd thought to hold on to my keys. I'd read they could be used as a weapon—if you're desperate. On high alert, I jumped when my bag began chirping wildly, and by the time my heart stopped hammering, I heard a familiar voice barking my name.

What was Koa doing here?

He was up ahead, rounding the corner of my building and talking into a handheld radio. He closed the gap between us in seconds. Underneath his usually stern expression, I could see concern and fatigue. "Are you okay? Where have you been? I've been calling you."

"My phone was off. I'm fine. I just got a little spooked. What is going on?"

Koa peered over my head. Frowning, he unclipped his badge and moved me out of the way. "Sir, HPD. I'd like to—"

The figure had done an about-face, speed-walking in the opposite direction. Koa motioned two uniformed officers over. "Chang, take Maya back to her apartment and stay with her. Morse, you're with me."

"Koa . . ."

But he'd already disappeared down the dark street.

* * *

I couldn't crack Officer Chang.

His smooth baby face pegged him as a rookie fresh out of the academy, but he'd already mastered the cop stare. Clearly, he'd been hanging out with Koa too long. In the elevator ride to my apartment, he gave up only the barest facts.

"There was an incident in the vicinity of the building."

No shit, Sherlock.

"What kind of an incident? Did anyone get hurt? Does this have something to do with the Waikīkī crime spree?"

Chang's solemn face remained impassive. "I'm not at liberty to say, ma'am."

"Call me Maya."

Silence. This guy made Detective Reyes look like Jessica Fletcher.

When we reached my apartment, he did a quick security sweep and insisted on standing watch outside, even though inside offered coffee, snacks, and a comfortable couch.

"Suit yourself," I said as the door shut behind me.

Alone, I had a dozen alerts to deal with. In addition to several missed calls from Koa, there were texts and messages from everyone he'd called looking for me.

Lani answered before I heard a ring on my end. "Where have you been? Koa's been calling all over looking for you. He said your phone was shut off—he was freaking out."

Unflappable, calm, poker-faced Koa? I didn't think so. "Exaggerate much? You forget I've known him longer than you."

"By one day. Anyways, you of all people should know how he gets. Why didn't you answer your phone?"

"I wasn't ignoring him on purpose. My phone was off—

"Oh, really?"

"I'm fine," I said, disregarding her implication. "Something happened near my building."

"I know. It's all over socials. A woman was attacked. Why do you think Koa was so worried? We all were."

I groaned, thankful my parents had disavowed all social media platforms. I would have to hope it wasn't big enough news to make the paper. After I promised to keep Lani posted, we hung up, and I quickly texted Kiyomi to let her know I was home safe.

Crisis averted, I checked my phone. Lani was right. Facebook posts were flying fast and furious over this latest attack in Waikīkī. I was hoping for more facts and less speculation, but all I could find was a brief on a TV news site about police responding to a reported purse snatching near Ala Moana Boulevard.

I tried to work but couldn't settle. I walked out onto the lanai, surveying the street below hoping to see Koa and Morse. Maybe I'd overreacted and the poor guy in the baseball hat was just trying to find his car or get to a hotel.

Restless, I went back inside and stared at the computer screen for a few more minutes until I gave up and went to the door, throwing it open. No surprise, Chang was standing guard, back erect and feet planted in a wide stance.

"Everything okay, ma'am?"

"Fine. Have you heard from Ko . . . Detective Yamada?"

For the first time, Chang's stern face seemed to soften. "He's downstairs talking to the lieutenant. He'll be up shortly."

The tension in my shoulders eased, and I breathed a sigh of relief. I flashed a grateful smile. "Thank you."

"You're welcome, ma'am."

"Maya."

"You're welcome, Maya."

To pass the time, I trawled the Internet for anything Kiyomi might've missed when she'd looked up Mark and his family. Other than an old Facebook profile pic and a few travel and hiking photos on Instagram, I didn't find anything new. But an online Yale alumni magazine articles confirmed his story about knowing Stephen from their days back east.

Hitting a dead end, I switched gears. I hadn't been able to find anything on the rumored mall in Kaimukī. Now I realized I'd attacked from the wrong angle. Moments later I was scrolling through the Instagram feed for a group of merchants who'd banded together to promote local businesses. I could read the subtext. Plenty of mom-and-pop shops had folded under the pressure of nationwide big-box chains and billionaire foreign investors. Now they were fighting back.

I started to click on a post from a recent meeting when a sharp rap at the door broke my concentration. Glancing at the time, I saw it was nearly nine o'clock. I opened the door to a scowling Koa.

Chapter Fourteen

He shouldered his way inside, giving the room a quick scan before checking the lanai.

"Chang already did that," I told him, but he pushed in the pocket door anyway. "Satisfied?"

"I would be if you'd answer your damn phone."

"I'm sorry." I genuinely regretted ignoring his call. "I was having dinner at my parents'. You know how my mom is about phones."

Koa's frown eased a fraction, leaving behind some lingering worry lines. "You're okay then, ya? No one's been following or watching you?"

"What? No, of course not. Why would you . . . what's going on? Did you catch the guy with the baseball hat?"

The scowl returned. "We lost him on Hobron. We're sending officers to check security videos. It's possible he got away in a white sedan. You sure you haven't seen one following you?"

"You don't think you might be overreacting? It might've been nothing."

"Then why'd he run?" He sighed. "A woman was attacked outside your building earlier tonight—"

"I know. Lani told me, but I don't understand what that has to do with me."

"The victim's at Queen's. It's bad."

A tiny prick of fear ran up my spine. Nothing online had mentioned serious injuries. I sank onto the couch.

Koa sat next to me. "It happened near the bike cage in the back. A tourist heard moaning and found the victim behind a dumpster. She'd been beaten—badly."

"Is she going to be okay?"

He paused for a moment before shaking his head. "It's touch and go." Reaching into his pocket, he took out his phone and tapped the screen a few times before showing it to me. "I was with the family at the hospital earlier. She works at a bar around here. Her name's Lauren Higa. You know her?"

The name wasn't familiar. I studied the driver's license photo of an Asian woman with black, wavy, shoulder-length hair, a year younger than me according to the date on her ID. I sucked in my breath, shocked to realize I recognized her—it was the woman who'd stopped and offered to call 911 after I'd been mugged.

"Yeah, I've seen her around a few times," I said, still staring at the image as I tried to take in the information. "I think the building manager lets her use the bike cage. When did it happen?"

"Around five o'clock."

"That's why you called? To see if I knew her?"

Koa ran a hand over his face, and I noticed how tired he looked. "The suspect took her purse, so there was no ID. The initial description . . . sounded like you."

I stared down at the driver's license again, this time taking in her vital stats: same weight give or take a few pounds, and roughly the same height, plus identical hair and eye color.

"I don't understand. You think whoever attacked the woman tonight is the same person who mugged me, because we fit the same general description? Seems a little far-fetched, don't you think? I mean, this is Hawai'i. It's probably just a coincidence."

"Or . . ."

"What?"

Koa shook his head. "It's nothing. I was worried. You never answered your phone."

"I'm sorry. Believe me, you have no idea."

A corner of his mouth curved in a faint grin. "I figured Lani could track you down. I could hear your phone blowing up from around the corner."

I suppressed a smile. "You want coffee? I can make a pot."

He nodded. "Yeah, I'd love some."

While I scooped beans and boiled water, he found cups and rummaged in the kitchenette for cream and sugar. I watched him burn his restless energy tidying the bistro table where papers, notebooks, and pens were scattered. By the time the coffee finished brewing, he'd organized my usual clutter into a neat stack.

"You haven't changed. I don't know how you find anything, let alone work here," he grumbled, sipping his black coffee.

I dug out the leftover shortbread cookies Mom had given me and pushed the container toward Koa, before doctoring my own coffee. "You sound like Mom and PoPo. When did you turn into a little old Asian lady?"

"Funny." His tone said otherwise, but there was a faint twitch of lips.

Dunking a cookie in my coffee, I thought for a moment. "Do you think one guy is behind the Waikīkī crime spree?"

There had been over a dozen incidents in the last month, ranging from pickpocketing on the beach to late-night robberies.

Koa gave me a sidelong glance. "Off the record? Our property crimes unit thinks a gang is behind all of it. The brass put together a task force."

"Does this mean you're off the Hamilton case?" I looked at him in surprise.

"Can't get rid of me that easily. I'm still lead on Hamilton."

"Then why'd you get called in on a robbery?"

His eyes slid away, and he tugged on his ear. "I wasn't."

"I don't understand. You were at the hospital, you said you were interviewing witnesses—"

He stood, taking our empty cups to the sink where he rinsed them out. "There's an alert on this place. Where's your dish soap?"

But I wasn't distracted so easily. "What do you mean, 'an alert?'" I demanded. "Do the police think the gang is operating out of the Ainahau?"

He shut the water off with a sigh. Turning to face me, he folded his arms and leaned back against the counter.

"It's nothing like that. I put out the alert. Dispatch calls me if we get a report from here."

I gaped at him. "You did what?"

Koa fixed me with one of his steely looks, but I didn't back down. "I talked to the detective in charge of the task force. Your mugging doesn't fit. For one, all the other cases happened late at night when the vics were drunk or distracted and leaving the bars. Not in broad daylight."

I opened my mouth to argue, but he stopped me.

"And this gang targets rich tourists. They got away with diamonds, Rolexes, and a couple of designer handbags. Nothing like what went down tonight."

This time, I did interject. "I had my laptop."

"There's no resale value in used computers. Your laptop is virtually worthless." He sighed and ran his hand through his hair. "I'm worried about you, Maya. Whoever killed Charles Hamilton is still out there."

We stared at each other, both too stubborn to stand down. Until the energy shifted into something familiar, and I remembered why I'd stayed away so long. I stepped back. "I'm not seeing a connection—"

"It's there." His voice was sharp with frustration, but I needed answers.

After a long pause, Koa spoke again. "At the moment, Stephen Hamilton is our main suspect. He has a lot to gain, and he deliberately misled us about where he was the day of the murder. We're keeping an open mind. But if he was involved, then he either snuck away from Nichols, or your boyfriend gave him a false alibi."

My face grew hot. I glared at Koa, lips pursed. I wanted to throttle him for butting into my personal life—and my work. Then I saw the tense line of his jaw and his worried, tired eyes. He had always taken care of the people around him—his dad, his little brother, me, ever since his mother left his family when he was a kid.

But I couldn't let myself be drawn back into that world. "You're out of line." I pushed past him and fished out a small container of dish soap, shoving it at him. "You're taking the whole 'protect and serve' way too seriously."

"I'm just doing my job," he said as he resumed dish duty.

"Why are you so focused on Stephen and Mark? A man like Charles Hamilton must have plenty of enemies. Shouldn't you focus on finding the fake gardener? He seems like a much more plausible suspect." But even as I said the words, I knew I didn't believe them. The guy I'd met didn't seem like a killer.

"We've canvassed the entire neighborhood, and so far you're the only one that saw him, so until we have an ID, there's not much we can do," he said. "Stephen, on the other hand, lied, or at least tried to mislead us. He said he was working with Nichols downtown all morning and was only at the estate for a short time around lunch. Then he went back to work until his dad called to break the news."

I thought back to the day of Charles's murder. "He's right. He stayed for lunch, maybe forty minutes or so. I think he said something about meeting an investor."

"Yeah, Nichols backed him too. Problem is, you said you saw a red Tesla at the house when you got there in the morning—"

"Let me guess. Stephen Hamilton is the registered owner of a red S Plaid? But Charles wasn't killed until late in the afternoon. Why does it matter where Stephen was that morning?"

"Then why lie about it?" Koa was silent for a moment. "His alibi for the afternoon is shady too. Nichols backed him up, but his secretary said they hadn't been working at the office."

"Makes sense to me. Mark lives in Kaka'ako, and I think Stephen has a place somewhere around there too."

Koa's lips pressed together. "Officially, he has a condo there, but Stephen stays at a beach house on the family estate a lot."

A mansion on the ocean wasn't enough of a beach house? I wondered what kind of place it was—pool house, or secondary dwelling unit? And where exactly was it situated on the Hamilton property?

The main mansion sat on a low hill facing the mountains, its back porch leading to a manicured lawn that sloped gently onto the beach. I hadn't seen any outbuildings or even a road or path to the ocean.

"Why do you think they were at the beach house?" I asked.

"Because I know the doorman at Hamilton's condo, and he didn't verify their story." He finished wiping the counter. "We're still trying to nail down where everyone was that day, but the Hamiltons and your boyfriend aren't cooperating."

"For the last time, he's not my boyfriend." Sure, I had my questions about Mark, but not telling me about his blue-blood family was a long way from conspiring to kill a defenseless old man. And for what? Money his own family already had in abundance?

"I think you're way off base. Stephen may be a cold fish, but I don't get killer vibes from either of them. Especially not Mark," I said.

Koa handed me a washed cup to dry. "Anyone's capable of murder given the right circumstances."

I debated telling Koa what I'd learned at lunch. Technically, my relationship with Mark was personal, and he wasn't one of the book's subjects. Up until a few days ago, I didn't even know he was involved with the family. The information was fair game, I reasoned, and not covered by the NDA since it hadn't come from any of my interviews with the Hamiltons.

"There was some bad blood between Parker and his father," I said slowly. "Apparently, Parker invested heavily in some projects that didn't pan out, and Charles was threatening to leave everything to Stephen instead of Parker. From what I gather, it's all been kept on the down low, probably for the sake of the business or maybe family relations."

I left out Parker's alleged youthful indiscretions—the girlfriends who had helped him cheat his way through Punahou and possibly into Yale—as well as his meeting with the mystery woman at Kawaiahaʻo Church.

"I wonder what was in Charles's will?" I mused aloud. "Parker probably had more to gain by Charles's death than Stephen. Especially if rumors about the Kaimukī mall project are true."

"What are you talking about?" Koa asked.

I opened my laptop and showed him. He peered over my shoulder while I scrolled through the Kaimukī neighborhood group's Facebook page. Flipping past images, I slowed when I got to pictures from a meeting posted a few weeks earlier.

People lined up behind a man signing something at a table, many of them laughing and talking as they waited their turn. Other photos showed a list of action items scrawled in red on poster board, a close-up of protest signs stacked on a table, and a wide-angled shot of a room filled wall to wall with worried residents and business owners.

I squinted, zeroing in on a tall, muscular man about my age with a deep tan and angular face standing off in the corner. I gasped, slapping Koa's arm and pointing to the screen.

"It's him—the gardener."

"What?" He bent to get a closer look. "Can you zoom in?"

After a bit of right-clicking and tapping, the image reappeared, this time filling the whole screen. I maneuvered the mouse to zoom in on the man's face and bumped it up even more.

"Send that to me," he said, already tapping a number on his phone. He went onto the lanai, presumably to talk to his partner in private, leaving me to continue searching through Facebook and Instagram. There weren't any more photos of the man I'd seen in the Hamiltons' garden, and even though I clicked on everyone tagged in the post, he wasn't one of them.

But I did see someone else I knew.

"It's too late to make the late news, but Amy's working on getting the photo out first thing in the morning," Koa said, coming back into the apartment.

"Or you could ask Luke."

"What?"

I clicked on a photo. Everyone's attention was focused on a speaker at the front of the room. Taken from behind, it showed the silhouette of a man holding a red marker in his hand. The lighting was bad, and his face was turned only enough to make out a vague profile. But I'd know Koa's cousin anywhere.

Chapter Fifteen

It would've been a major scoop if I were still a reporter.

I went straight to the primary source and got the story on the fake gardener less than twenty-four hours later.

"Hey, were you able to ID the guy in the photo?" I asked Luke the following night.

We were at the brew pub in Kaimukī for a casual evening of talking story, or so Lani had texted several times throughout the day. I had a feeling something was up but couldn't resist the chance to quiz Luke. As one of the organizers for the grassroots group dedicated to protecting the Kaimukī commercial district, he'd been front and center at the meeting I'd seen on Facebook. Surely, he'd know who the fake gardener was. Or he'd at least have access to the sign-in sheets.

The first to arrive, despite running ten minutes behind, I'd snagged the last empty table. I'd waited until he was halfway through his first beer and engrossed in the 'Bows game to ask him about the gardener.

"What? Oh, yeah. Adam something . . . Haus? No, Hale. Adam Hale."

"How's it spelled?"

"Why? You writing a story or something?"

"No. Of course not. I'm just . . . clarifying."

"Who're you talking about?" Lani asked. "What guy?"

We were seated near the patio, and the trade winds blowing through the open wall of folding doors cooled our heated skin. Luke's head canted awkwardly as he strained for a view of the large-screen TV above the bar.

Someone scored a touchdown, and he jumped out of his chair, pumping his fist in victory. The ensuing cheers drowned out Lani's question. I leaned in and gave her the scoop. When the noise faded, I tried to get more info out of her longtime beau.

"So . . . who is this guy?" I asked.

Luke raised his hands and shrugged. "No clue."

Lani and I exchanged looks. "Someone must know who he is. How'd you find out his name?" I asked, trying to hide my impatience.

"I looked at the sign-in sheets. Between me and the other organizers, we knew everyone on the list except him. It was a busy night, lots of people turned out. The community's up in arms about saving businesses. So no one noticed him. If he hadn't signed in, we wouldn't have known he was there," Luke said, his gaze never leaving the television screen. "Weird."

"He was weird?" I prodded.

"No. It's strange 'cause it looks like he only went to the one meeting. It wasn't like he was some kinda die-hard activist, ya? So what was he doing at the Hamilton place?"

So far, my hot lead was cooling wikiwiki.

"Did he leave an address or contact information?" I asked.

"Yeah, some place out in Hale'iwa. I heard he hasn't been seen around, though. Koa put a BOLO out on him."

Another touchdown knocked Luke out of the conversation—he stood and announced he was getting another round of drinks.

"Were you at that meeting?" I asked Lani. "Do you remember him?"

"Vaguely, and only because I'd never seen him before. You know, the quiet type, ya? Kept to himself."

That's what neighbors always say about serial killers.

I picked at my slider. "Did the police find him?"

"Here's an idea—ask Koa. I'll bet he knows." She put down her beer to arch perfectly plucked eyebrows at me. "What's with all the questions, anyways? Aren't you supposed to be writing a book, not investigating a murder?"

"I'm not," I said, sipping my wine. "I'm just curious. And I haven't been able to work on the book for obvious reasons."

Sign-in sheets typically included email addresses or phone numbers. I was debating the best way to get Hale's contact info out of Luke, when a high-pitched tweet sounded above the din. Lani made a grab for her phone, the hopeful expression on her face fading as she read the message on her screen.

"Everything okay?" I asked, watching with concern.

She shoved the phone back into her purse. "It's nothing. We put an offer on a house and got outbid."

I was caught off guard. I hadn't even known she and Luke were house hunting.

"Can you bid again? You know, what's it called, counteroffer?"

She shook her head. "It was already a stretch. This guy sounds like an investor. He can pay almost double the asking price—in cash."

"What was the asking price?"

"Nine fifty. For a two-and-one fixer-upper."

I sputtered into my wine. "A million bucks? For a fixer-upper?"

"A tiny fixer-upper. But cute, ya? Cozy. This guy is probably just gonna bulldoze it and build some ugly-ass McMansion."

"I'm sorry, Lani. You'll get the next one." I pushed a platter at her, offering the last furikake fry as solace.

"You've been gone a long time. It's bad out there." She sighed and picked up the fry, chasing it with the last of her beer. She surveyed the restaurant. "Don't say anything to Luke, ya? It's been a long week. Let him enjoy the night."

"I won't breathe a word," I said. Lani and Luke's nearly twenty-year romance was the sole reason I believed in the whole "meant to be" thing.

Luke returned with our drinks, expertly depositing three pints in the center of the table and a glass of rosé in front of me. He took his seat next to Lani.

"How's work, Maya?" he said, before I could ask him who the extra beer was for.

"One delay after another. I'm supposed to meet with Parker on Monday. I picked up another freelance job, though. You know anyone on Tinder?"

"Yeah, lots. Why?"

I told them about the story I had just under a month to write. "I need a fresh take. My editor wants me to set up an account"—I paused for dramatic effect—"with an airbrushed profile pic."

Lani sniggered. "You should talk to Koa."

"This is a women's magazine—I need a woman's perspective. Not a grumpy cop's."

Luke interrupted before Lani could protest. "That reminds me—you coming to the party next week? Everyone's been asking about you. You could bring your 'new friend,'" he said, using air quotes. "That'd be a first, ya? I don't think we've ever met any of your boyfriends."

Because none of them had lasted long enough to cross an ocean with. I didn't know if Mark would be any different, but I had good reason not to make him my plus one at Luke's party—even if he wasn't a murder suspect's alibi.

"You wait and see. We're not meeting this one, either," Lani said. "You wanna know why? He's not—"

"Koa," Luke cut Lani off midstream.

I looked at him in surprise. Luke usually made like Switzerland during these discussions, at least in front of me. But he was staring over my head, motioning someone over, and suddenly Lani's string of hard-sell texts designed to draw me out of my writing cave for dinner with her and Luke began to make sense. A quick backward look confirmed my suspicion, as a familiar figure moved through the crowded restaurant.

"Howzit going, brah?" Koa hugged his cousin and bent to kiss Lani's cheek. Off-duty and among friends, his accent thickened and he slipped into Hawaiian pidgin.

Taking the seat next to me, he greeted me with a nod and claimed the extra pint.

Lani smirked. "What do you know about Tinder?" she asked Koa after the preliminary greetings were over. I groaned inwardly.

Predictably, he grunted. "Predators and sex offenders love it. Makes it easy for them to hunt victims and lure them into their traps. Why?"

Make that grumpy, old-before-his-age cop.

"It's also how single adults date in the twenty-first century," I said, playing the devil's advocate.

He stopped mid-sip. "You're not serious?" Shaking his head, his jaw tensed. "What does your boyfriend think about you looking for dates on the Internet?"

"We're not exclusive." My relationship status was none of Koa's business, but I found myself defending my social life anyway, even if I wasn't on Tinder. "It's not like I'm swiping left all the time."

"Right," he said.

I glared at him. "I'm not."

"You're supposed to swipe *right*." He put down his glass and turned to frown at me. "What kind of dates have you been getting?"

Luke chuckled before I could answer. "Just like old times, ya, Lani? I missed the sound of these two bickering."

"You're careful, ya?" Koa said, proceeding to tick off a litany of unsolicited personal security advice. "Meet in public places. Don't go anywhere alone. Never get in a perp's—I mean, date's—car, and make sure you tell a friend where you're—"

"No worries. I got her back." Lani said. She took out her phone and tapped it, handing it to him. The screen showed a map and a blue dot pulsing directly over the brew pub. "See? I can track Maya in real time."

"More like I can track *you*," I said. "You're the one who got lost in Disneyland."

But an idea had wormed into my head. Maybe my story needed a grumpy cop after all. "Are there a lot of cases involving dating apps? You work any of them?"

"A few. Why?"

Lani didn't bother to hide her smug grin. "You're Maya's fresh angle."

Chagrined, he huffed. "This is for a story. Figures." He narrowed his eyes, drumming his fingers restlessly on the tabletop as he considered. "I guess an article could do some good. Okay, fine. I know people you can talk to."

Told you, Lani mouthed.

Dusk had come and gone, the cooling breeze turned chilly. Lani pulled a pareo over her bare shoulders. The color of old jade with feathery tendrils of red and gold flecks reminded me of the ohia lehua tree in her parents' yard.

"Yours?" I asked, nodding at the wrap.

The beam across her face told me she'd designed the pareo. "You cold?" she asked me.

Koa turned and surveyed the paperweight cotton tank I'd thrown on. "I've got a jacket in the car—"

"Thanks," I said with a quick headshake. "But I'll be fine. Back home it's fifty degrees. I think I can handle a little Hawaiian breeze."

Directly across, a single, scrutinizing brow shot up. Lani crossed her arms and cocked her head. "Hawai'i is your home."

"Not what her Cali driver's license says."

Lani and I slanted narrowed eyes at Koa while Luke ducked behind his pint glass. I never had any intention of staying on O'ahu—my life was in California. It had been for years.

But since when did being kama'aina have an expiration date?

Chapter Sixteen

A scrap of yellow crime scene tape clung to the bike cage early Sunday morning when I went for my run. Ominous dark splotches still stained the pavement. I made a mental note to ask Koa about Lauren's condition.

Unable to sleep, I'd emailed Deidre with my latest proposal for the dating app story. By the time my alarm went off, she'd given it an enthusiastic thumbs-up. There was one caveat: I had to get my detective friend to go on the record. Interviewing Koa was a wrinkle I hadn't anticipated.

I used a long punishing run up the beach to Diamond Head to put off asking. I composed a text in the elevator on the way up to my place, half hoping he'd pass me off to HPD's public information officer. Instead, I got a curt reply two minutes later.

I'll be there at eight.

Back upstairs, I streamed the morning news on my phone while I made coffee.

"Mr. Hale attended one business owner association meeting several months ago, but he is not a member of our organization. We support local law enforcement and are cooperating fully with the Honolulu Police Department's investigation."

A familiar voice sounded in my head. I peered at the tiny screen. The reporter was interviewing a man in a gray suit and pink tie, while a headline about the Hamilton murder crawled across the news ticker. The chief of police had released Adam Hale's name to the media in an effort to bring him in for questioning, and word got out about his association with the Kaimukī neighborhood group.

The slick, well-spoken attorney on TV was none other than Luke.

"I wouldn't have believed it if I hadn't seen it for myself," I told Lani an hour later as I picked out a black V-neck top at her shop. "I take it you dressed him."

Lani smirked. "Of course. Pretty funny, ya? Luke doesn't even sound like himself at these things. He sounds . . . like you."

My friend's shop was as sophisticated and modern as Lani herself—the soothing ecru walls and matching linen drapes serving as a perfect backdrop for the vibrant array of local craftsmanship.

Named for Kaimukī's main street, Wai'alae Avenue was sandwiched between the old crack seed store and an artisanal bakery. It had earned a reputation for showcasing local fashion designers as well as Island artists and other creators.

She shook her head at my selection. "Too boring."

I surveyed Lani's cream-colored cotton tank dress, which she wore with a simple gold necklace and the Hawaiian bracelets her parents and Luke had given her.

"Funny how it's 'minimalist' on you, and 'boring' on me. Only *Vogue* writers wear haute couture. The rest of us work in T-shirts and sweats."

Lani thrust several dresses at me. "You could use a little airbrushing, ya?"

She rummaged through one of the racks and held up a jersey wrap dress in a green palm leaf print. I loved everything but the cinched waist.

When you're barely half an inch over five feet and have a penchant for mochi, your body tends to vacillate between baggy jeans and swimsuit ready. But I'd rather reach for the last chichi dango than wear a bikini any day—even in Hawai'i where swimsuit season is 365 days a year.

"It'll look great on you—trust me," Lani said.

We chatted through the dressing room curtain while I tried on clothes. I filled her in on the night the woman was attacked outside my building, complaining about Koa's over-the-top tactics. "I think the job's getting to him. He put an alert on my building."

"He's always been—"

"Overbearing?"

"Protective. Ever since his mom left. You of all people should know that. Or have you been on the mainland so long you've forgotten?"

Lani was right, as always, but this time her delivery had an edge.

I finished tugging on my shirt and pushed open the curtain to face her. "This is about Luke's party, isn't it?"

"Try go find your accent, ya?" she said, hands on hips.

Dad had never acquired Hawai'i's uniquely singsong diction, and I'd grown up with a thinner accent than my friends. Kiyomi and I usually spent summers in California with his parents, and when we came home, it took a couple of weeks for our accents to follow. Mine had slipped in and out those first few years on the mainland before fading altogether.

"I had to hear from Jimmy that you and Koa hooked up—"

"First of all, we did not 'hook up,' and secondly, who's Jimmy?" I kept my tone light, stifling my irritation.

"The waiter at Kim Chee II. You'd know that if you'd bothered to visit once in a while." Lani exhaled and crossed her arms, studying me. "You finally come home, and it's like you're a tourist on vacation. Now Koa tells me you're going back to Cali as soon as the book is all pau."

Okay, whatever was bothering Lani definitely wasn't about Luke's birthday.

"There isn't a lot of work for me here," I said. Even to my own ear, I sounded defensive.

"You're a writer. You can work from anywhere. All these years, you've come home what? Two, three times? And we all know why."

I stiffened, starting to protest until she stopped me with one of her looks. When Lani spoke again, her tone was softer. "No matter how far you go, or how long you stay away, you'll always be kamaʻaina."

Swallowing the lump in my throat, I blinked back tears. Lani knew me better than anyone, but she wasn't right about everything. I turned away, shutting the curtain behind me.

"I don't care what your driver's license says," Lani called out.

Chapter Seventeen

I looked askance at Koa, unable to mask my disbelief.

"You're on Tinder?"

I'd spent the afternoon since returning from Lani's shop scrolling through dozens of dating app profiles—men's and women's—marveling at the lengths they'd go to get someone to swipe right. Cutesy profile pics and flirty bios didn't track with the Koa Yamada I knew.

"Decoy op to draw out a suspect," he said.

But that did.

In classic Koa fashion, he'd knocked on my door exactly when he said he would.

"I've only got about an hour. I need to get back to the station to relieve Amy," he'd said. Homicide detectives, I'd learned during my brief stint reporting on the cops beat, don't get time off during active investigations. Even if it was a Sunday night.

His bulky laptop swallowed much of the space on my makeshift desk, leaving little room for our coffee. I peered over his shoulder.

"In a zombie apocalypse, you'd write poetry while exploring the Pacific in a canoe?" I read aloud from his alter ego's bio, trying to stifle laughter. "Who was the suspect you were trying to catch—the poet laureate of Hawai'i?"

"Amy filled it out," he said, answering my unspoken question.

He flipped through users, pointing out ones he'd already identified as suspicious. One profile didn't have enough photos. Another had too many "stock" pics—a dead giveaway that the hot surgeon cuddling a golden retriever puppy while volunteering for Doctors Without Borders didn't exist.

"Basic rule of thumb: If the guy sounds too good to be true, he probably is," Koa said.

I thought fleetingly of Mark. "Were there any red flags in the assault case you worked?"

Koa leaned back in his chair, reaching for a file he'd left on the kitchenette counter. "A few. The perp had no social media presence other than dating apps. And he was too eager, pushed real hard to meet in person right out the gate." He handed me a stack of papers. "It's all there."

I skimmed the pages, which turned out to be a police report for the sexual assault of a twenty-one-year-old UH student who met her attacker through a dating app. I hadn't expected this—I'd been prepared to fill out a Freedom of Information Act request to see the report. Even though it was a closed case—the suspect was tried and convicted more than a year ago—a lot of law enforcement agencies tended to drag their feet on these things. But Koa had included witness statements and even screenshots of messages and texts the rapist sent her.

Koa took me through the case, explaining how the suspect initially communicated with the young woman through the app before exchanging phone numbers and switching to texts. It wasn't long before he'd persuaded her to meet in person, luring her to a secluded beach for a romantic picnic.

"She wanted to meet at a restaurant, but this guy was a real charmer, ya? And she liked him," Koa said. "So, here's my second tip: listen to your instincts. If something doesn't feel right, go with your gut."

Blue ink smeared the side of my hand as I jotted in my notebook. "How'd you get this case, anyway? It wasn't a homicide."

Koa averted his eyes and took a sip of coffee before answering. "I did a year in Sex Crimes."

I looked up, surprised. I thought he'd started in the Homicide Division. Then I remembered Lani saying something about Koa going through a rough time.

"That's when you considered leaving law enforcement," I said.

"Lani talks too much. But, yeah. I started wondering about the choices I'd made."

"You mean leaving law school?" I'd always wondered why he'd changed course with less than a year to finish.

But he shook his head. "No regrets there. Law school wasn't for me."

"And HPD is?"

"I like catching bad guys."

I finished scrawling and underlined the last sentence. Twice. "And I love a cop I can quote." *Crap.* Cursing silently at my unfortunate word choice, I flushed under his gaze. I shut my notebook. "I think I've got what I need from you. For the story, I mean," I said, cringing.

His lips parted as if to say something but changed his mind. "Yeah, I should get back," he said, but made no move to get up.

"Any promising leads?" I asked.

He shook his head, and I waited a beat. "It's weird, ya?" he said, as if thinking out loud. "We got a warrant to trace Hale's phone, but our tech unit says it's only pinged a few times since the murder. So, I chase down security footage from businesses on opposite ends of the island and spend all day watching videos. But there's nothing. He's nowhere. It's like he's invisible."

"You'd think with his name and photo being plastered all over the news and social media, he'd have surfaced by now," I said.

"Our tip line has been flooded. All false leads." He looked at me, frowning. "So far, you're the last person to see Adam Hale."

My arms broke out in chicken skin like when we'd tell ghost stories around the campfire as kids.

How does one man disappear on an island?

Koa glanced at his watch and stood. "I gotta get back and help Amy confirm everyone's alibis. Your boyfriend ever say where he was?"

I rolled my eyes. "He's not—no. He just said he was with Stephen most of the day." I thought for a moment. "I know you think Stephen lied about being at the estate that morning, but what if it wasn't his car I saw?"

Koa, who'd begun putting away his laptop, stilled. "What do you mean?"

"I just realized, there were two red Teslas at the funeral." I told him about seeing one speeding away long after Stephen had left the church.

"So what? There were probably four or five there. Maybe more." He paused. "But I'll look into it."

He zipped the laptop case. "What's your deadline for this magazine article? I don't know when I can meet—

"You don't need to be there. Just give me her contact info and let her know I'll be calling. I can reach out on my own."

Koa frowned. "She's been pretty traumatized. The press was brutal . . ."

I grabbed the empty cups and stood, pushing past him to put them in the sink.

"I'm not going to browbeat her. I know what I'm doing." I turned back to face him, crossing my arms across my chest. "Believe it or not, I'm good at my job too."

He sighed. "I know you are, Maya. I'm just trying to protect her."

Typical Koa—surly with a side of sweet. Detective Reyes should've put that on his bio.

Chapter Eighteen

I'd wheedled my way back onto the Hamilton estate by Monday morning, negotiating an agreement to trail Parker through his daily routine despite the family's resistance. I considered it a good sign when Mrs. Goto led me into Parker's office.

I should've known better.

We spent the first hour or so going over the Hamilton family history as far back as his great-grandfather's humble beginnings in the Whitechapel district of London. I was pulling out some old photos I'd copied while doing research at the Bishop Museum, when a soft knock sounded, and Elizabeth stepped in with Stephen.

"Well, look who's graced us with his presence," Parker said. "It's about time, son."

"I had a meeting with an investor. You know—actual work." Stephen's taut lips relaxed when Elizabeth placed a hand on his arm. He made apologetic noises, kissing his mother's cheek before she left the room.

To ease the residual tension, I showed them a photo I'd found of Charles Hamilton I standing among a group of wealthy, white businessmen flanking a seated Queen Lili'uokalani, Hawai'i's last reigning monarch.

"I've never seen this picture," Parker said. "I had no idea he'd met the queen."

"He had a peripheral role in the provisional government." I chose my words carefully.

"We need to play this up—lead with it. We can make it the overarching theme of the book," Parker said.

"I'm not sure that's a good idea," I said.

"Why not? My great-grandfather hobnobbed with the queen of Hawai'i."

Stephen tossed the photo on the coffee table, snorting in derision. "And was part of a government that put her under house arrest and took her throne. Maya's right. We only just settled with the Hawaiians over that heiau in Hawai'i Kai. Do we really want to piss them off again? Over a book?"

Luke had successfully represented the Native Hawaiians in a hard-won battle to save the ancient temple from bulldozers. I wasn't going to mention I knew him or that he was related to Koa.

"Well, it's my book," Parker said, sounding like a petulant child. "And we're putting it in. Maya will find a way to finesse it, right?"

I chose my words carefully. "I'll do what I can," I said. "I'm not a public relations expert, but it's probably better to acknowledge it. These days, the information will get out, anyway, so you might as well face it head on. I wouldn't make a big deal of it, though."

A bell chimed. I glanced at my phone sitting on the side table, but the screen was dark. Parker pulled his out and peered at it.

"Sorry to cut things short, but—" His device buzzed again before he could complete the sentence. He swiped the caller into voicemail. "Damn reporters. They're on my ass for a comment on Hale. How did those vultures find out he worked here?"

My jaw dropped. Did Parker just say the number one murder suspect was an employee? Koa had been trying to identify Adam Hale for days, and the Hamiltons had known him all along. I glanced at the only other person in the room for confirmation. Stephen openly studied me, thin-lipped and grim.

"How the hell were we supposed to know Mrs. Goto hired him to clean up the grounds a couple of times? Like we're supposed to remember everyone who's ever worked here." Parker's head snapped up. "You used to be a reporter, Maya. Can't you handle them?"

"That's a bad idea." I cringed at my unchecked reaction, but I had no intention of being a mouthpiece for the Hamiltons.

"What is? You handling the press or talking to them at all?" Stephen asked.

"Both. I was hired to be a ghostwriter, not a spokesperson. As it is, I'm a witness in the murder investigation. I don't want to muddy the waters. Let your attorney speak for you."

"He told us not to comment," Parker said.

The younger Hamilton uncrossed his legs and leaned forward. "Good advice. For once, you should take it, Dad."

Batting the air as if to swipe Stephen from his field of vision, Parker stood. "Let's break for lunch. I've got to take a business call. Meet back here in ninety minutes."

I sat back as the others got up to leave. "I'm supposed to shadow you, remember?"

"I'm sorry, Maya, but this is a very important call. Highly confidential."

"I signed an NDA."

But Parker was already shaking his head. "We'll pick up again after lunch."

I checked my watch, suppressing a sigh. So much for putting in a full day's work. At this rate, I'd be stuck in paradise permanently.

I picked up my tote and made my way to the lanai, where Mrs. Goto had set up a buffet of sandwiches and fruit for lunch. Stephen was looking smug.

"So, how's the book coming? You write anything yet?" he asked.

"I've started the historical background, but we're still discussing ideas I have for the first chapter."

"Call me crazy, but shouldn't it be chronological? You know, begin at the beginning?"

I poured myself a glass of iced tea and shrugged. "It's the conventional way to go. But I'd like to try out a few other ideas first. A compelling anecdote can really grab readers and draw them in, or a significant event in his life that sets the tone for the book. It makes a more interesting read."

"Well, you're the writer, I guess."

I had the distinct feeling Stephen wasn't a fan of his father's project—or me. His next words proved me right.

"Don't take this the wrong way, but I'm only cooperating with this farce of a book for my mom. I think Dad's sinking a lot of money into a puffed-up vanity piece that's probably going to end up doing the family more harm than good," he said.

Stephen didn't have much tact for a hopeful politician, I thought.

"Ever since this thing started it's been one crisis after another. Now the cops are accusing us of withholding evidence—"

"So Adam Hale really was your gardener?" I asked.

Stephen's coffee mug landed on the table with a thud. "Why does everyone think that? Our regular groundskeeper retired. Apparently, Mrs. Goto hired this guy to do some minor cleanup work. He was here once for a couple of hours, and she paid him under the table. I saw her giving him money. But it's not like I got a good look at the guy. How were we supposed to recognize him, let alone know his name?"

So had Mrs. Goto lied about knowing Hale or was it an innocent mistake? Detective Reyes had said my composite sketch could've been anyone. By all accounts, Mrs. Goto was a devoted employee. Why would she protect someone who might be Charles Hamilton's killer? My reporter's instincts kicked into high gear.

Stephen continued, "We told the police to check out the activist groups. They've been hounding us for years. Just last month we caught someone trying to break into the beach house. It was only a matter of time before one of them got violent."

"Your beach house?" I asked.

He shook his head absently. "It's the family's. We all use it."

"Any idea what Hale was up to?"

"Who knows? Probably trying to dig up some dirt." Stephen stopped, narrowing his eyes at me. "Kind of like you. Mark tells me you know that cop."

I met his hostile gaze head on, not taking my eyes off his but saying nothing.

"I believe he said you two dated, so I'm guessing you know him pretty well."

I kept my voice even. "Well enough to know he's good at his job. He'll catch the killer—whoever it is."

He nodded, not backing down. "I don't know the ins and outs of your contract with us, but I know our attorney wouldn't neglect to include a nondisclosure agreement."

Yeah, but I had a lawyer too, and Luke had made sure criminal investigations were exempt from the document I signed. I did have some standards. The Hamiltons could still fire me, though, so I'd have to tread carefully.

But I didn't like bullies.

"My contract is with your father. Not you."

I needed a walk to cool down. Turkey sandwich in hand, I followed the white pebbled path back to the Japanese garden, where I settled onto a wooden bench under the banyan. After a morning cooped up indoors it was good to stretch and breathe fresh air. It was cool in the shade of the banyan, and I could feel the gentle trade winds on my face as I took in the surroundings. There was a low lava stone wall with bright red Hawaiian ginger growing beside it. Even the cacophony of chirping birds could not drown out the surf. Large gold, white, and black fish swam lazily around the base of a low waterfall in the koi pond. Scraps of bread from my sandwich whipped the Japanese carp into a frenzy, their bodies turning into a squirming mass in the water as their mouths gaped open in search of crumbs.

I checked the time. I still had twenty minutes before I was due back at Parker's office. I decided to explore the grounds, so I made my way back to the pebbled walkway.

Chicken skin broke out on my arms as the temperature dropped in the shade. A breeze parted the banyan's tendrils, revealing a break in the stone wall. Curious, I went to examine it. At first, it looked like a few stones had fallen, but as I drew closer I realized it was actually designed to make way for a narrow, unpaved trail nearly hidden by foliage.

I stepped onto the red, volcanic dirt and began following the path. I wasn't great with directions, but as I picked my way through overgrown ferns, I guessed the trail cut through the dense trees and shrubs bordering the estate. At first glance, it didn't appear the route was used much, until I noticed footprints in the damp earth.

A few minutes later, the path ended abruptly at a gate. I peered through the wood planks into the side yard of a small, raised bungalow situated above the shoreline. *The Hamilton beach house.*

I pressed my palm against the gate. Clacking footsteps approached the front of the house, and instinct made me duck back onto the path, where the trees shielded me from view. A door slammed, and I peeked again through the wooden slats.

Heels tapping on the veranda told me the visitor was a woman, but I could only make out a fleeting glimpse of lavender. I reached into my tote, searching for my phone to zoom in for a closer look. My fingers scraped bottom before I realized I'd left it behind in Parker's office.

The footsteps stopped, and I heard the front door rattle, then a light rap. But no one answered. Irritated huffing was followed by fumbling noises as the woman rummaged around in her purse.

"How could you do this to me, Parker? I rearranged my entire day to be here." She was apparently talking on her phone. She listened, but his response didn't seem to pacify her. "Whatever. I fixed your permit, but now my guy wants more money. Quick, ya? Before he changes his mind."

I still couldn't see her, but it had to be the woman in the teal dress. She resumed walking, so I crept along the wall to hear more. I stepped on a large twig, and the snap seemed to thunder. I froze.

"Hold on. I thought I heard something," she said into the phone. "I gotta go. We'll talk later."

I didn't breathe, hunched under the cover of trees, until eventually her footsteps receded. My ears pricked at the high-pitched, intergalactic whirring I now recognized as a Tesla, until that too faded.

Chapter Nineteen

I was tempted to check out the house now that it was empty, but I retraced my steps back to the mansion. I was picking leaves out of my hair as I hurried through the garden and past the pool, my mind reeling.

The shortcut linking the estate to the beach house blew apart Stephen Hamilton's alibi—maybe Mark's as well. Stephen, who'd lived on the estate his entire life, must've known about it. The footprints I came across were proof someone used it. He could've easily run to the main house, killed Charles, and made it back to his place in under five minutes.

I didn't like Stephen much, but his grief at Charles's funeral seemed genuine, and I just couldn't see Mark vouching for a killer.

It was still early, so I passed time by picking at the fruit and pastries on the lanai, every once in a while looking over my shoulder half expecting to see Parker's mistress barreling through the shrubs.

"You like a soda or what? We have Hawaiian Sun too, ya?"

Silent in her zoris, Mrs. Goto seemed to materialize on the lanai. All pretense of formality dropped, her pidgin shone through like her relaxed, easy smile. Instead of a mu'umu'u, she was wearing a loose-fitting shirt dress, the abstract white lines against deep purple somehow still forming an obvious Hawaiian print.

"Mahalo, auntie." Faint traces of my old accent slipped in as I accepted the cold can of guava juice. "You've worked for the Hamiltons a long time, ya?"

"Since Parker was a keiki. I started in the mailroom, worked my way up to Mr. Hamilton's personal assistant. Now, I manage the estate."

I did the math. By my rough calculations, Mrs. Goto had been working there for close to fifty years.

"No plans to retire?" I asked.

She shook her head. "I don't know what I'd do with myself if I didn't work. Besides, I practically raised my daughter here. It's like home, ya?"

I remembered Parker's former classmate had told me at the funeral that Mrs. Goto's daughter died years ago. I wondered if she stayed in part to feel close to her only child.

"I have a grandson." Mrs. Goto produced a wallet-size folio and thrust it in my face. "Cute, ya?"

I made the appropriate noises as I flipped through several pictures of a sleeping infant. The edges were worn, and it was clear she frequently removed the photos from the plastic protectors. Her hand trembled, and I looked up to see her smile had faded. The photos disappeared back into her dress pocket. She sniffled.

"Are you—?"

Mrs. Goto brushed aside my question by pointing to a large manila envelope on the table. "Mr. Hamilton asked me to put together family photos. I had copies made."

"Thank you." I opened the envelope and pulled out several photos of Charles Hamilton with his wife and son. "He must've thought very highly of you."

"He was a good man. Difficult, but fair."

"And Parker?"

Mrs. Goto didn't reply, but her eyes said it all. My eyes fell on the cracked pavings as I remembered the crumbling wall and overgrown Japanese garden. Minuscule details were often telling.

"What really happened to the gardener?" I asked, looking up.

"He . . . quit."

"So you hired Adam Hale to do some work around here?"

She frowned. "No. Who told you that?"

"Stephen—"

"Well, he's wrong. It was Mr. Charles. I only paid him."

I gaped at Mrs. Goto. "If you saw Adam Hale here, why didn't you identify him to the police? They think he might be the killer."

"He's not." Mrs. Goto's vehement response took me by surprise. "He . . . seemed like a nice boy. He wouldn't hurt Mr. Charles."

I had more questions, but I never got to ask them. Heels rapped briskly on flagstone, and the estate manager resumed stacking dishes as they drew closer.

"Mrs. Goto, Parker would like his tea soon. And please be sure to clear the lanai by dinner," Elizabeth said, her lips thin and tight. She turned to me, adding, "Parker has to take an overseas call. It'll be a little while longer."

Disappointed I couldn't question Mrs. Goto further, I checked my watch. "Fifteen minutes okay?"

"Better make it one o'clock. These things tend to run long," she said, smiling apologetically.

I nodded, chastising myself for once again leaving my phone behind. So instead of catching up on emails, I passed the next half hour going over notes. Promptly at one, I climbed the steps onto the wraparound porch and headed to the east side of the mansion, hoping to prod things along.

Low, tense voices carried through the open French doors leading to Parker's office. I hung back, wondering if I should go back to the lanai.

". . . not codicil. Holographic . . ."

I could barely make out Parker's voice, but Elizabeth's came through loud and clear.

"Couldn't we contest it? You're in bed with everyone at city hall. You must know a judge or two."

"Maybe if you hadn't blown millions on that damned foundation, we'd be in a better position," Parker said.

"That foundation helped a lot of kids." There was an iciness in Elizabeth's voice I'd never heard before. "You need to clean up your mess before it's too late."

A light tap on the interior office door signaled the arrival of Parker's tea. By the time I made my entrance, Mrs. Goto was pouring the steaming liquid into a porcelain cup edged with gold leaf. Elizabeth dismissed the older woman with a wave of her hand.

"Don't forget about the foundation gala tonight, darling," she said, handing him a teacup.

A muffled buzzing from the leather sofa caught my attention, and I remembered my missing phone. I crossed the room and reached for the glowing screen, realizing immediately the phone wasn't mine. Two missed calls, but only one name jumped out at me—the Honolulu district attorney. Had there been a development in the murder investigation?

"Is this yours?" I picked up the device and held it out to Parker.

Patting his pockets, he said, "How'd that get there?"

"It's a mystery, darling," Elizabeth said. "Thank you, Maya. My husband is always losing his phone."

I found my own device right where I'd left it on the side table. The screen lit up with missed texts from Mark confirming when he'd pick me up for our dinner date at a downtown restaurant. I smiled at the reminder. We'd made plans days earlier, and it had slipped my mind. My finger hovered over the thumbs-up icon, remembering the path to the beach house. Koa's voice echoed in my head.

Watch your back.

"I'll meet you there," I texted instead.

Stephen didn't make another appearance. I wrote with Parker hovering over me for a couple hours before there was a knock on the door.

Elizabeth swept in without waiting for a reply. The long skirt of her pale pink gown swooshed across the polished wood floor. Shiny baubles glittered at her throat and wrist.

"Darling, it's getting late. We have to be at the hotel by five o'clock," she said.

Parker let out a low whistle, and she flushed with pleasure.

"Still the prettiest girl at the party," he said, standing to kiss his wife's cheek. "Maya, will you take our photo?"

I framed the shot, zooming in on the picture-perfect couple. A click of the shutter captured the Hamilton illusion.

Chapter Twenty

Back home, I kicked off my shoes and sank onto the couch. I'd debated what to do with the information I'd learned at the Hamilton estate, and the short drive from Diamond Head to Waikīkī helped me reach a decision—of a sort.

I texted Luke for his advice, but in my heart I knew I would end up spilling everything to Koa. I had to trust my friend and pro bono lawyer to protect me from getting sued for my conscience. I doubted he could save my job.

While I waited to hear back from Luke, I opened my laptop to check a hunch.

In the short time I'd known the Hamiltons, I'd spent almost more time walking their property than working, and I knew there was only one road leading from the gate to the main house. But I'd distinctly heard the woman opening and closing a car door, and from the glimpse of red I'd caught I guessed it was the Tesla I'd seen the morning of Charles's death.

I suspected the beach house wasn't part of the original estate. I checked Google satellite images and found what I was looking for—a small, residential street with two beachfront homes, including one directly adjacent to the Hamilton estate.

My suspicion confirmed, I reached for my bag and dug out the manila envelope, spilling its contents on the coffee table. A quick sift through the photos revealed nothing new. I'd seen most of them before, either on the grand piano in the parlor or in newspaper clippings, but the last two caught my eye because they appeared to be original prints, unlike the others.

Ruffled tuxedo shirts and empire waist gowns dated one photo of Parker and his friends to their '70s senior prom.

The second was a candid shot of Stephen as a tow-headed toddler, sitting on a blanket next to a young woman in a purple muʻumuʻu, the trade winds whipping shoulder-length black hair across her face. Probably Mrs. Goto. Someone had scrawled a barely legible date on the bottom right corner: *Sept. '88*. There were also a few baby photos, like the ones Mrs. Goto had shown me, and I wondered if some of her pictures had somehow gotten mixed up with the Hamiltons'.

Next, I took out the articles I'd copied at the library, sifting through the papers until I found a business story about Hamilton, Inc. At the time, Charles was at the helm with Parker poised to take over the multimillion-dollar family business. In addition to the development company, Elizabeth Hamilton was head of a charitable foundation, and the family had real estate holdings throughout Hawaiʻi.

In other words, there was a crapload of money at stake. Supposedly.

It was too soon for the will to have been recorded with the county, but from the news clippings, it was assumed Parker would inherit the bulk of the wealth with his son and wife benefiting indirectly.

My concentration was broken by my beeping phone.

"My client canceled our afternoon meeting. Any chance you can meet earlier, say in an hour?" Mark asked.

"Sure. See you in a bit."

I hung up, placing the photos on top of the pile and went to get ready. I'd neglected to account for how long it would take me to primp for our date, and I was running behind schedule when my phone rang again.

The caller was unknown, and I was tempted not to answer, but I did anyway.

Silence.

"Hello?" I repeated.

A beep told me whoever it was had hung up.

When I arrived at the restaurant, Mark was already waiting for me at a table by a wall of windows overlooking King Street. His eyes widened in appreciation when he spotted me, and he smiled, standing and kissing me on the cheek.

I'd worn the dress I'd gotten from Lani's shop, only this time I'd ditched the cardigan and paired it with slinky black heels. He spent the first few minutes telling me about his day off hiking across the Kilauea Iki crater.

"It was incredible, exactly the way you described. I thought I was on another planet," Mark said.

The waiter arrived with our entrees, and after a few bites, he asked, "So, how's the book coming?"

I'd barely started this book, and I already hated that question. I raised my shoulders in a hapless gesture and told him about the argument between father and son. I wasn't telling him anything he didn't already know about the Hamiltons. "What Stephen said made a lot of sense, not that I think we should ignore the issue, but Parker wants to play it up like it's a badge of honor. I think it could backfire on him," I said. "I'm bumping into factual issues too, which could also bite him in the ass."

Mark huffed. "Sounds like Parker. He has a tendency to, shall we say, embellish? He likes to weave a good story, doesn't mean it'll be the truth. It's how he got into hot water over a couple of projects."

"What happened?" My journalistic Spidey-sense tingled.

"He had an idea to build a big arena and concert venue on the Big Island, attracted some major investors from all over the world with his plan to bring pro baseball to Hawai'i and build the next Waikoloa-type resort town."

"They've been trying to bring pro sports to Hawai'i for years, but it's not a big enough market," I said, puzzled.

"Exactly. The numbers didn't add up. But Parker wasn't having it, and he blew through what was left of his money trying to make it happen."

"I don't understand. Are you saying the Hamilton fortune is gone?"

Mark finished sipping his wine. "Not the Hamilton money. Parker's mom left him a tidy sum—enough to keep most people in the lap of luxury for the rest of their lives."

"But not Parker," I said.

"He blew it all, which is why Charles controlled the Hamilton purse strings until the day he died."

"I don't remember hearing anything about the arena deal, and nothing came up in my article search."

Mark lifted his brows. "That's because Charles spent a pretty penny to hush everything up and pay off the investors. It hadn't gotten very far in the planning process, so there wasn't an official paper trail, just a lot of expensive land use studies."

Maybe his rumored Kaimukī mall would meet a similar fate. I pushed the thought aside and played another hunch.

"Did Charles leave a holographic will?"

Mark didn't have much of a poker face for an attorney. His jaw drop was all the confirmation I needed. He cleared his throat, wiping his mouth with the cloth napkin. "Not that I know—I mean, he threatened to. Supposedly, he was going to cut Parker out."

"And leave everything to Stephen?"

He shrugged. "Guess so."

I sipped my wine, letting the information sink in. With his own money gone, Parker stood to lose everything to his son. He had a better motive for doing away with Charles than Stephen did.

A beep sounded from the vicinity of Mark's pants. Looking abashed, he reached in his pocket to check his phone, peering at the screen. He tapped it a few times, then shut it off and put it away.

"Sorry about that. It was . . . work."

I pushed my food around on the plate. "You haven't said much about what you're working on. Exactly what kind of case do you have on the Big Island?"

He gave me a sheepish look. "It's pretty boring stuff. Even puts me to sleep sometimes. Environmental impact reports and corporate investments aren't exactly scintillating dinner conversation."

"So why don't you talk about your family?" I said.

To his credit, he didn't bat an eyelash. "Knowing your line of work, I'm surprised it took this long to come up." He put his fork down with a sigh. "They're kind of the reason I took the job here. Bad breakup with a woman who'd been more in love with the idea of my family than with me. She didn't realize I'm the black sheep, and glad of it. I'm not interested in politics. So, when it all came to an end, I decided I needed a change of scene."

"People here don't know who your family is?" I asked.

"Nope. I'm just another haole in a suit." He paused, studying me closely. "Look, I really like you, and I want to see where this goes. I know things are a little complicated right now. So for the time being, I'm going to assume whatever I say is on the record and could possibly reach a certain homicide detective's ear."

It was more than fair, and I was reminded again why I liked him. It had been a great—not to mention informative—date, and for a moment, when he kissed me, the whole, messy murder investigation thing faded from my mind.

Then he invited me back to his place, tempting me with promises of a nightcap and great ocean view, and I heard Koa's warning in my head.

"Maybe next time," I demurred. He took the rejection gracefully with a nice goodbye kiss before shutting my car door.

Fifteen minutes later, I entered the Ainahau's lobby, bumping into the building manager's wife.

"Kinda early night for a date, ya?" she teased after looking at her watch. "Not a keeper, huh?"

I raised my hands as I headed to the elevator. "Not sure yet, Mrs. Lopez. Too soon to tell." I fished for my keys during the ride up to the twelfth floor. But I was still empty-handed when the elevator pinged a few minutes later. Cursing my cavernous tote, I stepped into the landing and blindly made my way down the corridor while rooting through pens, notebooks, phone cord, gum, and the occasional dried-up lip balm. Nearing my door, I realized I was squinting, and my breath quickened.

Something was wrong.

The security lights were out, leaving half the hallway pitch black.

My fingers brushed metal, and for the second time in less than a week I found myself clutching keys as a makeshift weapon. The slinky heels I'd taken such care in selecting earlier clacked noisily against the tiled floor, announcing my progress.

I paused when I reached my apartment. *What would Koa do?* No doubt lecture me to walk away and find help.

Pursing my lips, I reached for my phone, tapped the flashlight tool, and scanned the darkness. It was empty save for a skittering gecko.

I let out a breath, chiding myself for overreacting. I inserted the key and gave it a turn, giving the door a push.

It didn't budge.

I twisted the key again, and this time the door popped open. *Had I forgotten to lock up in my rush to leave for dinner?*

I stepped inside, ignoring the faint alarm bells. Papers and photographs were strewn across the floor, fluttering in the breeze coming in through the open window. Dangling cords and a gaping space on the bistro table were all that was left of my laptop.

I swore, my face hot. I started to dial 911 when I hesitated. My finger hovered over another number on the screen.

The air behind me shifted, the sour smell of sweat and something vaguely woodsy filling my nostrils. I tried to scream, but it was too late. An arm wound around my neck, choking off my air and turning my cry for help into a muffled gurgle.

I clawed at the arm, desperately trying to sink my nails into skin, but got only cloth. Flailing, I kicked at my attacker, but he tightened his hold, nearly lifting me off my feet.

I couldn't breathe. Bursts of light flashed behind my eyelids. Summoning the last of my strength, I reached up behind me and clawed at his eyes.

I hit my target. The arm loosened, and I wrenched free, heaving in gulps of air.

Breathing cost me. I was too slow on the offense. I turned to kick at my attacker, but my head erupted in pain.

Knees thudded on carpet, and as I crumpled to the floor, I thought I heard Koa's voice before everything went black.

Chapter Twenty-One

I woke to a blinding light, and a voice shouting in my head.

"Ms. Wong! Ms. Wong, are you okay?"

I squinted and tried to sit up, groaning when the pain hit me.

"Your friend called the paramedics. They'll be here soon. Can you sit up? Are you hurt anywhere else? What happened?"

The questions were coming too fast, and I had a few of my own. Like where was I? And who was shouting at me?

When my vision came into focus, I found myself staring into the worried eyes of Brent Lopez, the building manager's son. Smart and studious, he was on track to go to med school at UCLA. Now he aimed a small flashlight in my face, pressing his fingers into my right wrist.

I opened my mouth and croaked, my throat burning.

Then I remembered. The mess in my living room, my missing laptop, and the sickening smell of sweat.

"Can you tell me your name?" Brent asked. "Who is president?"

Irritably, I shook him off. "Give me a sec." I finally managed to get out, my voice hoarse and raspy. "My head . . . hurts."

I raised my hand, tentatively touching the back of my skull. Feeling something sticky, I looked at my bloodstained fingers, fighting back nausea.

"Head wounds bleed a lot, even minor ones. Can you stand? I called 911, but we need to leave, ya? Get you somewhere safe."

Brent gently helped me off the floor, holding me steady until I got my feet under me, and we made our way to the elevator. Never letting go of my arm, Brent resumed his questions during the ride down to the ground floor, where his parents occupied a three-bedroom unit.

"Do you know your name?" he asked.

I told him, throwing in my middle name, then rattled off the year and name of our commander in chief as further proof I was firing on all cylinders.

Mrs. Lopez took charge the moment she threw open the door, ushering me to the floral print sofa in a cozy living room. I sank onto the soft cushions, wondering vaguely if I'd be able to get up again.

Mrs. Lopez hurried into the kitchen, returning with a glass of water and a cold compress for my head.

"Drink," she said, leaving no room for argument.

I did what I was told. The cold liquid soothed my aching throat.

"Your friend is on his way," Brent said.

"My friend?"

Footsteps sounded in the hallway, followed by a rap on the door and the answer to my question.

"Jesus, Maya—are you okay? What happened?"

Koa crossed the room in a few long strides, squatting as he peered at me, a frown etched on his face.

"I checked her vitals. They're good," Brent said. "She was disoriented at first, but she was coherent in the elevator and was able to answer basic questions."

Koa nodded, glancing up at the physician-in-training. "Good work. Thanks." He reached up, gently tilting my head so he could examine the wound.

"What are you doing here?" I rasped.

"What's wrong with your voice?"

"I asked first."

"I've got a badge."

Haltingly, I told him everything, the effort further weakening my voice. Koa sucked in his breath and swore. I was about to repeat my question, when I remembered the alert he'd put on the Ainahau.

"How'd you get here before anyone else?" I asked instead.

"You called me."

"No, I didn't." I tried to force certainty in my voice, but my thoughts were fuzzy.

His cop's eyes raked me up and down, the lines on his brow deepening. I squirmed.

"How long was she out?" he asked Brent.

"I'm right here, and I'm fine. I didn't call you—" A memory jogged loose. "I was going to call 911," I amended lamely.

"How long was she unconscious?" Koa repeated.

"I can't be sure, but it wasn't long, A minute or two, tops," Brent said.

Vigilant since the attack on Lauren, Brent had noticed the darkened hallway when he came up to the twelfth floor to work on a unit near mine. He'd called out, but it had taken a few moments for his eyes to adjust to the dim light.

"Ms. Wong's door was wide open, and I could hear you on the phone, so I went inside and found her lying there." Brent frowned. "I think I might've heard the stairwell door shut. It's kinda loud, ya? I should've checked. But I thought Ms. Wong had an accident or fell—nothing like this has ever happened at the Ainahau."

Koa stood and placed his hand on Brent's shoulder, reassuringly. "You did good. Do me a favor? When the officer comes down, show him whatever security cameras you've got."

Turning to me, he said in his no-nonsense-cop voice, "You're going to the hospital."

The stinging pain at the back of my head had already dulled to an ache. The last thing I wanted was to spend hours in an uncomfortable chair waiting to be seen by a doctor who would only tell me what I already knew.

"I'm fine. I just need some rest."

Footsteps thudded in the hallway, and soon paramedics were tromping into the Lopez apartment. One of them, a woman, greeted Koa and he moved aside. While he briefed her on the situation, she bent to flash a penlight in my eyes.

"Miss, can you understand me?" she asked, staring into my pupils.

Again, I rattled off my name, the date, and leader of the free world while she parted my hair with gloved fingers and examined my head.

"Chokeholds can be pretty nasty. Are you having trouble breathing?" She pressed a stethoscope to my chest.

"Only when there's an arm around my neck," I said. I took a deep breath and exhaled slowly. "See? I'm fine now."

"That's for me to say, ya? Open wide." She shone the penlight in my mouth and examined my throat. "You have a mild concussion. You were lucky. I've seen a lot worse—"

"See, Koa? I told you. I'm fine."

She arched her brows. "You two know each other?"

"Long story," Koa said.

"Aren't they all? Well, I was going to say, you need to get checked out, anyway, to make sure there wasn't any damage to your trachea, ya?"

"I have the right to refuse transport," I said.

They exchanged glances.

"That's true," she said. "I can't force you to go to the hospital for treatment."

Koa folded his arms across his chest. "But I can."

I scoffed. "How?"

He bent to look me in the eye, his lips curving in a smug grin. "I've still got Auntie Linda on speed dial."

Chapter Twenty-Two

It was a cheap shot.

"Worked, ya?" Koa said, when I told him as much three hours later.

"This stays between us. My mom will freak if she hears what happened."

Clad only in a worn hospital gown, my bare backside covered in chicken skin from the overly air-conditioned exam room, I was in no position to bargain. And he knew it.

We'd been at the medical center for close to three hours by then. The hospital corridors were crawling with patrol officers, guarding the waiting room, taking my statement, or talking to Koa in hushed voices. Someone hauling a large caddy came by to swab my neck and hands for DNA, even collecting my clothes as evidence. When I was finally whisked off to see a doctor, Koa had flashed his badge at the nurse and insisted on accompanying me.

Now he was slumped in the hospital chair, his long legs stretched out in front of him. Eyes closed and shielded by dark sunglasses to block the harsh fluorescent lighting, he could've been asleep. If it weren't for the faint, upward tug on his lips.

"You, me—and HPD."

"Koa—"

The grin faded. He sat up, took off his glasses, and narrowed his eyes at me. "I won't tell your parents you were attacked in your own apartment and nearly killed. But don't you think you should?"

"Nope."

He sighed and slouched back in the chair. "Have it your way."

A nurse in blue scrubs pushed open the accordion door that served as a partition between exam rooms. Pretty with dark hair and salon-kissed highlights, her face brightened as she smiled and batted eyelash extensions at Koa.

"Nice to see you, Detective. You're working late, ya? Caught a bad case or what?" she said, not even glancing my way.

"Just making sure Maya's okay. She's had a rough night. Any idea how much longer?"

She sat at the computer terminal and began tapping the keys. "Are we admitting her?"

"No," I said.

"Depends on the doc." There was an unmistakable note of warning in Koa's tone.

She looked up from the screen to eye us curiously. "We've ordered an MRI, and she's next in line, so it shouldn't be much longer."

"I'll be fine, if you need to leave," I said after the nurse had gone. I winced at how the words sounded. We'd been waiting an hour, but truthfully, I didn't want to be alone. Koa's presence was comforting.

Back at the Ainahau, I'd watched him issuing orders to the other officers, efficiently managing the crime scene and search for the culprit from the makeshift command station in the Lopez apartment. In addition to collecting security tapes, I knew they'd already interviewed a tourist staying in one of the units who'd seen a figure in dark clothes running from the rear stairway exit.

"Amy's got it covered. How's your head?"

"Better. Thank you."

"Just doing my job." He looked away, then suddenly turned back to me. "You said, 'he.' What makes you think the perp was a man?"

I hadn't gotten so much as a glimpse of my attacker. "Just a feeling, I guess. Whoever it was wore long sleeves, like a sweatshirt or something, but the arm seemed . . . big. Which means nothing. It could've been a tall, really buff woman."

"What about a voice? Or smell?"

I closed my eyes and thought back, trying to organize a jumble of scattered thoughts and impressions. And then I remembered.

"Bergamot," I said. "I smelled cologne."

"Okay, that's good. Definitely male," he said. "Recognize it from anywhere?"

I shook my head. "Not really. No."

"Tell me again, what happened tonight?"

I gave him a rundown of my activities. I'd left my apartment at about a quarter to seven and arrived at the restaurant on the hour. Mark and I were there until shortly after nine o'clock. By the time I got home it was nine fifteen.

He listened closely but didn't take notes. "Who else knew you'd be out?"

I thought for a moment. "No one. I may have mentioned it to Lani, but that's it. Why?"

Koa shrugged. "Just covering all the bases. You came straight home after dinner? You didn't go to Nichols's place?"

I shook my head. "He asked, but I said no."

As soon as the words escaped my lips, I understood Koa's line of questioning. I wondered how my life had gotten to the point where I avoided being alone with a cute, smart, funny guy because my ex suspected him of protecting a killer—or worse.

As if reading my mind, Koa said, "If he cares about you, he'll stick around."

It was like a stab in the heart. A rush of memories I'd buried years ago hit me. Once upon a time, I thought Koa would stick around. I couldn't have been more wrong.

Eventually, an X-ray tech came to get me, and when I returned to the curtained-off exam room, my purse and a small duffel sat on the seat next to Koa. Before I could ask, a doctor came in and promptly declared I was free to go.

"You have a mild concussion," he said, rattling off a list of symptoms I should watch for. "The swelling in your throat should go down after a few days. Take some Tylenol for the pain and be sure to get plenty of rest."

I threw Koa an I-told-you-so look, but he ignored it.

"I had an officer pack some things for you," he said. "I'll drop you off at your parents' house."

"What are you talking about? I'm going back to my place."

"You can't stay there tonight. The lock on your door is busted. Your apartment is a crime scene. It's not safe. I'm taking you to your parents or Lani's, whichever you prefer."

I sighed, too exhausted to argue.

* * *

Koa was silent as we drove through town. I waited until he pulled onto Kalaniana'ole Highway to prod him.

"What aren't you telling me?" I asked.

He stayed mum until I repeated my question, this time more forcefully. "Tonight doesn't fit the MO of the other cases. Those were petty crimes—pickpocketing, a few thefts, and a couple street muggings."

"No burglaries?" I asked, skeptically.

"Not on the twelfth floor of a building with a twenty-four-hour front desk. There're too many risks for your typical burglar. This wasn't a crime of opportunity. It was intentional."

He stopped short of mentioning the assault outside my building.

"Are you saying I was specifically targeted? Why?"

Koa sighed, running a hand through his hair. "There's no proof of that, but—"

"What?"

"I don't believe in coincidence, so let's play it safe, ya?"

Niggling doubts crystalized. "Mark got a text."

He glanced at me, not understanding.

"I didn't tell anyone about tonight. Not even Lani," I said. "I couldn't because I forgot we had a date. No one else knew I'd be out of my apartment."

The passing light flickered across his impassive face, but the muscles in his arm tensed as he tightened his grip on the steering wheel.

"What time did he get the text?"

I thought for a moment and shrugged. "It was after our entrees were served . . . sometime after seven thirty. He said it was work."

"What'd he do next?"

"Nothing. He answered it and put his phone away."

"He didn't take any calls or leave the table?"

I shook my head. Maybe it was the knock on the head, but suddenly other coincidences seemed to fall into place.

"Everything happened so fast after the murder—I didn't put two and two together," I said. "I had breakfast with Mark the next day. I told him I was going to the library and planning department for research."

His face grim, Koa said, "When you were mugged." His fists clenched when I nodded. "I don't want him anywhere near you."

I waved off his concerns. "He's on the Big Island for the next few weeks."

I couldn't believe I'd been wrong about Mark. Or was I letting Koa's suspicious nature get to me? I knew there was something else I'd forgotten, but my skull had begun to ache again. I touched the back of my head. After tonight, I was willing to entertain the possibility Koa was right about someone targeting me. But I had no idea why.

The car came to a stop, and when I looked out the window, I was surprised to see we'd already arrived at my parents' green stucco house. There was no traffic this late at night, but I'd been too preoccupied to notice. He put the SUV in park and opened his door.

Then I remembered the beach house.

"I found something at the Hamilton estate," I said, watching as he shut it again. I told him about the path between the garden and beach house, and the woman Parker stood up. "From what I heard, she's more than his mistress. It had to have been her car I saw that day. You didn't find the path when you searched the estate?"

Koa shook his head. "No. Our warrant was only for the pool and lanai areas."

"Stephen has to know it's there. He could've easily gone back and forth from the beach to the estate the day of the murder." I cut him off before he could deliver another lecture. "I was going to tell you, but I wanted to talk to Luke first. I signed an NDA, remember?"

"There's more." I ignored the choking sound he made and told him about Parker's tense encounter with Elizabeth. "It was something about a holographic will. The development company alone is worth millions, and the family has a bunch of other businesses all over the country. There's a lot of money at stake."

Koa swore. "Have you ever considered they're watching you as much as you're watching them?"

"I was careful, and it wasn't like I was looking for any of this—it just came up," I retorted. Hastily, I added. "I know what I'm doing."

"You're a *writer*, Maya. Not an undercover cop."

"I was a reporter. I covered my share of dangerous stories," I bluffed.

"You covered city council meetings and the occasional wildfire."

I gaped at him. "You said—"

"I've known you my whole life. We went out for three years. Of course, I looked up your stories. We have Internet in Hawai'i, you know."

Koa had an innate knack for being annoying and endearing at the same time.

"It's my job to catch the killer—not yours," he said. "You just need to stay alive."

Chapter Twenty-Three

High-pitched chirping slowly penetrated my muddled brain. Blindly, I reached for my phone, desperate to stop the noise, but nothing I did would shut it off. I nearly hurled the device across the room until I realized the twittering was coming from outside.

Where was I?

The dull pain at the back of my head was a quick reminder. I fell back onto the pillow, the birds still chirping away outside my window with the view of Koko Head.

"Damn mynahs," I cursed.

I lay with my eyes closed, willing myself back to sleep, but memories of the previous night invaded my thoughts. Koa seemed convinced Mark had something to do with Charles's death and the break-in at my place. But my gut told me he was wrong. A detective on a home invasion I'd covered once told me the simplest solution was usually the answer. Even if he wasn't the killer, Hale had to be the key.

Voices sounded from the other side of my bedroom wall, and my eyes popped open when I realized they weren't my parents' usual hushed tones.

We had company.

And there was something all too familiar about the visitor's low, calm timbre.

I groaned and lurched out of bed, putting on the same denim shorts and linen shirt I'd changed into at the hospital. After stealing a quick look in the bathroom mirror to make sure my hair covered the lump on the back of my head, I hurried down the hall. Taking a deep breath, I turned the corner.

Koa sat at our dining table chatting with my parents over a steaming mug of coffee, glass of guava juice, and plate of eggs and breakfast fried rice. From their rapt expressions, he was keeping them entertained—something about a car chase story from his rookie days on the street.

"I told my TO to turn right, so when he turned left, I yelled, 'Other right, other right!'"

Apparently, they found this hilarious. I could barely make out my mom's question through her chortling. "What's a TO?"

Stifling a groan, I said, "Training officer." Three pairs of eyes swung to me, and I had a sudden flashback to our college years, when he'd pick me up for class. Koa had been a fixture in our house since we were kids, and by the time we'd started dating they treated him like the son they never had.

"What's wrong with your voice?" Mom asked, frowning at me with concern.

"I'm, um, catching a cold," I said, shooting a glance at Koa. "What are you doing here?"

"Still not a morning person, ya?" he said pleasantly before sipping from his mug.

"No, she isn't. But that's no excuse for being rude," Mom scolded. "He came to give you a ride back to Waikīkī. Wasn't that nice of him?"

"I thought we agreed I'd take Uber."

"I was in the area. Besides, I called a friend of mine who can fix your . . . sink." He looked at me pointedly over his mug. "He'll give you a deal. We're meeting him at your place."

My parents had woken up at my unscheduled, late-night arrival, and I'd told them a pipe burst in my apartment. I was relieved Koa had caught on and hadn't given me away.

Grudgingly, I sat down next to him in the only empty chair.

"Maya hasn't told us much about what's going on with the Hamilton case. I don't like the idea of her working for them when there's a killer on the loose. What do you think, Koa? Is it safe?" Mom asked.

Thankfully, Dad derailed the conversation. "I heard the case is all but solved—it's just a matter of finding Hale. Or at least, that's what the press says."

Koa grunted. "The press is wrong. He's a person of interest, but the investigation is ongoing."

"Maya isn't in any danger working for them, is she?" Mom asked.

Koa took his sweet time answering. "As long as she sticks to writing and keeps her nose outta my case, she should be safe." He shot me another withering look before turning to Mom. "I'll make sure of it, Auntie Linda."

She visibly relaxed, sinking back into her chair and smiling at Koa fondly.

"See, Linda? Nothing to worry about. Koa will protect her," Dad said.

I gritted my teeth. I knew I was being stubborn, maybe even unreasonable. But I didn't want anyone to protect me, let alone Koa. I held my tongue because I knew saying anything would bring up the attack on me.

Thankfully, he and my dad moved on to discussing the latest 'Bows game, and after several minutes I saw Mom try to nudge Dad under the table.

"Come, Mike. I want to get to Home Depot before it gets too hot, ya?" she said when her attempts failed.

"Home Depot?" Realization slowly spread across his face. "Oh. Right."

Koa stood, and Mom reached up to hug him. "It was lovely seeing you again. Don't be a stranger, ya?"

By the time they were gone, my head had begun to throb again. "I need . . ." The last word trailed off as Koa handed me a full mug of coffee. Silently, I stirred in cream and sugar.

"We're not meeting my friend for a couple hours, so you have time to eat." Peering at me, his brow furrowed, he added, "How's your head?"

"Fine." I took a long sip of coffee, pausing to let the caffeine take effect. "Shouldn't you be at work?"

"You are work, Maya."

"You're getting paid to chauffeur me around town?"

"Something like that."

I suppressed a sigh of frustration. I once thought I could read Koa like a book, but I learned when we broke up there were things he had never shared with me. The years had made him even more enigmatic and reserved.

I took another gulp of coffee and stood. "I'm not hungry. I'll get my things, and we can go."

But he reached over and put his hand on my arm. "Relax and drink your coffee. There's no rush. You should eat something."

Ten minutes later, the coffee had my synapses firing away, making connections I hadn't been able to the night before.

"The Hamiltons might've known about my date with Mark," I said, explaining how I'd left my phone in Parker's office during lunch. "For that matter, he could've easily mentioned it to Stephen. And another thing, he moved the time up at the last minute, which might be why I interrupted the burglar."

Koa's jaw tightened. "Until we clear this up, I don't want you alone with him. Better safe than sorry, ya?"

"Don't you think if Mark set up the break-in, he would've warned the burglar I was on my way home? There was plenty of time—"

"Or burglary wasn't the perp's real objective.

His words chilled me. Nothing made sense. *Why would anyone want me dead?*

The coffee burned in my stomach. I stood and poured the rest down the sink.

* * *

Driving into town from Hawai'i Kai during the morning rush hour nearly doubled our travel time, but it was nothing compared to California's Bay Area traffic. While Koa drove, I shopped for a new laptop on my phone. Unlike a big city on the mainland, Amazon Prime did not offer two-hour delivery to O'ahu, so I quickly found a laptop at a big-box electronics store that would be ready for pickup in an hour.

"Where is the Best Buy at Ala Moana?"

"Why?"

The growing car culture of the 1950s had influenced the design of Ala Moana, best described as an outdoor mall surrounded by a two-level parking deck. What it lacks in curbside appeal it makes up for in size, and even locals have been known to lose their cars. I was debating whether it would be simpler to take the bus or ride my bike than drive when Koa repeated his question.

"I bought a new computer. The locksmith doesn't need me, does he?"

"The parking structure near Best Buy is closed—they're working on another expansion."

"That's fine. I'm probably going to take the bus, anyway."

Koa swore. "Are you kidding me? You were mugged on the street, attacked in your own apartment, and now you want to run around town with a brand-new laptop? When will it be ready? I'll take you."

Scrolling through my phone had given me an idea for finding Adam Hale, but I needed to ditch Koa first. "I don't need a police escort to go shopping. I'll drive myself."

"*What. Time.*"

It wasn't a question. My skull throbbed as I tried to figure a way out of my dilemma before deciding it wasn't worth the headache. My search for Adam would have to wait.

"It's easier if we go straight there." I could grab breakfast at the mall.

"Fine. The crime scene guys haven't finished processing your place yet. There was a robbery on the other side of the island, plus a multi-vehicle accident this morning."

Best Buy was faster than I'd expected, and a little more than an hour later we were back at the Ainahau. Koa's phone had beeped several times along the way, but after glancing at the screen, he ignored whoever was texting him. Now, as we got into the elevator, it chimed again. Reluctantly, he withdrew it from his pocket to peek at the screen, then shoved it back in.

"Everything okay?"

"Yeah. It's nothing." He paused. "Did you and Lani have a fight or something?"

"No." I sounded defensive, even to my own ears. "Why? Did she say something?"

Koa arched his brows. "No, but you just did. Why else would she bug me to see if you're coming to my place Saturday? She says you haven't RSVP'd yet. Did she send engraved invitations or what?"

Lani said Luke's birthday would be "nothing big," but I'd forgotten how Island parties worked. A small gathering meant your fourth cousins once removed who lived in Maui wouldn't be there. Probably. But everyone else—all the aunties and uncles, not to mention friends and neighbors, who didn't have to hop a plane—were fair game.

Lani and Luke's rental cottage a few blocks from her shop was too small, so of course the party was at Koa's.

"Everyone has been asking about you. The whole gang is coming."

Translation: Lani was laying on the Asian Guilt pretty thick.

I let him off the hook. "I've got a lot of writing to do, and I need to get started on that Tinder piece. Wish Luke a happy birthday for me, though."

The elevator dinged. I started to walk out until I realized he hadn't followed.

"Try telling him yourself," he said, reaching out to block the closing door. "Don't you think you've avoided us long enough?"

It was true. I dreaded facing everyone from back home. Especially all the aunties and uncles inquiring about my status. No husband. No home. No real job.

"Dad and Matt would love to see you. Come on," he cajoled. "It'll be fun. Like old times."

I narrowed my eyes even as I found myself relenting. "Lani coach you or what?"

"Maybe."

"Thought so. I guess I can take the night off."

"Good. Now will you please RSVP, so she'll stop texting me?"

Chapter Twenty-Four

The crime scene techs were already inside collecting evidence when we got to my place.

"They're still dusting for prints, so don't touch anything," he said, handing me a pair of rubber gloves. "Put these on just in case. We need you to go through the rooms and tell us if anything else was taken."

My tiny apartment was in total disarray—papers and books strewn about the floor—only now there was also a fine black powder coating doorknobs and every surface the suspect could've touched. I took an inventory of my work areas, but other than the upended files, the only thing missing was my computer.

The pile of notes and articles I'd left on the coffee table appeared untouched.

"I don't think he looked there," I told the technician, who'd started to dust the surface.

"How can you tell?" Koa asked, as they both looked at the area where I ate and worked. A book on Hawaiian history teetered open on a stack of more files and mail. Articles I'd printed about dating apps lay scattered nearby, some stained with coffee rings.

"Ha, ha. It's a mess, I know. But it's how I work."

Koa nodded at the tech. "Print it anyway," he said.

He donned a pair of gloves and began examining my door, squatting to get a good look at the lock. He stood, turning to survey the living area and kitchenette.

"Did you touch anything?"

I shook my head. "Just the door when I came in. After that, I was careful. I figured I had to preserve the crime scene."

"You binge-watching true crime shows again?"

I was too absorbed watching him work to answer. I could see he was processing the information in his head, trying to work out the details, and I wondered if he'd come up with any answers.

I followed him to the alcove where a technician was examining the half-opened pocket door. I hadn't looked at the bedroom the night of the burglary, and now my stomach churned at the ransacked room—clothes, bras, and panties were strewn on the floor, the contents of my nightstand dumped onto the bed.

I looked for the small cloth bag I'd kept under a manicure kit. It wasn't long before I had to accept it was gone. The burglar had taken the only jewelry I'd brought with me from California, earrings and a necklace that were more sentimental than valuable.

I turned away and felt Koa's watchful gaze follow me.

"You okay?"

His gentle tone unnerved me almost as much as the violation to my home. My throat tightened.

"He took some jewelry."

"Insured?"

I shook my head. "No. It wasn't worth anything."

Koa called in one of the crime scene guys and directed him to the drawer I pointed at. The team worked quickly and efficiently, taking swabs and brushing hard surfaces with more fine black powder. From the monotone murmurings, I gathered they didn't find much.

When they left, Koa texted his locksmith friend while I searched my cleaning supplies for something to wipe off fingerprint powder.

"You got an empty spray bottle?" Koa asked. He filled the one I gave him with lukewarm water and added some dish soap, giving it a shake. "This'll do the trick."

Together, we wiped down the surfaces of my apartment, working in companionable silence. Dark particles were scattered on some of my papers and books, and I shook them into a trash can.

"Were you ever able to find out where everyone was the day Charles died?" I asked.

Koa snorted with derision. "They lawyered up. Everyone was coming and going throughout the day. It's been impossible to nail anything down. They were pretty vague in their initial statements."

"Shocker." I told him about Parker's tardiness the day of our first interview. "He didn't show up until hours later—something about an important meeting or overseas phone call."

I suddenly remembered my notes.

"What is it?" he asked.

"I might be able to help with your timing problem."

Koa stopped wiping the counter and narrowed his eyes. "How?"

"Not so fast. What's in it for me?"

"The satisfaction of being a good citizen."

I threw a paper towel at him, and he caught it midair with one hand. I hid my grin by rummaging through the stack of papers and files on the kitchen counter.

"What are we looking for?" He scanned the surface and lifted a file covering a stack of bills.

"My notebook," I said. "I record my interviews, especially the ones I know are going to be long. When I know I'm going to want to refer back to something, I make a note of the time so it's easier to find in the audio recording later. Where did I put it?"

We searched for several minutes, the silence broken only by sifting papers and the occasional clink of a cup or plate. I gathered the used dishes and moved them to the sink, turning back to find Koa holding up a narrow, spiral notebook.

"This it?"

The number one had been written on the cover and circled in red.

"Where was it?"

"Under a potholder. Where else would a notebook be?"

Flipping it open, I perched on a bar chair and scanned my scrawled writing, trying to recall the sequence of events.

I'd already covered my arrival and when I'd finally met the Hamiltons during my first meeting with Koa and Detective Reyes. According to my notes, I'd started the recording app on my phone at 1:32 PM.

"Stephen left a few minutes before that," I said as I flipped pages. "Elizabeth went inside, and I didn't see her again until about three thirty, when Parker left for his meeting. That's when I ran into Charles. Parker and Elizabeth rejoined us maybe thirty minutes later. I stopped recording shortly after that."

"Back up." Koa had abandoned cleaning and was taking his own notes in a pad much like mine. "What meeting? I thought Parker was with you the whole time."

"No, he had to take a phone call from the mayor. He was gone about forty minutes—in his office, I assume."

Koa's notebook snapped shut. He ran his hands through his hair and expelled an agitated breath. "This gives all my suspects the perfect window of opportunity to—" He stopped as if he'd said too much.

"Let me guess—it was poison? I'm right, aren't I? Why else would the 'window' be while Charles was still alive and kicking?"

He glowered at me, then sighed in resignation. "Off the record, ya?"

"I'm not a reporter anymore, remember? I couldn't write about this if I wanted to, but if Parker is a murderer, I need to know."

Satisfied, he said, "Charles was on digitalis for his heart, but someone gave him an extra dose—or three. According to the medical examiner, it had to have been minutes before he went into the pool."

"What about the bruises on his body?"

"The ME thinks he was held underwater while he was having seizures from the digitalis," Koa said. "Pretty brazen, but it would've only taken a couple of minutes."

"He ingested the digitalis shortly before going into the pool, but I'm guessing it could've been put in his drink or food at any time," I said. "He took some kind of protein supplement. I heard him ask Elizabeth to order more."

Koa groaned. "This case is a frigging nightmare."

A knock on the door signaled the arrival of the locksmith. I set up my new laptop, and Koa worked on his own computer across from me while his friend installed my new lock.

I opened my cloud account and downloaded the last file I'd been working on. I noticed one of the folders was empty. I clicked on it, confirming my suspicions.

The recording of my interview with Parker was gone.

I opened the other folders, then did a quick search, but it had disappeared. Hurrying to the kitchenette counter, I lifted a pile of folders, chortling when I found a zippered cloth bag. I opened it, riffling through the contents—pens, a small pair of scissors, a few pieces of wrapped Japanese coffee candy, and a small flash drive.

Koa lifted his head and gave me a questioning look.

"I thought I'd lost a file," I said.

Slipping the flash drive into a port, I opened a folder to check my files for the recording. No one would ever call me fastidious, but after the man in the baseball hat stole my phone, I started taking extra precautions.

"What's on your laptop anyway?"

I looked up to see Koa watching me, his face thoughtful. I shrugged and continued typing. "Notes, outlines, a few audio recordings."

"Let's try this: is there anything on there someone would want?"

I stopped. Now he had my full attention. Slowly, I shook my head. "No. Native Hawaiians probably won't like the Hamiltons portraying themselves as a 'founding family' of Honolulu, but there's nothing explosive about Parker's biography. This isn't a best-selling tell-all. It's basically an eighty-thousand-word puff piece, and it hasn't even been written yet, aside from drafts of a few chapters."

"What about your research? Anything interesting there?"

I shook my head. "Everything's readily available at the library or the Bishop Museum. Nothing remotely earth-shattering or even newsworthy."

"And the file you were so anxious to find?"

"My interview with Parker," I said.

Koa rubbed his brow. "I thought you told me you lost it when your phone was stolen?"

"I did, but it was automatically uploaded to the cloud."

"So, what's the problem?"

"It's not there now. Luckily, I saved it to a flash drive. The thing is, I listened to it and there's nothing interesting on it. I can't for the life of me figure out why anyone would want it."

Koa nodded, deep in thought. "I don't suppose you'd send me a copy of that file?"

"Not unless you have a warrant." I was skirting dangerously close to the boundaries of my NDA with the Hamiltons. There was no way I could hand over the recording of my interview with Parker.

He frowned but dropped the subject. "The lock will be done in a few minutes. I called some cleaners. Fingerprint dust can be a bitch to get out of carpeting."

"You didn't have to do that."

He shrugged. "I know a guy."

My lips curled into a smile on their own volition. And then I had a sudden thought. "I don't suppose you know a sound guy?"

He looked at me quizzically.

"Someone who could clean up an audio file?"

"The audio file you won't let me listen to?"

"No comment."

Shooting me a chastising look, he took out his phone and made a quick call. "He'll contact you in the next day or so," he said, scribbling a name on a piece of paper and handing it to me.

I arched my brows, impressed. "If you weren't such a pain in the ass, you'd be pretty handy to have around."

"Remember our deal. You'll let me know if there's anything on that file I need to know about."

"I remember."

A dull throbbing began at the base of my skull, and I reached up to rub away the pain. Koa retrieved the medicine bottle and handed me two pills along with a glass of water. "Lock up and get some rest," he said.

I crashed hard. Any plans to dig into Adam Hale's background were abandoned the moment my head touched the pillow. I was roused from a deep sleep when the phone rang. Sunlight streaked through a crack in the drapes. I tapped the answer button, still groggy, not bothering to check the number.

My perfunctory greeting was met with silence.

"Who is this?" I asked, by now irritated.

A few puffs of breath came through the speaker before the caller hung up.

Chapter Twenty-Five

Koa tried to warn me.

"You sure you want to stay here? Why don't you crash at Lani's for a few days, just until things settle down?" he'd said, after inspecting the new state-of-the-art lock and security bolt for a second time. "These things affect people differently. Sometimes . . . there's a delay."

"What are you talking about?"

He'd turned concerned eyes on me. "You got lucky last night, Maya. Maybe it hasn't sunk in yet, but it will, and it'd be better if you weren't alone."

I'd felt like a spinster auntie—an implication all the more humiliating coming from him.

"I can't stay with Lani indefinitely. You may never catch this guy. I'll be fine."

But the hang-up calls had me spooked. I shook the jitters by restoring order to my temporary home. I picked clothes up from the floor, stuffing them into a laundry bin, then put away cosmetics and toiletries. I even reorganized my papers. I found an old shoebox and began picking up the photos left strewn about the living area, figuring I'd sort them later.

It didn't take long to clean the tiny condotel. I checked the time, dismayed to see I'd lost a full day of work. I texted Parker confirming our meeting the next day, then emailed Deidre to negotiate more time for the Tinder piece. Like everyone I was working with lately, Koa's contact was ghosting me. The UH coed who'd been assaulted by her date hadn't returned any of my phone calls. I hated to admit I might need Koa's help after all.

With the paying gigs out of the way, I opened my laptop and checked social media, hoping to find out more about the mysterious Adam Hale. A little cybersleuthing would hardly interfere with Koa's investigation—it was public information, available on the World Wide Web, after all.

As far as I could tell, Hale wasn't following the Kaimukī activist group on Facebook or IG, but with thousands of users hiding behind cryptic handles it was impossible to know for sure. Tracing them all would take days. Facebook was usually a better source of intel, but only when it came to people of a certain age. Last year a college student I interviewed told me she and her friends created Facebook accounts "because otherwise it'd be like we didn't exist." But they rarely posted anything on the platform.

I was banking on Hale being closer to my demographic. But he appeared even cagier than me. No one from the Kaimukī group had tagged him in any of their photos, and judging by the frequency of his posts he rarely used Facebook. Other than a hometown of Hale'iwa and some photos of a bookstore, he hadn't filled out any information about himself. No relationship status, no school affiliations, not a selfie in sight. Even his profile pic was a surfboard stuck in the sand. Nothing more than two years old.

This was going to be harder than I thought. I continued scrolling through his timeline, which consisted mostly of other people's posts he was tagged in. They stopped altogether after only a few swipes on the mousepad. Frowning, I checked and saw the oldest entry dated back only two years.

I closed my laptop. This wasn't getting me anywhere. On impulse, I grabbed my purse and headed out the door, typing the bookstore's address into my phone.

Time to knock on some doors.

* * *

It took Siri a while to get her bearings. The further west I drove on Highway 1, the more she struggled to pronounce the Hawaiian locations until she gave up and resorted to spelling them instead.

Once I hit Pearl City and merged onto the H2, I settled back and began to enjoy the scenery. A small mountain range rose in the distance from the lush Mokuleʻia Forest Preserve. As I drove past sugarcane and pineapple fields, I caught flashes of green vegetation against red volcanic earth.

Koa said Hale's phone had pinged in Haleʻiwa a couple of times. Maybe someone from one of his old haunts could give me a lead, and the bookstore from his Facebook page seemed like the perfect place to start.

Almost an hour later, I pulled into the little town on Oʻahu's North Shore, famous for its shave ice and stunning beaches, where sea turtles and surfers alike flock. I passed the town center, crossing the Rainbow Bridge, and pulled in front of an Old West style building complete with a covered porch and tin roof. I slid into a spot directly in front of a large storefront sandwiched between an ukulele studio and surf shop.

You have arrived at your destination, Siri announced.

I looked up, peering at the empty window display through my dirt-streaked windshield. A red "closed" placard hung upside down from the door.

Crap.

I got out and slammed the Civic's door in frustration. Digging into Hale's past was going to be harder than I thought. Determined not to waste the trip, I surveyed my surroundings. A café on the corner looked promising, judging from the foot traffic.

I jogged across the street to the popular Island chain selling Kona espresso drinks and açaí smoothies. I ordered a guava croissant and the fussiest drink on the menu, a frozen macadamia coconut latte, so I could chat up the barista.

"The bookstore closed over a year ago. The owner retired and moved back to the mainland. Somewhere in Oregon—Portland, I think." He eyed me over the steam from the hissing espresso maker. "You don't look like a cop. You a reporter or what?"

"Sort of," I said, handing him my business card, which he stuck in the pocket of his apron. "Do you know Adam Hale?"

"Just to say hi. He's a regular. Doesn't talk much, though. He'll order a coffee and sit over there for hours reading or working on his computer."

He jutted his chin toward the far corner of the café where a young woman was sitting at a table sipping coffee and watching us. I smiled, but her eyes slid back to her mug.

"When was the last time you saw him?" I said.

The barista topped my drink with a heavy cloud of whipped cream, then finished it with flecks of coconut as he considered the question. "Maybe a week. Hard to say. The days kind of blend together, ya know?"

A few more questions yielded similar results, so I thanked him and got my croissant to go. I glanced at the corner table, but the woman was gone.

Back in the car, I called Luke. "Can you text me a photo of the sign-in sheet from the meeting Adam Hale went to?"

"Sure. Hold on—what're you up to, Maya?"

I didn't answer. His deep sigh was followed up by a trill on my end. I checked my phone screen and zoomed in on the photo he'd sent. Hale's address was clearly visible.

"Thanks, Luke." I paused. "Don't mention this to Koa, ya?"

"I don't know what you're talking about."

I was still grinning as I pulled out of the parking spot and followed Siri's directions to a small apartment complex off Waialua Beach Road. I wasn't so upbeat once I discovered no one in the four-unit building was home. So much for knocking on doors. I slipped a business card in each mail slot and headed back to Waikīkī.

It was late by the time I got home, but I was wide awake thanks to the long nap and sugary espresso drink. I fixed myself a sandwich and went onto the lanai to work on Parker's manuscript.

I was writing a note in the margins when a flash of movement caught my eye. A panel of the sheer, white curtains in my sleeping alcove fluttered in the wind through the open window.

I froze, my heart racing as I fought off panic. I could've sworn I'd closed the window before I left for Hale'iwa. I went inside, yanking it shut and jamming the latch in place. Telling myself I was overreacting, I mimicked Koa's security sweep anyway.

Back outside, I went to the railing and surveyed the street below, then the nearby hotels and apartments, before grabbing my laptop and retreating inside.

Two days in, I remembered Koa's advice to stay with Lani.

It started with little things. A scratching sound I thought was someone trying to pick my new lock turned out to be a plastic bag fluttering in the breeze. A faint trace of cologne in the elevator. The air conditioner running full blast when I thought I'd turned it off.

And when I woke up in a cold sweat, I blamed it on having to lock the windows at night.

Back home in California, I'd relished the quiet, uninterrupted peace of living alone. These last few weeks, even my tiny Waikīkī condotel had become an oasis. But now, looking down at the people passing below or standing on their balcony across the way, I couldn't help but wonder if someone was out there. Watching.

I'd ignored my inner warning bells out of obstinacy, but now I was forced to admit Koa might be right. Too many coincidences. Too many close calls. The next time I turned a blind eye could be deadly.

It was days before I ventured onto the lanai again.

Chapter Twenty-Six

"Would you like to go to the hospital gala?" Parker asked.

I'd awakened to a pounding headache, but with the looming deadline I couldn't afford to lose another day of work. So I'd picked up a bottle of Tylenol at a nearby Long's on the way to Parker's office downtown bright and early the next day. I'd spent all morning trailing after him as he flitted in and out of meetings, shaking investors' hands, making small talk with city officials, and flirting with staff. Especially the young, pretty, female ones.

I didn't complain when he called it a day shortly after lunch so he could squeeze in a round of golf.

I zipped up my laptop sleeve, remembering the Hamiltons had been no-shows for the museum fundraiser.

"You said you wanted to shadow me. The gala is the perfect opportunity. All the foundation board members will be there. You have something to wear, right?" Parker said.

A fancy fundraiser wasn't exactly the normal-everyday-routine scenario I had envisioned to get a glimpse into what made Parker tick, but then again, I wasn't a millionaire developer. Black-tie shindigs were probably normal for them.

"I can find something," I said, opening my Google calendar. "When is it?"

"Seven o'clock."

My head jerked up in surprise. "Tonight?"

"You have to forgive Parker. He has absolutely no clue what it takes to get ready for one of these things." Elizabeth had quietly slipped into the room, clutching a bouquet of flowers. "My dear, we heard what happened. I came as soon as I could. How are you feeling? Are you sure you're up to working so soon? Parker and I want you to take as much time as you need to recuperate."

I accepted the arrangement of purple orchids and monstera fronds, and together we made our way to the bank of elevators. "I'm fine, believe me. It's nothing a little Tylenol can't cure."

She didn't look convinced, but said, "Very well. I'm sure Parker is pleased to be moving ahead on this book." Giving a small shake of her head, she sighed. "Waikīkī used to be so safe. It's terrible what it's become. Are the police close to arresting anyone? Surely, they must have an idea who's behind these thefts."

"Actually, they're not sure it's related to the other Waikīkī cases."

Elizabeth's eyes widened in surprise. "Really? But what else could it be?" She grew quiet, a crease forming above her nose. "Maya, I need you to be honest. Are you involved with anything . . . illicit? I'll be candid. Stephen can't afford any bad publicity."

I started to laugh, until I realized she was serious. "I assure you, I'm clean. Do a background check if you want. You won't find anything beyond a few parking tickets."

"Then why would someone break into your home?"

"I have no idea. The police think it has something to do with Charles's murder."

She gasped, a hand plucking at the pearls around her throat. "You mean, it was Adam Hale who attacked you?"

I shrugged. I wasn't convinced Hale was the killer, but no sense pointing that out to Elizabeth. "I didn't see him. But the crime scene techs were there earlier, so hopefully whoever it was left fingerprints or DNA."

She nodded. "Well, I won't keep you. Take care of yourself, and we'll see you tonight," she said as the elevator dinged. Turning, she placed a hand on my arm. "You're very lucky you weren't hurt. Please be careful, Maya."

* * *

It took me almost an hour to get ready for the gala, not counting time in the shower. It was double my usual twenty-minute prep, and without Lani it felt like an eternity.

It was too late to get a haircut or have my hair styled, so I had to make do with smoothing my shoulder-length tresses with a flat iron. I stuck to the basics, eyeliner and shadow, forgoing the lash curler and mascara. Luckily, I'd packed my only cocktail dress—a simple, black, knee-length sheath—for just such an occasion. A check in the mirror reflected a sleeker, more polished version of my usual self.

Slipping my phone into the tiny clutch I still hadn't returned to Lani, I hurried out the door, a pair of black strappy heels dangling from my fingers as I padded down the hall in my bare feet. I hadn't even made it to the elevator when my phone buzzed in my hand.

I didn't recognize the local number, but I'd given out a dozen or more of my business cards since I'd been in Hawai'i, and the reporter in me felt compelled to pick up. My greeting was curt.

"Are you the lady who was in the café asking about Adam?" The woman on the other end of the line sounded young. And scared.

I stalled for time, glad I'd listened to my instincts. "Yeah, that was me. I'd never been there before. Great coconut lattes." I was babbling to try and put her at ease. I tapped the voice memo app on my phone and hit the record button. I didn't know if it was legal to record someone without their knowledge in Hawai'i, but who was watching? For once, Koa was nowhere in sight. "Is Adam a friend of yours?"

"Um, yeah. Kind of."

I waited.

"We met at the café and got to talking."

"What about?"

"Just work stuff. We're both in finance. Look, the only reason I'm calling you is because I'm worried about him. Something's not right."

"Well, he *is* evading the police—"

"That's not it." Her breath hissed in my ear. "The texts. They don't sound like him."

Koa had said Hale's phone had been pinging all over the island. Of course HPD had been tracking Hale's texts. I took my time replying. "What did he say? Do you have any idea where he is?"

"Never mind. I gotta go."

"Wait. We should talk. Tell me your name and—"

The answering beep told me she'd hung up.

* * *

Elizabeth coached Parker in the limo during the short ride to the hotel.

"The Kleins had a Silicon Valley start-up that they sold for billions and retired to Hawai'i. Stephen knows their daughter—"

"The blonde with the legs? Didn't they date back in Yale?"

Elizabeth sighed. "That was Meredith," she said, then cocked her head toward me. "Actually, she and Mark were a thing for quite a while. The Kleins' daughter lives in California. But we digress. It's important to note the Kleins are very active in politics. They were major contributors to the governor's campaign in the last election."

"How much did they give to the hospital?" he said.

"Five."

Five thousand didn't seem like enough to warrant a seat at the head table—but a beat later I realized she'd meant five *hundred* thousand. Half a million. Dollars. The Hamiltons swam in a different tax bracket than anyone I'd ever known. And it sounded as if Elizabeth was angling for a sizeable donation to Stephen's campaign.

It was becoming clear who really ran the family.

Between the rubber chicken dinner and chalky mousse, Elizabeth cued Parker from behind her cloth napkin, sometimes with a discreet nod or twist of her diamond solitaire ring. I wished again I was writing her biography instead of Parker's.

"How long have you been Parker's PA?" asked the Honolulu city councilman seated next to me.

"Research assistant," I said. "Just a few weeks. I'm helping him document the Hamilton family history for the book he's writing. What part of the island do you represent?"

Parker's table was a mix of people with deep pockets and those with influence. The councilman, a public school teacher in his early forties, had the deciding vote on an upscale, mixed-use housing project in Kaka'ako. Parker had taken out his phone to show us an artist rendering of the planned community when the lights dimmed, signaling the start of the auction.

Bidding started slowly. O'ahu's wealthiest philanthropists weren't in the market for a week at a Mexican timeshare, and the rest of us couldn't afford it. But our servers kept the drinks flowing, and paddles were flying by the time a dinner with Honolulu's hottest chef went on the block.

The bid had reached ten grand when Parker glanced at his phone and slipped away. When the others were distracted by the auction I murmured an excuse and made my own escape. I followed his route along the edge of the ballroom and exited through a set of double doors into an empty hallway.

Where did Parker go? Shadows at the far end of the corridor caught my attention, and I walked toward them as fast as I could in my flimsy heels, grateful the floor was carpeted. As I got closer, I could see Parker was talking to a dark-haired man in a tux. One of the high-ranking city officials I'd been introduced to earlier, I thought, but I couldn't be sure. It was dim, he had his back to me, and I'd just left an entire ballroom full of dark-haired men in tuxes.

Parker handed the man an envelope before walking away. I turned and hurried back down the corridor, ducking into the women's restroom before he could see me. I let several minutes pass before I ventured out again. I slid into my seat as the mayor's wife won the dinner with the celebrity chef.

The band struck up an orchestral rendition of "Dancing Queen," and the table emptied as couples took to the dance floor. I reached for my phone to pass the time, surprised to see I had a message from Kiyomi. Her decoded pictogram was a reminder to bring dessert to Luke's party.

What was it my anonymous caller had said? *The texts. They don't sound like him.*

I wasn't much of a texter. Most of my messages consisted of one or two words, usually to confirm times, dates, and locations. Kiyomi communicated primarily with emojis, and Lani was heavy on exclamation points. Is that what Hale's friend from the café meant? He wasn't sending the texts? But who else could it be? I shook off my doubt. It didn't sound like they'd been close.

My phone chirped, alerting me to a new text message.

Koa: Meet me in the lobby.

Biting back a sigh of irritation, I drained the last of my wine and said my goodbyes. He was standing under the porte cochere talking to a hotel security guard.

"How'd you know where I was?" I asked when we were alone.

"I saw you on one of the security cameras. Hale's phone pinged within a couple hundred yards of the hotel. Imagine my surprise to find *you* here. You didn't see him, did you?"

I shook my head, glancing over my shoulder, wondering if Hale was there watching us.

"Yeah, well, no one did," Koa said. "He's here one minute, gone the next. Like a ghost."

Chapter Twenty-Seven

With my deadline looming for the Tinder piece, I hunkered down to write. The day of Luke's party, I emerged from behind my laptop and realized I didn't have a dish to bring. Showing up to someone's house empty-handed is the number one Asian sin, worse than standing chopsticks upright in a bowl of rice or forgetting to take your shoes off at the front door.

Salad and a bottle of wine were safe bets on the mainland, where parties were rife with vegetarians, vegans, and friends on a cleanse. But no one brings salad—least of all one bought in a bag—to parties in Hawai'i unless noodles, crunchy or cooked, are involved.

An idea hit me. I took out my phone and tapped out a quick text. Moments later, it chirped alerting me to a new photo from Mom. I instantly recognized the worn pink index card, stained with grease and splatters of coconut milk.

A quick trip to Foodland yielded everything I needed to make butter mochi. I couldn't remember the last time I'd eaten the chewy, cakey mashup of mochi and Filipino bibingka. I'd never made it, but it turned out to be ridiculously easy.

I emptied a box of Mochiko rice flour into a large bowl and added melted butter, coconut milk, evaporated milk, and sugar. Taking care to whisk out any lumps, I poured the batter into a large baking dish, banged it on the counter a couple times to get rid of air bubbles and popped it in the oven.

Twenty minutes later my humble condotel started to smell like home.

While the butter mochi baked, I drifted back to my laptop, where curiosity got the better of me. An hour of searching various mutations of the name Adam Hale produced zero results, other than a review for a bed and breakfast on Maui and a nonprofit organization for foster youth, reminding me that *hale* was also the Hawaiian word for "home."

The oven timer dinged, and I reluctantly pried myself away from the computer to check the butter mochi. It was a perfect golden brown, and when I pierced a toothpick through the center, it came out clean. I shut off the oven, leaving the pan to cool on a wire rack. Showered and dressed an hour later, I was cutting the mochi into squares when my phone buzzed.

"Maya, I need your help."

"Luke?" I'd never heard my laid-back, go-with-the-flow friend sound so anxious. "What's wrong? It's not Lani—she's okay, ya?"

"Oh, yeah. Nothing like that. But I need you to get something from her shop for me." He was whispering, and I realized this probably had something to do with one of their elaborate practical jokes or gift-giving schemes. "It's a surprise, so don't tell anyone."

"You hid a surprise for Lani in her boutique?"

"Genius, ya? It's the last place she'd look for it."

Especially since Lani's birthday was six months away. "Okay, but why can't you get it? You live two minutes from her shop . . . on foot."

"I'm not at home. I'm at Uncle David's getting ready for the party. Lani's here, and I don't want to bother Koa. He's on the other side of the island. Can you stop by and pick it up for me?"

What was Koa doing on the North Shore? I wondered if it had anything to do with the case.

"Maya?"

"Sorry. Yeah, no problem. But how am I supposed to get in the store? She doesn't keep a key under the mat or something, does she?"

Luke breathed a sigh of relief. "Mahalo. You're saving my life."

Leave it to Lani to have a backup plan. She kept a spare key with the bookshop owner a few stores down. All I had to do was stop by and pick it up.

"I'll text you the security code. Don't set off the alarm, ya? One more false call and not even Koa can get us out of a fine."

I hung up and checked the time. I had to hurry and pack up the mochi if I didn't want to be late to the party. Then I remembered. This was Hawai'i. I had plenty of time.

* * *

The bookshop owner, an aging hippie named Monica, was busy with a customer when I stopped by, but she'd given her assistant a heads-up because the young woman produced a key as soon as I told her my name.

A few minutes later, I unlocked the glass front door and went to disarm the security system, carefully typing the passcode Luke had given me. When the beeping stopped and the red light turned green, I expelled a breath, looking around my friend's boutique.

I crossed the showroom floor and unlocked the door to the staff area. The small sealed package was exactly where Luke said it would be—at the bottom of a file cabinet drawer under a stack of fashion magazines.

I dropped the box in my tote and left the store, taking care to lock up and set the alarm.

Monica was alone and getting ready to close when I got back to the bookstore. She tossed gray curls over her shoulder as she dropped Lani's key in a bowl behind the counter next to burning incense.

I took the opportunity to glance around the brightly lit shop with displays featuring local authors and Hawaiiana on tables fashioned out of old surfboards.

"This is a great store. How long have you been here?"

"A couple years now. I used to manage a shop in Hale'iwa until I finally had enough money to open my own place."

A bookstore in Hale'iwa? It was a long shot, but this was O'ahu. "By any chance, did you know Adam Hale?"

Monica's smile flickered, her demeanor shifting. She shoved a manila envelope with green certified mail stickers into a drawer. "Hale?" she said, pronouncing the name the way I had. "Why do you want to know? Are you with the cops?"

I hesitated. Unlike cyberstalking from the safety of my own apartment, I knew I was dipping my toes into Koa's investigation. But I did it anyway.

"No. I'm a writer. I guess I want to hear his side of the story."

She looked at me for several long moments before shrugging. "Yeah, he was a customer. He's quiet, keeps to himself. Kinda shy, but nice. Smart."

"Do you know his family? Or where he's from?"

Monica shook her head and walked to a table, where she straightened books. "No. I only met him a couple years ago when he moved to Hale'iwa. He came into the shop a lot. We didn't talk about anything personal."

Weird. Even small talk usually reveals some personal information like family background, school, or hobbies.

I pulled out a business card and handed it to her. "Well, if you think of anything, or want to talk, give me a call."

The bell above the shop's door jangled. We both turned, and I groaned inwardly when I saw the new arrival.

Detective Amy Reyes's face darkened, mimicking one of Koa's patented scowls. "Ms. Wong. What are you doing here?"

Feigning a bravado I didn't feel, I jutted my chin. "I'm helping a friend. Why are you here?"

Her lips tightened, eyes narrowed. "Police business." Turning to Monica, she flashed her badge. "Is there somewhere we can speak privately?"

And with that, I was dismissed. I quietly slipped away, suddenly dreading the party.

Koa was going to skewer me alive.

Chapter Twenty-Eight

I was running late even by laid-back Hawaiʻi standards, and by the time I pulled onto the quiet, residential street in Aina Haina there was already a truck and a black SUV in the carport and several more cars parked along the curb. I found a spot about halfway down the block, where I sat for a moment before finally emerging, shoulders squared.

I gripped the platter of butter mochi, the cool ceramic edge biting into my palms as I made my way to Koa's house, a place I'd once known as well as my own.

He still lived there with his dad. Uncle David had suffered a heart attack at the age of fifty-three, and by the time he made a full recovery Koa's younger brother was L.A.-bound with a full ride to USC law school.

So Koa stayed, surprising no one.

Raucous laughter and lively conversation poured from the Yamada home, the merriment growing louder as I drew closer. Perfect timing. By now there were too many guests for Koa to yell about interfering in his investigation. I had no doubt Reyes would have been on the phone with her partner the moment she left the bookstore.

Time to rip off the Band-Aid. Reluctantly, I quickened my pace, slowing only when I'd reached the bottom of the steep driveway. I looked up at the house, pushing away memories of another party more than a decade before, the last time I'd been at the Yamada home.

Back then, it was still the same sunny yellow Koa's mom had chosen when we were kids. I knew in a glance who'd picked the new color, boring beige. The mango tree we'd spent hours climbing as children looked smaller than I remembered, the vibrant red Japanese maple fuller. But otherwise, Koa's home was unchanged right down to the gash in the lava stone wall where his brother Matt had scraped the family car backing out of the driveway. Trudging past old memories, I headed for the garage.

I didn't bother with the front door. This was Hawai'i—the party was outside.

Guests spilled out of the open garage onto the driveway, their hefty paper plates sagging dangerously as they hovered around long tables covered with trays of chow mein, spam musubi, lumpia, and teriyaki chicken. Who could resist piling on one more piece of sushi, scoop of mac salad, or another kakimochi cookie?

I didn't recognize anyone mingling on the front lawn, so I made my way through the garage to the backyard. More guests, including a smattering of familiar faces, sat at tables eating and talking story. My parents were already here, chatting with Koa's neighbor. I waved, and Mom nodded back, a pleased smile spreading across her face.

Pivoting on my heels, I made a beeline for the patio, where I knew I'd find the dessert table and cooler full of drinks. I had a feeling I'd need one. I dropped the mochi platter on the table with a bang, which was drowned out by chatter and laughter. A deep voice interrupted my tussle with the cling film. Something about the accent, timber, and boyish pleasure sparked a memory.

"You look like you could use a drink," Matt Yamada said, grinning as he offered a plastic cup. "Be careful, ya? It's one of Lani's concoctions."

The last time I'd seen Koa's little brother, he'd been a skinny high school kid with braces. I barely recognized the dark-haired man who towered over me, smiling from ear to ear. I sniffled, brushing away sudden tears as I reached up to hug Koa's younger lookalike.

"Glad you're home, Maya," he said, kissing my cheek. "Everyone's been asking about you. They're in the usual spot. Koa's around somewhere. He got a call and disappeared."

I tipped back my head and gulped a generous swig of Lani's infamous liliko'i margarita. The tequila warmed my knees and made my nose tickle. I coughed. It'd been a while since I'd had one of Lani's drinks.

I scanned the yard for Koa, wondering half-seriously if I could avoid him the rest of the night. I turned back to Matt. "Congrats on getting hitched by the way. I hear you're both lawyers. How'd you two meet?"

He launched into a love-at-first-legal-battle story and judging from the way his face lit up, it was the real deal. I smiled, my eyes misting again. Apparently, some love stories do have happy endings.

I raised my cup for another sip of Lani's margarita when a brown, muscled arm wrapped around my neck and squeezed. I jerked in fright, dropping the cup in my hand. It bounced on the ground, its contents splashing my bare legs—and Luke's.

He let go and stepped back. "Whoa, it's just me. You okay? Why so jumpy?"

Matt and Luke hovered over me, and I waved away their concern, not able to speak. Out of the corner of my eye, I saw a familiar figure approach.

"Maybe you should quit sneaking up on people, ya?" Koa said to his cousin. He handed me a napkin, scanning my face.

Flustered, I covered my embarrassment by wiping off the sticky remnants of the margarita. "It's nothing. I'm just a little tired."

"Why? Aren't you sleeping okay?" Koa asked.

Matt filled another cup and gave it to me, which I accepted gratefully. "I'm sleeping fine," I said, taking a long sip. "It's just work."

His eyes narrowed, and I knew he didn't believe me.

"Try go easy on Maya, ya?" Luke said to Matt, fearlessly draping an arm around my shoulders. "She's a lightweight. See—her face is already turning red." He chuckled when I nudged him in the ribs.

Koa turned to me. "We need to talk."

"Oh? What about?"

His eyes narrowed. "You know what."

"Look—"

"Sorry, brah. You're gonna have to wait," Luke interrupted, shooting his cousin a warning look. "Maya's helping me with something."

Koa's jaw clenched, but he backed off. Luke grasped my elbow, pulling me toward the open sliding glass door. "Let's go inside, ya? Lani's back with everyone else, and she's been looking for you."

Aside from a few texts, we hadn't spoken since the day I'd tried clothes on at her shop. As we slipped off our shoes, leaving them on a mounting pile on the lanai, I heard Koa call out. "Have you eaten? You should make yourself a plate."

"I will," I said, waving behind me.

"You gonna tell me what that was about or what?" Luke asked when we were inside.

"Watching too many scary movies, I guess."

Luke gave me a funny look. "I thought you said you were working late. Anyways, I meant what's with you and Koa?"

"Nothing. It's just a work thing."

"His bark is worse than his bite. You know he's just worried about you, ya?"

"He forgets I bark back."

The kitchen and den bustled with guests, so Luke gestured for me to follow him down the hallway. Grasping my elbow, he propelled me through the first door we came to.

Like its owner, Koa's room hadn't changed much in the last decade. The same pale wood furniture stood in the exact same spots. A double bed, covered in a perfectly made blue duvet, sat under a row of jalousie windows, flanked by a matching bookshelf on one side and a desk on the other. The old soccer and basketball trophies were gone, replaced by framed photos neatly arranged on dust-free surfaces.

There was one of his mom and a more recent picture of the three Yamada men—from Matt's wedding, judging by the tuxes. I wasn't surprised by the group shot of our old gang, but the close-up image of my own smiling face startled me. The memory of when he'd snapped the photo flashed in my head.

I gulped my drink, shaking away the ghosts as I pulled the package from my tote and handed it to Luke. "What's with all the cloak and dagger? I thought it was your birthday, not Lani's."

Prying open the box, he dug through the contents and took out a cloth jewelry bag, which he opened with a snap. Smiling, he held out a slim Hawaiian band delicately etched with scrolls and plumerias. A sparkling diamond perched on top.

"You're her best friend—whaddya think? She'll say yes, ya?"

Suddenly, all was right in the world. My oldest, dearest friends—two people I'd known and loved nearly my whole life—were getting their Happily Ever After. For the second time that night, I found myself wiping away tears.

"Of course, Lani will say yes. Are you crazy? Why wouldn't she?" I reached up and threw my arms around him. "I'm so happy for you guys."

Hastily, he swiped at his eyes as we broke apart and grinned sheepishly. But he quickly sobered. "The timing's not great. Her shop's finally breaking even, but with everything that's been going on, who knows how long she'll be able to keep it open. And forget about buying a house."

I thought of Lani's beautiful boutique—the chic styling, her sophisticated take on Hawaiʻi fashion, the way she always showcased local artisans. I knew how much it meant to her. I also knew many of Luke's clients were pro bono.

Guilt washed over me. I'd been a lousy friend.

"So why not hold off for a little while?" I asked, inwardly resolving to be better.

He shrugged. "I can't keep putting our lives on hold. For what? Security, more money? I have Lani, and that's all I really need."

Wordlessly, I squeezed his hand. "Wait. You're not going to propose here, in front of everyone, are you?"

Luke shook his head. "Nah. She'd hate that. I'll pop the question tonight at home, when we're alone."

I nodded in approval. "And the ring?"

Aside from being glittery, I knew nothing about diamond rings. But as with anything fashion related, I suspected my friend had strong opinions.

"She's always liked heritage jewelry. We've been together sixteen years. You think I don't know our Lani?"

Chuckling, I watched as he replaced the jewelry bag and closed the box.

"You got any tape in that giant purse?" he asked.

"No, but—" I walked to Koa's desk and opened one of the side drawers. A tape dispenser lay in plain sight in a wire tray.

"It's like you never left," he said, taking it from me to reseal the box. "It's good you're home. We all missed you, ya? Especially—"

"I know what you're going to say, and you're wrong."

"Am I? 'Cause he's been spending a lot of time in Waikīkī—"

"Not with me. I told you, it's just work. He said so himself, so don't give Lani any ideas."

"Hey, I'm only trying to return the favor," he said, holding his hands up in surrender. "But which is it? He's not with you, or he is, but it's 'just work.'"

I ignored him. "If you really want to help me out, you can tell me what you know about Monica."

Luke dropped his eyes, busying himself with hiding the package behind a large frame on Koa's shelf. "Why do you want to know about her?"

"Because I think she knows more than she's saying, like maybe where Hale's hiding."

He turned to me, arms crossed. "Look, it's like I told Koa, there's only so much I can say, ya? It's like you two never heard of attorney-client privilege or something."

"She doesn't seem to trust the police much," I ventured.

Luke smirked. "Koa's right. You are a pain in the ass." He smiled affectionately. "But we love you anyway. Even—"

"*Luke.*"

"Okay, okay. Monica's cool. She's from Cali, moved to Hawai'i to surf. She's from that whole anti-establishment generation, ya? Hates the Hamiltons. And cops." He paused. "She refuses to answer their questions about Adam Hale because she's convinced they won't give him a fair shake."

"Koa would never let that happen."

Luke flashed a smug grin, but he quickly grew serious again. "It won't be up to him. The Hamiltons have a lot of sway on the Islands. Rumor has it they met with the chief of police yesterday. How much you wanna bet they put pressure on him to charge Hale?"

"Whatever the truth is, once it's out, there's nothing the Hamiltons can do about it, and I'm not a cop," I said. "Think you can get Monica to talk to me?"

Luke leaned forward, conspiratorially. "Is Koa okay with you poking around in his case?"

A loose floorboard creaked. Too late, we both realized Luke had forgotten to give the tricky door an extra hard tug.

"No. I'm not."

Chapter Twenty-Nine

Luke jumped at Koa's angry bark, but I'd braced for the inevitable.

"Ease up, brah. Maya and I were just talking story—"

He silenced Luke with a look. "She's in way over her head. I need to talk to her. Alone."

Loyalties tested, Luke conceded to me. "Maya?"

I nodded, and he reluctantly started to leave. Placing a hand on his cousin's shoulder, he murmured, "Be careful. Don't say anything you'll regret."

As soon as he was gone, Koa folded his arms across his chest and lit into me. "You can start by explaining why the hell you were at the bookstore today."

I parted my lips to tell him where he could stick it, when I spied the box Luke had left behind and remembered the ring was supposed to be a surprise. *Did Koa know?* To err on the safe side, I lied. "I needed a last-minute birthday gift."

"Yeah, right. Then why were you asking questions about my murder suspect?"

I sidestepped his question. "How long has Adam Hale been in Hawai'i? Everything I've found on him only goes back a couple of years. Weird, don't you think? Have you ever considered he might be using an alias?"

His silence told me they hadn't put the two together. I shot him a smug look. "What would you do without me?"

Rubbing his face, he sighed. "Sleep better for one. Life was a lot easier when you were on the mainland."

I looked away, heat creeping into my cheeks. *Why did I let Koa get under my skin?* "I promise, as soon as I'm done with this book, I'll be on the first plane outta here," I said, my voice clipped. "I should go say hi to Lani."

Slipping past him, I flung open the door, startling a tall, gray-haired man, his arm poised to knock.

"Uncle David," I stammered. Flustered, I hastily added the only thing I could think of. "Hi."

Kind, dark eyes so much like his son's widened in amusement. "Well, this is unexpected. Is this what they call déjà vu?"

My cheeks burned.

"Maya and I were just talking, Dad," Koa said.

Uncle David raised his hands, shaking his head. "It's none of my business. You kids are all grown up now, ya?" He smiled at me. "But I do want a hug. It's been far too long."

Relaxing, I stepped into his familiar bear hug. I sniffled against the rough cotton of his T-shirt, wishing I'd thought to bring tissues.

"Our Maya, home at last," he said, patting my cheek when I pulled away. "Prettier than ever, ya, Koa?"

His son muttered something unintelligible. I looked away and emptied my cup.

Koa frowned. "Have you eaten?"

"I was just about to grab a bite. Want to get a piece of cake with me, Uncle?" I asked, offering him my arm.

I made the rounds with Uncle David, avoiding Koa by chatting with friends I hadn't seen since high school. I caught up with local gossip, shook hands with spouses I'd never met, and oohed and ahhed over everyone's adorable kids. I saw more hugging, cheek-kissing action in an hour than I had in the last dozen years. I'd somehow forgotten how tactile the aloha spirit was, and Luke's party was a vivid reminder.

By the time we toasted Luke, the only thing I'd eaten all night was a sliver of liliko'i coconut cake from DeeLite Bakery. But when I spied Lani in our usual spot with the rest of the gang, I bypassed the garage to join them. I caught her eye, and she nodded, smiling.

Willa sprang from one of the chairs, a pink and yellow plumeria lei dangling from the crook of her arm.

"Now it's official," she said, draping the flower necklace around my neck and pulling me into a warm embrace. "Welcome home, Maya."

Safely ensconced in our usual corner of the yard, it felt as if no time had passed. I relaxed into the cushioned swing, gently rocking it with my toes. The weight of the lei was cool and satiny against my skin, and the plumerias' sweet perfume triggered memories of birthdays, graduations, airport reunions, and family celebrations.

A homey peace settled into my bones as my friends' familiar voices washed over me. The guys were having an animated debate over a Warriors game, while Willa and Lani made plans for a weekend trip to Maui.

"You're coming too, ya, Maya?" Willa asked.

They looked at me expectantly, Lani's expression dubious.

"I wouldn't miss it," I said, realizing I meant it.

We were comparing dates on our phones when Koa showed up. He sat next to me on the swing and handed me a plate piled with tekka maki, karaage chicken, chow mein, lumpia, and musubi. Two pieces of my butter mochi teetered on top in their white paper cupcake liners.

"You need to eat," he said, extending a pair of disposable chopsticks.

I flashed a smile and accepted his olive branch. "Thanks. I'm starving."

"I figured," he said, a corner of his mouth curving upward.

He reached over and took a mochi, popping it in his mouth. I watched as he savored the last bit and offered him the remaining piece. Ignoring Lani's watchful gaze, I dug my chopsticks into a mound of noodles, bean sprouts, and char siu.

"So, did Reyes burst a blood vessel or what?" I asked when it appeared my nosy girlfriends weren't listening.

"I can handle Amy."

"For the record, I didn't go to the bookstore to ask about Hale. The opportunity came up, and I ran with it."

Koa sighed and nodded. "Luke told me. I knew he was gonna ask her, but why hide the ring in her shop?"

"'Cause it's Luke and Lani."

His face split into a grin, and we laughed.

By the time I'd finished the sushi, he'd grown serious again. "I don't care about the people at work. It's you I'm worried about. We're at a standstill with the Hamiltons, and Hale's in the wind. I can't protect you—"

"You don't need to. I'm not your responsibility. I'll be fine."

"Like you were the other night? I saw your face when Luke grabbed you. You were terrified." He paused. "I've seen this kind of thing before with other crime vics. Trouble sleeping, panic attacks—"

My hands were suddenly clammy, and I was grateful when Willa broke in, waving us over for a group selfie.

"Together again," she said, holding up her phone. "You have any idea how long it's been? Forever. Okay, smile, everyone."

A few clicks later, she checked the screen, her smile telling us she was satisfied.

"So, Maya, we ever gonna meet this new friend of yours or what?" she said after texting the photo to everyone.

I tried to picture Mark, in his polo shirt and chinos, hanging out under the mango tree with my friends, and somehow the image never materialized.

"It's complicated," I said. "Maybe next time."

Koa took a long pull of his beer, then lowered the bottle. "I met him. Seems okay."

Lani glanced between us. "Complicated. Right."

Chapter Thirty

It was late by the time I got home from the party. I changed into a tank top and boxers, but I couldn't sleep, so I took out the shoebox where I'd stuffed the papers and photos Parker had given me the day of the burglary.

I started sorting photos into one pile and papers in another, organizing them chronologically with the earliest ones on top. I frowned, leafing through the pictures again. Something wasn't right.

Slowly, I examined each image one by one, starting with childhood photos and family vacation shots, then jumped to one of Parker standing in front of a red brick Gothic revival building—Yale in the fall, judging by the architecture and leaves carpeting the ground.

Some photos were missing. I knew I'd seen several pictures of Parker's high school years. I skimmed through the pile again, then rustled through the stack of papers with no luck. I searched under the sofa and behind furniture, in the hopes they'd fallen during the burglary, but again found nothing.

I thought back to the last time I'd gone through the manila envelope Mrs. Goto had given me and realized it was right before my date with Mark. I tried to remember the photos I'd seen—some sports team pictures and school portraits thrown in with society party images—nothing out of the ordinary. Except for two original photographs.

Wishing I'd taken the time to look at the photos more carefully, I jotted down what details I could remember, including the date written on Stephen's baby picture. Then I mentally retraced my movements after the burglary. I was sure I hadn't put any photos in another place. Was it possible a crime scene technician had taken them as evidence? Koa hadn't mentioned it, leaving one other possibility: the burglar had stolen Parker's photos along with my laptop and jewelry. But why?

Before I could come up with a reasonable explanation, my phone beeped. I frowned at the screen: Koa texting to make sure I'd made it home safely. I debated whether I should mention the photos. I knew what he'd do—overreact. But I asked about them anyway.

My phone bleated a few minutes later.

"There aren't any photos listed on the crime scene inventory. I'll be there in ten," he said.

"Koa—"

"Don't. Move."

The line went dead before I could get out another word.

Sighing, I went to change back into street clothes. His rap on the door sounded ten minutes later. On the nose. "The peephole's there for a reason, you know," Koa said when I opened the door.

"Who else would it be? You think a burglar's gonna ring the bell?"

Ignoring me, he performed his security ritual while I made coffee. It was brewing by the time he sat down. I pushed a plate of butter mochi at him—the unsightly, slightly tougher, browner edges I'd saved for a snack.

"I've been home for hours. If someone was in here, he would've shown by now," I said, pouring him a cup of coffee.

He grunted and took the mug I offered.

"You got here fast. Don't tell me Detective By-the-Book broke the speed limit."

"I wasn't home."

"Oh." I considered for a moment, wondering where he'd been. Had there been a break in the case, or had something personal come up?

"So, what happened?" he asked. "Why do you think the perp stole your photos?"

I told him about the shoebox, explaining how Mrs. Goto had given me a manila envelope of old photos Parker thought I could use for the book.

"It was on the coffee table when I left that night. Afterward, I put everything in an empty shoebox to sort through later. It never occurred to me to check if any of them were missing. I was focusing on valuable items." I paused, shaking my head. "Maybe we're jumping the gun here. The balcony door was open. They could've blown away." But even I didn't believe it. What were the chances of the only two original photos blowing away and not the others? On the other hand, why would a burglar steal photos?

Koa stared at me. "You never said anything about the door being open."

"I didn't?" Everything had happened so fast, and some of my memories were a little fuzzy. I thought back to the papers scattered on the living room floor, fluttering in the wind. I remembered hearing the vertical blinds flapping against the sliding glass door. "It was open. Is that important?"

He frowned. "Maybe."

"So, they could've blown away." When he didn't respond, I said, "But you don't think so."

Slowly, he shook his head. "I know a guy at Bishop Museum. You said you first met Nichols at a fundraiser there, ya? The Hamiltons bought two tickets—yours and his. I'm guessing he didn't mention that, did he?"

"No." My voice was flat, resigned. I'd wondered why Mark hadn't told me he knew the Hamiltons, but hearing Koa's discovery chilled me. What I'd once thought was a random meeting turned odd coincidence now appeared to be a cold, calculated setup. But why?

I'd been off my game since the moment I'd stepped off the plane in Hawai'i.

Being home came with pressures I didn't have in California—Mom and Dad, Lani, Koa, my mugger, Koa's murder investigation. But my instincts were usually spot on, and there was something genuine about Mark I'd liked right away.

"Hear me out, okay? You said to listen to your instincts, and mine tell me Mark is a straight shooter. He's not like—" I stopped myself. "He might be hiding something, but I don't think it's murder. I mean what's his motive?"

Koa scowled. "I don't know, but his best friend and business partner inherited a lot of money, and greed is pretty high on the motive list." He paused, his jaw tight. "They won't give us a statement, or even a timeline of where they were the day of the murder. In my experience, that's a big red flag."

"Stephen Hamilton would've inherited a lot more money if Charles had lived long enough to change his will."

Koa sat up. "What are you talking about?"

"Apparently Parker went through all the money his mother left him, and Charles had to pay off a bunch of people to cover up bad investments Parker made. He'd been threatening to leave the Hamilton fortune to Stephen instead."

Koa's expression was unreadable, but he seemed to consider my argument. "Look, I get it. You really like this guy—"

"That's not why—"

He held up a hand. "Whatever. This isn't about us. I wouldn't be doing my job if I didn't at least warn you to be careful around Nichols. You can't assume it was Hale. I don't buy how a total stranger could've known where you live and when you'd be home."

I suppressed a shiver, suddenly relieved Mark was still on the Big Island for work.

"Look, there's something else you should know," Koa said. "You remember Lauren, the vic from the other night? We found her things in a rubbish can a couple blocks away. The suspect got away with cash, didn't touch the credit cards. But her driver's license was out."

"I don't understand . . ."

"He took the time to remove the driver's license from the window in her wallet, but then tossed it with the rest of her stuff. Like he was checking her ID."

I felt a prick of dread. "That doesn't prove—"

"Not in a court of law, but it's enough to convince me. Now these missing photos link everything that's been happening to the Hamilton case. The mugging, Lauren, you. None of it was random."

I turned away, not wanting him to see my fear, and busied myself stirring my coffee. Staring at my hands, I tried to keep them from shaking. Long, warm fingers closed over mine and steadied me.

"I won't let anything happen to you, Maya."

His voice, low and resolved, instantly soothed me even though I knew it was a promise he couldn't possibly keep.

But I knew he meant it.

I offered a shaky smile and met his gaze, where I allowed myself to linger for the first time since we broke up all those years ago. The kind, serious eyes I'd once known as well as my own were exactly as I remembered. A familiar tingle warmed my skin, and suddenly a new fear crept into my heart.

Blinking, I eased away, reaching for my mug. "You're pretty good at the whole 'serve and protect' thing. But I've been on my own, in the big, bad city, for a long time now."

He sighed, resigned. "I've got a unit making regular patrols by your building. Call me if you need anything—I don't care what time it is, ya?"

"Okay."

Unconvinced, he grasped my hand and leaned forward so our eyes met.

"Promise me, Maya."

"I promise. I'll call you."

He stood to leave. "Send me a list of the missing photos. And be sure to lock up after me. Use the latch."

"Yes, Detective."

He flashed a quick smile. "Good night, Maya."

"'Night, Koa."

Chapter Thirty-One

I spotted a unicorn on my jog the next morning: Twentysomething and fit, an Asian man sitting at a bus stop across the street from the Ainahau was reading a newspaper.

No one under the age of seventy read real newspapers anymore. Especially not a Gen Zer. Not without an electronic device. I would know.

I was still feeling the effects of Lani's margaritas and a long, restless night by the time I reached Kūhīo Beach. Normally a fast walker, I'd opted for a leisurely stroll instead. I hadn't even had my coffee yet. The park was empty save for the surf shop owner and an early morning walker, a man wearing a zipped-up hoodie, khaki cargo shorts, and running shoes.

I took my time stretching my calves and hamstrings, hoping to get the blood flowing to my brain as much as my legs, before starting my lope along the beach. Several minutes into my run, it hit me.

A rolled-up newspaper had been sticking out of Hoodie Guy's back pocket.

Was it the same man from the Ainahau? I couldn't remember what he'd been wearing. It was a gorgeous day in Waikīkī. The sun was shining, and temperatures were already pushing mid-70s. So, what was he doing wearing a sweatshirt zipped up to his chin?

I fought panic and quickened my pace, sprinting along the mostly deserted beach to the Hilton Hawaiian Village, where workmen were clearing fallen palm fronds and debris. When I reached the lagoon, I took advantage of the curving walkway to surreptitiously check behind me. To my relief, the path was clear.

I told myself I was being paranoid, and I blamed Koa. The spate of mysterious hang-up calls didn't help.

Resuming a more relaxed speed, I didn't stop until I reached the Prince Waikiki, where I could treat myself to a good cup of coffee. I let my heart rate gradually return to normal, watching the boats in the harbor while the warm breeze dried the sweat on my skin. Balancing on one leg, I pulled my left ankle behind me and stretched for several long seconds.

I turned to switch sides, and my arms broke into chicken skin.

Hoodie Guy was rounding the lagoon at a brisk clip. He slowed abruptly when he caught sight of me.

A faint whoosh from the hotel's automatic doors alerted me to incoming tourists. Using the crowd as cover, I ducked inside. Maybe I could hide in the women's bathroom. Heart pounding, I abandoned the idea when I saw it was located at the end of an isolated hallway. I was better off where I was. No one would try to attack me in a busy hotel lobby, in full view of the doorman, desk clerks, and early risers already gathering at the café.

Risking a glance through the glass doors, I could see the man loitering outside near the entrance, pretending to look out across the harbor at the fancy boats moored along the docks.

Slipping my phone from the belt at my waist, I dialed Koa's number.

"Maya? What's wrong?" he asked, his voice ragged and bleary.

"I-I think someone's following me." I took a deep breath, steadying my voice. "No. I know someone's following me."

"Where are you?"

I told him, and just like the night before, his calm, confident tone reassured me.

"Stay where you are. I'm on my way."

I took cover behind a large wooden sculpture near the café, sneaking quick peeks through the glass doors. The man took out his phone and held it to his ear before pocketing it and walking away.

Cautiously, I looked outside, scanning the street. But the man had vanished.

My phone buzzed. I knew it was Koa without looking, and suddenly everything clicked.

"I can't believe you had me tailed!" My angry hiss drew curious glances from people nearby.

Koa sighed deeply. "He wasn't tailing you. He was guarding you. I wanted to make sure you were safe."

"He scared the crap out of me!"

"I know. I'm sorry. He's a rookie and got a little overeager. Stay put. I'll be there in ten minutes to take you home."

"I don't—" I tried to tell him to go to hell. I was perfectly capable of walking across Ala Moana Boulevard by myself. But he'd already hung up.

I swore, flushing as the woman in front of me turned to give me a dirty look. Desperation for coffee kept me from slinking off in shame. Ten minutes later, the barista was handing me a large, Kona peaberry pour-over when Koa walked through the lobby doors.

I strode angrily toward him, not even bothering to doctor my coffee, prepared to lay into him.

Then I saw how haggard he looked. His eyes were red, face unshaven, and his rumpled clothes—the same ones he'd worn last night—looked as if they'd been slept in. My outrage dissipated. He'd promised to keep me safe, and I knew more than anyone how seriously he shouldered his responsibilities. Even if they were misguided.

"You look terrible," I said, handing him my coffee. "Bad date?"

He didn't answer, just accepted the hot beverage gratefully and took a long gulp.

"Seriously, Koa, were you up all night or what?"

Still ignoring me, he downed half the cup while I waited in line again, and by the time I'd added cream and sugar to my second order—this one iced—he was sitting on the faux leather couch in the lobby. I sank down next to him, and we silently consumed our much-needed caffeine.

"Since when do you jog, anyways?" he grumbled.

Rolling my eyes, I let him avoid my question. "Since I moved to the mainland. I needed . . . It gave me something to do. Sitting in front of a computer screen can do a number on your waistline."

He barely glanced my way. "You look fine, Maya. You always do."

"Flattery will get you nowhere."

This elicited a slight grin. He rubbed his face and finally looked at me. "Thanks for the coffee. I'm sorry I scared you."

"I'll admit, I've been on edge, lately. Ever since the attack. Plus, someone's been calling me and hanging up." My voice trailed off as I suddenly realized who my so-called prank caller was.

"What? Jeez, Maya, why didn't you tell me? Give me your phone, and I'll have it traced—"

"No. I'm pretty sure I know who it is. She's not trying to scare me. She's the one who's frightened. If I'm wrong, I'll let you trace the calls."

Koa hesitated, so I continued. "You have enough on your plate with this murder investigation. You don't need any more obligations. Least of all me."

He stood and held out his hand, which I took, letting him help me out of the sunken couch.

"Maya—" he said, not letting go of my hand.

Simultaneous chirps from our phones interrupted whatever he was going to say. I flashed him a questioning look, but he was as puzzled as me. Until we saw the text from Luke. We grinned at each other and read aloud in unison.

"*She said yes.*"

* * *

We left the Prince Waikīkī together. His unmarked car was parked illegally in front of the hotel, and he slipped the valet a few bills before opening the door for me. I didn't even try to dissuade him from escorting me into my apartment.

"Are you hungry?" I asked when he'd finished checking for intruders.

"Starving."

I fished out a half-carton of eggs from the mini-fridge and a small container of leftover rice. He leaned over and peered into the metal mixing bowl I was using.

"You cook?" he asked, his voice skeptical.

I flicked my wrist, cracking an egg on the tile counter, expertly splitting the shell open single-handed. The egg slid cleanly into the bowl with a soft plop.

"Yes," I said, unable to resist a smug grin as Koa's dubious expression faded.

Not that I could blame him. I'd once blown up his microwave after school when I'd tried to defrost a chicken wrapped in foil. Uncle David had come home to a screeching smoke alarm, a hysterical Matt, and Koa dousing the microwave with a fire extinguisher. That night, the four of us had gone to Zippy's for dinner.

He'd never let me near a kitchen again.

"Wait. You're the one who brought the butter mochi to the party? It was really good. So, did you or your mom make it?

"Me, smart-ass."

Chuckling, he cleared the table, which was cluttered with my usual assortment of papers, notebooks, and pens, while I sliced Portuguese sausage.

"Where do you keep your bowls?" he asked.

I pointed my knife at the cupboard next to the stove. He rummaged around until he found two rice bowls and pulled some chopsticks from a blue Japanese ceramic vase on the counter. He heated a pan and started frying sausage while I chopped cabbage. I added the container of leftover rice, and he tossed everything together while I carefully poured splashes of shoyu until the white grains were tinted with bits of orange and brown.

"This'll be your first wedding," Koa said when we sat down to eat.

"What?"

"You haven't been to any of the other ones."

"Oh. Right."

Willa had asked me to be a bridesmaid when she got married a couple years after I left, but I'd just scored an important internship that I hoped would turn into a permanent job, which it had.

When the invitation to Matt's wedding arrived in the mail, I'd debated right up until the RSVP deadline before finally deciding against going. Over the years, other classmates and friends had gotten married too, but those nuptials had been easier to avoid, especially living three thousand miles away.

There was no way I could get out of going to this one.

"Lani would kill me if I missed her wedding," I said.

"No joke."

As if on cue, my phone rang, and I grinned knowingly. "Speak of the devil," I said, tapping the answer button. "Hi, Lani. I hear—"

Koa's frantic hand gesture stopped me mid-congratulations. Leaning close, he whispered in my ear. "Act surprised."

His breath felt warm on my cheek, and my skin tingled. I suppressed a shiver, taken off guard by my body's reaction to his nearness. I nodded brusquely and stood, walking to the couch. He started clearing the table, dishes clattering as he put them in the sink.

"Is that Koa?" Lani's voice was a welcome distraction.

How did she know? "Um, yeah. It's nothing—long story. So what's new?"

"Luke told you, didn't he?"

"There might've been a text. I'm so thrilled—"

"That's not why I called. I'm going over to Monica's shop later, and I thought you might want to come with. Luke said you wanted to talk to her. How soon can you get here?"

I glanced up at Koa. "I just got back from a run, give me a chance to shower. I can't wait to try on bridesmaid dresses."

Hanging up, I turned back to Koa. He leaned against the kitchenette counter, arms crossed with one eyebrow arched at me.

"Since when do you like trying on bridesmaid dresses?"

Chapter Thirty-Two

Lani's briefing began the moment she unlocked the door to her shop.

"Whatever you do, don't mention Koa, ya?" she said, gesturing me inside. "Monica hates cops."

"But Koa's so warm and cuddly. How can she resist?"

Lani stopped and looked at me over her shoulder as she locked the door. "I dunno, Maya. You tell me."

"I have immunity."

"Yeah, right."

Something flashed in the bright Hawaiian sunlight pouring through the store's windows, and I remembered my friend's news.

I drew her into a hug. "Congrats, ya?"

Lani sniffled, and when we pulled apart, I noticed what looked suspiciously like a tear. "Look who got her accent back," she said, swiping it away. "Come, I gotta grab the snacks."

A few minutes later, we were in the bookstore's staff lounge, sitting at a surfboard table piled with books and stacks of vinyl "hang loose" shaka sign stickers. Incense hung in the air.

Lani opened the box of malasadas, bear-shaped buns, and pink and purple waffles.

"Ube mochi waffle?" she asked me.

I shook my head "Thanks. I had breakfast."

Lani arched her brows. "We'll talk about that later, ya?"

Monica put down her grinning bear bun and glanced between me and Lani. "You want to tell me what's going on?"

"I'm sorry, Monica. Lani's heart was in the right place, but she reads too many bad detective stories." I glanced at my friend, who had the grace to look sheepish. "I was hoping you'd tell me about Adam. Like about his last name."

Monica stilled, and I took advantage of her hesitation.

"We've been saying it wrong. He uses the Hawaiian pronunciation—*hah lay*, doesn't he?" I said. When she didn't say anything, I continued. "Look, this is off the record. I won't tell anyone—"

"Oh, really?" she said, crossing her arms. "I heard you're working with that detective."

"You can trust her, Monica," Lani interjected. "She won't say anything to Koa, ya, Maya?"

"Not unless you say it's okay."

Monica looked at Lani, then me, as if trying to decide before relenting. "I don't know Adam's real name. When I met him, he was already using Hale. But I had my suspicions, same as you."

"How did you meet?" I asked.

"Just like I told you, at the bookstore where I used to work. There was a café, and he came in every day, working away on his laptop. He seemed kinda lonely, and he reminded me of my grandson back in California. So I made friends with him, introduced him around." She pointed her pastry at me. "He's a good kid. When I opened this place, I didn't have a lot of money, and he offered to handle my accounting for free. I insisted on paying, of course, but I know he charges me a fraction of what he could."

Monica told us Adam was a finance guy, a whiz with numbers, with clients all over the United States. It explained how he could afford a place in Hale'iwa, but not why he had been working as a day laborer at the Hamilton estate.

"He's not kama'aina, you know. He blends in as a local because he's hapa, but you can tell. He sounds kinda like you and me." She peered at me over the rim of her tortoiseshell glasses.

He'd barely spoken that day in the garden, but I'd suspected as much. "Where was he from?"

Monica shook her wiry gray curls. "No idea."

"Surely you must have a work history, Social Security number, something like that?"

"Nope. Paid him under the table. All I know is, he came to Hawai'i for a job. Everything else is just stuff I put together on my own, guesses, really. So there's nothing to tell the cops."

"What made you think he was using an alias?" I asked.

She bit into her pastry, lifting her shoulders in a shrug as she chewed.

"He's a private guy. Doesn't say much," she said when she finished. "But one day, after he left work, I had to use the store's computer. He forgot to close down the browser, and there was a website for adoptees looking for their families. It got me thinking about his name—"

"Because *hale* is Hawaiian for home," I said.

She nodded. "Kinda on the nose, ya?"

"So how'd he get involved with the Kaimukī neighborhood group?"

Monica snorted as she ripped off the head of another teddy bear bun, chocolate oozing out. "He wasn't. I told the cops that, but they won't listen. The only reason he was at that meeting was to bring the snacks. I was running late, and he did me a favor 'cause that's the kind of kid he is."

Lani's head bob confirmed Monica's statement. "We've had several meetings, and I'd never seen him before."

"He signed in and stuck around long enough to end up on a Facebook post," I said.

"The secretary likes to keep accurate records. She probably made him sign in," Monica said. "I'm telling you, Adam had no skin in the game. There was no reason for him to go after the old man, let alone kill him." She sat back, brow furrowed. "I'm worried about him. He was going to hang out with a few of us the day of the murder, but he never showed at the bar. I didn't think much of it, but then he didn't respond to any of my texts, which is unusual. The store got busy, so it was a couple days before I had a chance to drive up to Hale'iwa."

A pile of newspapers on the doorstep had heightened her concern. She'd used the key he'd given her and found his cat, Nekko, hadn't been fed.

"She was like his child. There's no way he would've left her alone like that." Monica paused, and I could see her knuckles turning white as she gripped her cup. "I went back to his apartment yesterday. I think someone had been there."

The mail and newspapers had been picked up and placed neatly on a table. Even the cat bowls were full.

"But I took Nekko home with me the first day," Monica said, gesturing to a clear plastic bin on the floor filled with a bag of cat litter and food. "If Adam had really come back, he would've called to find out what happened to her."

"Maybe it was the police," I said.

She shook her head. "I don't think so. It was too neat. Not like the place had been searched."

"Did you tell any of this to Detective Reyes yesterday?" I asked.

"How do I know they won't twist what I say to suit their bullshit case?" Monica said. "I'm not doing anything to help them hang Adam. I know he didn't kill Charles Hamilton."

I realized Monica had an agenda of her own and maybe a blind spot when it came to Adam Hale. But it didn't mean she was wrong.

"If Adam is innocent, he doesn't have anything to worry about," I said.

Back at Lani's shop, I nibbled on a purple waffle and tried not to think about how pissed Koa would be if he found out about our meeting. Though technically not evidence, Monica and I were withholding information in a murder investigation.

"I hear Koa didn't come home last night. Care to explain why he was doing your dishes this morning?"

I paused midbite, trying to process the information and wondering crazily if my friend had somehow read my mind. "I have no idea where he was last night."

Her lips curved in a knowing smile. "If you say so."

"I don't. I swear." Her look said she was unconvinced. "He was at the hospital visiting a crime victim, and then he came over, but it was for work. He left around midnight."

"You two running pals now or what?"

"That was a misunderstanding. Have you ever thought maybe he's got a girlfriend?"

Lani looked askance. "What? You think I wouldn't know if he did?"

I couldn't argue with her there. Lani knew everything about everyone, especially our group of friends. Then I remembered how Koa looked when he'd shown up at the hotel—uncombed and wrinkled, like he'd just gotten off an oversold red-eye flight, or . . .

"Son of a—"

"What?" Lani asked, alarmed.

"Nothing." I had just figured out where Koa had been, and it was time to change the subject. "I think Monica should talk to Koa. He's an overprotective pain in the ass, but he's a good detective. We both know he'd never let an innocent man rot in jail for a crime he didn't commit."

Lani arched her perfectly shaped brows, fixing a pointed stare at me. "I suggested talking to Koa already, but it was a hard no," she said. "Figured you were the next best thing."

"If Koa finds out about this little meeting, I'll be the one in jail."

"It's okay. I'll come visit, ya?"'

We laughed like we were kids again. I threw a wadded-up napkin at her, and she batted it away, the light glinting off her new bling.

I caught hold of her hand, exclaiming over the slender gold band with delicately etched plumerias crowned by a tastefully sized diamond.

"You knew Luke was going to propose, didn't you?" I said.

She smiled, lifting one shoulder. "Of course."

"You two were always meant to be." It came out more wistful than I'd intended. "Well, it's about time. I'm so happy for you, Lani. I can't wait for this wedding. Have you set a date yet?"

Slowly, Lani shook her head. "We're probably going to hold off making any plans. The local economy hasn't been great, and I'm still carrying a lot of debt on the store. If a mall goes in, I could lose this place. Luke and I don't need to pay for a wedding on top of everything else."

My heart ached for Lani. I knew how long she'd dreamed of having her own boutique and how hard she'd worked to make it happen. I hated that circumstances beyond her control were jeopardizing not only her dream, but her future with Luke as well.

"We may be in luck. An investor from the Big Island is interested in doing a smaller shopping center, more friendly to mom-and-pop type businesses."

She showed me a document with the development company's primitive-looking symbol, some kind of stick figure, next to its name, NHR, Limited Liability Corporation.

"So you could be getting hitched sooner than you think, ya?"

Lani's face brightened, and she smiled. "I did sketch a few ideas for your dress. Wanna see?"

Not waiting for an answer, she disappeared into the shop, giving me a few minutes to consider what she'd told me. A memory niggled on my brain's periphery, but I couldn't grasp it. I looked at the document Lani had left on the table, staring at the company's name. I reached for a malasada, hoping a little sugar would jog it loose, when Lani returned with her sketchbook.

She flipped through the pages and pointed to an ink drawing of a sleeveless gown in a translucent aqua the color of Hanauma Bay. Elegant and sexy, it draped in a deep V to the breast bone, nipping snugly at the waist before falling to the floor in a swirl of fabric.

"It's gorgeous, Lani," I said, hastily pushing away the Portuguese doughnut. I'd need to cut out a few sweets if I wanted to fit into my bridesmaid dress. "Maybe a long engagement is a good thing."

* * *

Back home, I headed straight to my laptop to take another look at Adam's Facebook page. One by one, I clicked each profile on his friends list, scouring every post for mentions of Hale for hours, but came away with nothing aside from a few animated birthday GIFs. All his friends seemed to be local, except for a tousled, blond-haired, blue-eyed surfer dude type.

He turned out to be the owner of a successful chain of surf shops located up and down the California coast. Curious how the two knew each other, I looked through the entrepreneur's posts until a picture of a surfing competition caught my eye. A woman stood out because of her bright pink tank top bearing a popular Hawaiian surfing logo.

It was probably nothing, I told myself. Plenty of mainlanders wore Hawaiian T-shirts. Especially surfers. But I clicked through the list of women tagged in the photo anyway. And hit pay dirt.

It was one of those group shots so big you could barely see anyone's faces. They were standing in the back, their arms wrapped around each other, his face half hidden by her hair. No one named Hale was tagged in the photo—or any subsequent posts—but Adam Whittaker was.

Chapter Thirty-Three

It was late afternoon by the time I had enough to warrant a trip downtown. I didn't call ahead. I knew exactly where he'd be.

I pulled into the parking lot and slid into an empty space. Grabbing my purse and a manila envelope I'd tossed on the front seat, I hurried across South Beretania Street. At the public counter, I gave the receptionist my name, and a few minutes later, a uniformed officer admitted me through the security door.

I signed in, flashed my California driver's license in exchange for a laminated guest badge I was told to wear at all times while on the premises. After passing through a metal detector, the officer escorted me up three floors, through a warren of hallways to the Homicide division.

Koa's desk was wedged into a corner of a large nondescript office divided by low cubicle partitions. He'd arranged his workspace so he had a clear view of the entire division.

Detective Reyes barely looked up from her nearby cubicle, mumbling a greeting without a pause in her keyboard tapping. Koa ended a call, slamming down the receiver as I approached.

"—fucking ghost," he said, slumping back in his chair.

"Hale?" I used the monosyllabic, Western pronunciation. The reporter in me couldn't resist digging. "Not finding much?"

I must've caught him in a moment of weakness because he said, "The guy hasn't got a record anywhere—no driver's license, no social, not even a freaking parking ticket. It's like he didn't exist before—"

"Two years ago?"

Crossing his arms, he eyed me, one brow raised.

"What're you doing here, Maya?" he asked.

"Helping you with your case." I held out the envelope, where I'd stuffed printouts of everything I'd found online. "His name's Whittaker, not Hale."

Reyes shot out of her chair and scowled. "What the—"

"Amy, I got this," Koa said, pulling rank with a warning look before she could protest further. "You mind telling me how you came up with that? I told you to stay outta my case."

"It was just a little Internet research."

A few more minutes of digging was all it had taken to stitch together Adam Hale/Whittaker's backstory. I'd taken care to omit anything Monica had told me in confidence, sticking to what I'd dug up using social media, Google, and my reverse directory subscription.

He eyed the envelope as if it were an incendiary device, while his partner fumed.

"His ex can probably fill you in—her name and number are in there," I said, tossing the envelope on his desk before turning on my heel to leave.

I made it past the cubicles but hesitated when I hit the main corridor, trying to remember which way the elevator was. Koa appeared beside me, grasping my elbow as he steered me to the left and down another long hallway to the elevator.

"I'll walk you out," he said, pushing the call button.

"You don't have to. I can manage."

"We don't let visitors wander around the station by themselves."

"Oh. Right. 'Course not."

"Look, Maya. Give me—"

The elevator dinged, interrupting him. The door slid open.

A woman in a fuchsia sheath dress, lined and tailored to hug curves and nip her tiny waist, stood inside. Dark brown hair was pulled into a low, sleek ponytail. She flashed her pearly whites at Koa.

"Glad I caught you, Detective. Amy said you were on your way down, and I wanted to speak with you before you left," she said, heels tapping as she stepped out of the elevator. "I need an update on the Hamilton case. Conference room?"

Koa blocked the door before it could slide shut again and nudged me inside, his hand warm on the small of my back, before following close behind.

"Start without me. I'll be there in a few minutes."

She gave a faint frown, glancing my way. "The prosecuting attorney believes we need to get ahead of this latest development."

"Amy can fill you in. She knows everything I do," he said, cutting her off with a punch of the ground floor button.

The polite smile faded as we began our descent.

"What was that about?" I asked.

"Nothing."

I waited a few beats, knowing he'd say more.

"Politics and the DA's bullshit agenda," he said.

The pressure was on for Koa to close the case. "I'm not trying to cause any more problems, but you need to take a look at what I found. I'm not sure Adam Hale—Whittaker—is your guy."

I braced for a scathing lecture, threats of incarceration, or at the very least a warning about where I stick my nose, but none came. If anything, I thought I saw Koa's shoulders and jaw ease a fraction.

The elevator stopped. Koa nodded a greeting at the two officers who stood aside as we exited, then escorted me to the security desk, where he waited for me to sign out and return the guest pass.

"I'll walk you to your car," he said, leading me through the lobby where we drew a few interested glances from his colleagues. He remained silent as we picked our way through the public lot, stopping well out of earshot at my Civic. "We need to talk, but not here," he said. "Have you eaten? We could meet at the Wailana, say around six?"

It'd been one of our favorite late-night hangouts. We'd spent countless hours there, talking, laughing, and eating into the wee hours of the morning, usually with Lani and Luke and the rest of the old gang, sometimes just the two of us.

I hesitated until my stomach rumbled, and turned to open my car door. "Sure. See you there."

"Maya—" Koa's voice had taken on the familiar warning tone.

"Before you start lecturing me, I told you, it was just a little cybersleuthing—completely legal and totally safe."

I slipped into the driver's seat, and he shut the door, leaning against the frame. "Somehow, that doesn't make me feel better."

"See you at six," I said, wiggling my fingers at him as I backed out of the parking spot.

* * *

Koa was twenty minutes late, a rarity for him. He'd texted me from the station and again when he was on his way. By then I was already at the restaurant, so I ordered a Coke and reviewed the notes I'd made for my upcoming meeting with Parker. We needed to have a serious talk about the difference between fact and fiction, and I was dreading it. A few minutes in, I found myself drifting back to Facebook.

I'd spent hours digging into Whittaker's online life, clicking posts, his friends, and friends of friends, wondering if it was all a waste of time. But I'd emerged from the rabbit hole with a synopsis of a life.

Adam Whittaker was a UCLA grad who listed Pacific Beach, a suburb north of San Diego, as his hometown. A financial wunderkind, he loved surfing and playing the ukulele, and was just as social media shy as his Islander alter ego.

I'd managed to find one decent photo of him posing on a SoCal beach, laughing animatedly with an arm draped around the woman from the surf shop, presumably his girlfriend, the other arm clutching a surfboard. A few more clicks confirmed my hunch, and a brief search on a professional network site resulted in her place of employment and contact information.

I'd stopped short of calling her myself.

Now I wanted to see if there was any more information to dig out. Sure enough, one of his friends had mentioned him in a comment, inviting him to join a private group for adult adoptees. An idea popped into my head. It was a long shot, but I knew I couldn't let it go.

My phone buzzed, and I glanced at the screen. It was my unknown caller again, and this time I was ready for her.

"Don't hang up. I know who you are. You're the UH student, ya?" I paused, remembering how fluttering curtains had sent me into a panic. "I know you're scared, but if you hear me out I think your story could help other women."

I held my breath until I heard a quiet, "Okay."

We arranged to meet the following week. I was putting the date in my calendar when Koa slid into the chair across from me. "Sorry I'm late. I had to deal with something," he said, looking bleary-eyed and haggard.

I almost felt sorry for him, until I remembered why he was so tired.

"You look terrible. You should get more sleep," I said, sipping my Coke.

Our waitress came by, and Koa ordered coffee. She immediately produced a carafe, pouring him a generous cup and flashing a smile at his polite "Mahalo."

He caught my tone and glanced over the table at me. "I'm guessing Lani told you I didn't come home last night. It's not what you think," he said, gulping down half his cup. "How does she know this stuff, anyway?"

I had no clue, but I never doubted my friend's intel. Leaning forward, I met his stare. "Oh, it's exactly what I think. You spent the night in your car outside the Ainahau. You stalk all your friends, or is it just me?"

A corner of his mouth quirked. "I don't have to *stake out* my other friends—none of them get in trouble the way you do."

The waitress reappeared to take Koa's order.

"I'll have mac nut pancakes with eggs and Portuguese sausage." He handed her the menu, looking sheepish as he turned back to me. "I didn't have breakfast. This is the first meal I've had all day that didn't come out of a vending machine. You having your usual?"

I nodded, mildly annoyed he knew my order. The Wailana was a better breakfast joint than dinner, so I typically got another local favorite—a hamburger patty over rice, topped with brown gravy and a perfectly fried egg.

"I'll have the loco moco," I said to the waitress. "So what did Whittaker's girlfriend tell you?" I asked when we were alone again.

Koa peered at me over his coffee mug. "You don't know already?"

"I swear, I didn't call her." He hesitated, so I jumped in. "Let me guess, he's adopted."

"I thought you said—"

"Facebook. How d'you think I found the girlfriend in the first place?"

Koa sighed, shaking his head as he rubbed his brow. Our food arrived, and he reached for the guava syrup, drizzling it over his pancakes, before absently cutting off about a quarter slice and slipping it onto my plate.

"Sorry," he said, realizing what he'd done. "Force of habit."

It was on the tip of my tongue to point out it'd been twelve years since we'd eaten together at the Wailana, but I was starting to realize our friendship was a force of habit neither of us could break. Maybe that was a good thing.

I scooped part of my hamburger, rice, and egg onto his plate, and he grinned at me crookedly.

"So Adam Whittaker is adopted. Does that have anything to do with why he came to Hawai'i?" I asked between bites.

"Yes and no. Turns out he was born here. The Whittakers adopted him while his dad was stationed at Hickam, and he's lived on the mainland since he was ten." Koa forked a piece of burger, swiping it through gravy and runny egg yolk and eating it with a scoop of rice.

Eager for the full story, I tapped my foot impatiently while he finished chewing.

"His parents died a few years ago, and that's when he got into the whole ancestry thing, according to the girlfriend. He took one of those DNA tests, which is how he found out he's hapa. Can you imagine going your whole life not knowing what you are?"

"He doesn't know anything about his biological parents?"

He shook his head. "It was a private adoption. But a couple years ago, a new client offered to bring him here for a big project. So, he took it, figuring he could dig up more information about his family, look up hospital records, that kind of thing. She heard from a mutual friend that he had a lead. They broke up, so that's all she knows."

I huffed under my breath, sinking my fork into a pancake and swirling it in pink syrup before raising it to my lips.

Koa eyed me. "How'd you know she was his ex if you didn't talk to her?"

I gave him a pointed look. "He's been here for two years, and yet she's still where? San Bernardino? Please." I speared another bite of pancake and jabbed the air for emphasis. "If they were really in love, they'd be living in the same time zone by now."

Koa frowned and pushed food around on his plate.

"So did she say anything else?" I asked.

"No. She hasn't talked to him in a while." He sat back and drained his mug. Our waitress was quick to refill it.

"It explains a lot," I said, after she left. "Why he changed his name, living below his means, off the grid, so to speak. He's reinventing himself, trying to figure out who he is."

"Right now, he's looking like a pretty good suspect." Koa's tone didn't match his words, and I knew he had his own doubts.

I played with the paper straw in my soda. "He had kind eyes."

"What?"

"In the garden, when we met, he seemed . . . nice. I get why he's the logical suspect. But the more I find out about Adam Whittaker, the less he seems like a killer."

"Yeah, well, I need something more concrete than your feelings if I'm gonna take this case to the DA," Koa said. Reading my silence, he lowered his half-raised mug, his expression dark. "What've you got?"

"Nothing 'concrete.' And I can't prove it because the photos were taken from my place."

"Just tell me."

"Okay, remember the one of Stephen when he was a kid?"

He nodded, squinting as if trying to recall the details. "You said he was with Mrs. Goto, ya?"

"Yeah, only I don't think it was Mrs. Goto. Someone wrote the date on it—September '88. She would've been about forty-five or so. The woman in the picture was in her late twenties, tops. I think it was her daughter."

Koa put his fork down. "You gonna show me her Facebook profile or what?"

I shook my head. "I've never even heard anyone mention her name. Parker's old high school buddy said she died years ago. I think she was Stephen's nanny. Adam was born in February of '89, right?" I already knew the answer. I'd seen all the well-wishers on his Facebook timeline. "She was wearing a pretty big mu'umu'u—what if she was pregnant?"

Koa's silence left me hanging. I took the plunge.

"And Parker Hamilton cheats on his wife." At Koa's look—first puzzled and then incredulous, I added. "You're the one who doesn't like coincidences." I knew it was a big leap.

Koa rubbed his forehead. "You know what I really don't like? Nosy civilians playing armchair detective. That's a huge leap with no evidence to back it up. And if anything, it means Whittaker would've had a claim on Hamilton's money, which means he had motive."

"Why would Adam kill Charles before he'd changed his will? If anyone, Parker had more motive to kill his father to stop him from cutting him out."

"Parker is the only one of my suspects who has a solid alibi—the mayor of Honolulu and you," Koa said. "And anyway, even if Whittaker was his grandson—and that's a big 'if'—he could've realized Charles never planned to follow through on his promises. Maybe the rejection sent him over the edge, and he killed him."

He drummed restless fingers on his coffee mug. "Most criminals aren't that smart. Nine outta ten cases, the obvious suspect is the killer. Right now, the guy who used a fake name, trespassed onto the estate the day of the murder, and then disappeared is looking pretty good for this."

I had to admit, it made sense. But then I thought of the ukulele-playing surfer guy, who'd come to Hawai'i searching for his family, and cared enough to help a bookstore owner keep track of her finances for free. I wasn't buying it.

Something told me Koa didn't either.

He put his fork down, pushing the plate away. "Look, there's something else I need to tell you."

A tug on his ear triggered déjà vu, but I reburied the memory. While I had no delusions of domestic bliss in California, there was plenty of fodder for other bad news. I braced myself.

"You were right about Nichols. We cleared him."

The words penetrated, but their meaning had a delayed response. "What?"

"Your 'friend.' He's no longer a suspect. He came in. Gave us a detailed timeline of his day, even passed a polygraph." Koa cleared his throat. "He was on a video conference call from three to six. His buddy Stephen too. They recorded it and everything. You could hear the ambulance siren."

"Why were they being so cagey?" I asked.

"Hamilton doesn't want his dad to know about some business venture he's working on."

"So, he lied to you about where he was?"

"Turns out he was downtown that morning. We got ahold of his building's security video, and his car was parked in his reserved spot until he left to have lunch at the estate."

Koa also confirmed Mark had told the truth about the phone calls he'd received while on our date at the restaurant. "They were from his firm in California," Koa said. "He even had an explanation for how you two met. Stephen was supposed to go to the museum fundraiser and represent the family but bowed out and asked Nichols to go instead."

I frowned, mentally going over the dwindling list of suspects. "So you're saying Adam Whittaker is the only suspect now that Stephen and Mark have been eliminated."

Koa's brows arched as he peered at me over his coffee mug. "Funny, I thought you'd be happier to hear your boyfriend isn't a killer."

Chapter Thirty-Four

Monday started out promising—a double rainbow with my coffee on the lanai. What could go wrong?

Turns out, a lot.

I had a meeting with Parker, and for once he didn't keep me waiting.

"We need to talk about your run for state senate in '97." I looked at my notes to check the date.

We were in his office, the windows and plantation shutters thrown wide open so the trade winds could breeze through. Parker sat back in his chair behind an antique koa wood desk, elbows propped on armrests.

"The other guy ran a dirty campaign. I tried to rise above it all, but there's no telling what voters will fall for."

According to the press clippings I'd read, that wasn't quite the story. The Hamilton political machine had been first to sling mud, but the local Gulf War veteran from Hilo had risen above the fray, trouncing Parker. Reading between the lines, the state senate seat was meant to have been a stepping stone to the governor's mansion and beyond. Instead, Parker's single, disastrous foray into politics had been his last.

Stephen was the family's last hope to put a Hamilton in office.

Parker checked his Rolex impatiently. "Skip it. Ancient history no one remembers. What else do we need to discuss?"

Glossing over issues was one thing. Lying about them was a line I wouldn't cross. I put down my pen and met Parker's gaze. "Fine. If that's what you want. But we have to talk about some . . . inaccuracies in the manuscript you gave me."

"What inaccuracies? I wrote the damn thing myself. Are you trying to say I got my own story wrong?"

I'd anticipated Parker's bluster. "No. But memory is a tricky thing," I said, giving him a way to save face. "You're a public figure. You don't want a reader Googling something you wrote about and questioning you or the integrity of your book."

With or without a byline, I didn't want my name associated with a pack of lies. I was prepared to walk away.

Parker steepled his fingers and glared at me, but I held my own, never looking away.

"I suppose I may have misremembered a few things," he said after a long pause. "Everything's on the Internet these days, most of it garbage. It's probably best to be prudent."

I should've been relieved, but I was looking for an out too. I nodded and picked up my pen.

"Your book could also use a more personal touch. Like a funny story or memory, something readers can relate to." I decided to appeal to his love of sports cars, hoping to salvage our interview. "Tell me about your first car."

Parker's face broke into a nostalgic grin, and the decades fell away. "It was a red Mustang convertible. Man, I loved that car. My friends and I went everywhere in it—we got into a lot of trouble."

"Like what?" I asked, sensing a good story.

He thought for a moment. "You know about Pele and Old Pali Road, right?"

I glanced up from my notebook, intrigued. Everyone knew bringing pork on the steep abandoned road up the jagged Ko'olau mountains to Nu'uanu Pali would risk the wrath of the fire goddess.

"Naturally, we didn't believe any of that stuff, so we thought it would be a blast to see what would happen if we did," Parker said. "We snuck out of the house with some leftover Chinese takeout. We got about halfway up the Pali when the engine started sputtering and died. I'm talking total system failure. Not even the headlights worked. That car was brand spanking new."

He paused, staring unseeing at the horizon as if lost in memories.

"What did you do?" I asked.

"Everyone was shouting and screaming. I was totally panicked. Dad would've killed me if it hadn't been for—"

I waited, but when he didn't continue, I said, "What happened?"

"What? Oh, Catherine threw the pork over the side of the road." He chuckled, shaking his head. "The damned car started all on its own, just like she said."

I stopped scribbling and looked up. Keeping my voice neutral, I asked, "Who is Catherine?"

A creak made me jump. Elizabeth stood in the doorway, shoulders set, her face mottled pink. In a flash, the fury in her eyes disappeared.

"Just some local girl, right, dear?" she said, smiling coolly at her husband.

* * *

We broke for a long lunch when Parker had to take another private conference call. I grabbed a couple of finger sandwiches and followed the sound of the ocean.

Where green lawn gave way to white sand, I slipped out of my sandals and walked to the water's edge, letting the warm waves slap against my ankles. The water was calm, but I knew better than to turn my back on the sea.

This part of the island was rockier than Waikīkī, and large patches of ancient lava bed spotted the white sand beach. I passed the raised bungalow Stephen used as an occasional crash pad and decided I had time to explore a little further.

Salt air mingled with the sweet scent of ʻawapuhi, and I breathed in deeply as I wandered the shoreline. Once I'd gone another hundred or so yards, an outcrop of rocks jutting into the Pacific blocked my progress. Rather than scramble over sharp lava, I started to turn back when it hit me.

The sickly sweet smell of rotting flesh.

I took out my earbuds and scanned the beach, but there was only surf, sand, and the occasional driftwood. Whatever the source, it had to be big, judging by the stench and swarm of insects I heard before I could see. It was coming from the rocks.

The smart move was to leave and call 911.

But I wouldn't be me if I'd walked away.

I slipped my sandals back on for better footing as I scrabbled for a firm grip on the porous rock. Wishing I'd worn my trusty sneakers, I gingerly picked my way across the ancient lava bed where thousands of years of pounding surf had carved treacherous crevices.

I covered my nose and mouth as I drew closer to a tidal pool buzzing with flies. By the time I reached the edge, I had to squint, but I could see it was a deep fissure partially blocked by something caught on the rocks. Peering closer, I could barely make out a silhouette covered in seaweed and writhing creatures.

A swell crashed through the blowhole, spraying salt water and critters. I caught a glimpse of a gray Local Motion T-shirt and empty eye sockets where a crab clung.

I reeled back, falling on the sharp, black lava rocks, the scream rising from my throat drowned out by the surf.

Chapter Thirty-Five

"You have a thing for dead bodies or what?"

I glared at Detective Reyes from across her desk in the squad room. I'd lost track of time, but over an hour had lapsed since I'd reported finding the missing Adam Whittaker. A uniformed officer had shuttled me away from the crime scene, leaving me to cool my heels in the chilly police station until Reyes had shown up.

The adrenaline rush was long gone, and the only thing fueling me was annoyance. But it didn't seem to faze Reyes. She didn't back down until Koa's shadow loomed over us.

"I think we've got what we need for now," he said.

She clicked her pen and stood, tucking it into her back pocket along with her notebook. "Yeah, sure, brah. I gotta go talk to one of the techs."

Koa leaned against Reyes's desk and handed me a bottled water. He'd ignored me until now, letting his partner question me while he spoke with the Hamiltons, and for some reason I was more pissed off at him than Reyes. I sipped the cold water, then downed the rest in a couple of gulps, eager to rinse away a lingering taste of bile.

I'd managed to make it back over the rocks without falling again, taking off in a sprint the moment my feet touched sand. I'd run as far as the bungalow before finally stopping to call the police, barely noticing the stinging cuts on my hands. By the time the first patrol car had pulled up, I was heaving into the bushes.

"She has a point," Koa said. "You've been around a lot of bodies considering you've only been in town what? A couple months? Why the hell didn't you just call 911?"

"I did." I tried unsuccessfully to keep the edge out of my voice. I was sick of explaining myself to cops.

"Before you went traipsing through a crime scene—"

"And do what? Report a bad smell on the beach?"

Koa ran a hand through his hair in frustration. "What were you thinking, Maya? You promised to quit—"

"I was thinking I'd go for a nice walk on the beach. I wasn't thinking I'd find your dead murder suspect. But you're welcome." My voice rose in volume and pitch, and I wasn't sure if the quaver at the end was out of anger or horror as the image of Adam's battered face suddenly flashed before me.

Several heads turned our way. I crossed my arms over my chest, suppressing a shiver. I couldn't get the stench of decaying flesh out of my nostrils, and I imagined it clinging to me like sand.

I looked down and noticed streaks of dried blood on my arm and dress. My fall on the rocks had banged me up more than I'd realized. The pale pink T-shirt dress I'd worn for my meeting with Parker had gotten soaked in my dash along the beach, and the material clung to my thighs. Salt water and sand had ruined my leather sandals.

Koa grabbed a zippered hoodie from the back of his chair. He draped it across my shoulders, and I pulled it tight around me, ignoring its familiar scent.

He disappeared, returning moments later with a first-aid kit. He knelt in front of me and took my hand, examining the gash on my palm. Gently he cleaned off the blood and applied antibiotic ointment before bandaging the cut.

"I'm sorry," he said when he'd finished. "You've had a bad shock. I'll take you home, and you can sign your statement in the morning, ya?"

Koa's gentle, sweet side was worse than the gruff detective I'd learned to tolerate. Tears pricked my eyes, and I bit my lip to stop it quivering. As if sensing an impending breakdown, he grasped my elbow and led me to a deserted hallway, where I promptly burst out sobbing. Koa pulled me to him, letting me cry into his shirt as he murmured soothing words.

It had the opposite effect. Ugly, wrenching sobs devolved into snorts. I was too distraught to be mortified. Images of a living, breathing Adam Whittaker in the garden flashed in my head and mixed with ones of his corpse, teeming with bugs and sea animals.

When the crying jag finally subsided, Koa reached into his pocket and produced a tissue. This time, I accepted it gratefully, knowing full well my face was a hot mess. I blew my nose. His mouth curved upward at my noisy honking, and I flushed.

"Koa." Reyes appeared at the other end of the hall. She motioned him over, and he jogged to her.

Over the tissue, I watched as his partner handed him a plastic evidence bag, which he examined for a moment before holding it up and peering at what looked like scraps of green paper through the fluorescent light.

I caught snippets of conversation—something about a male and a wallet. Abruptly, the tone changed. Koa's posture stiffened, his voice grew tense and words like "mayor" and "prosecutor" were enough for me to guess which way the trade winds were blowing.

"You're not buying that 'accident' bullshit, are you?" I asked later when we were out of earshot, safely ensconced in his unmarked Dodge Charger.

He didn't answer, turning onto South Beretania toward Waikīkī.

"The body had on the same clothes I saw him wearing that day in the garden. He's been dead all this time, hasn't he? He couldn't have killed Charles."

Koa remained silent for several moments. "Between decomp and the sea life, the cause and time of death are going to be tricky to determine. There's no way to know who died first. He could've circled back to the house and poisoned Hamilton."

"Then who killed him?"

"No one," Koa said, grimly. "Not according to the Hamiltons—and my superiors. The working theory is Whittaker killed Hamilton and fell on the rocks while fleeing the scene, bashing his head and drowning. Pretty convenient, huh?"

"But you don't think so."

Koa shook his head. "It doesn't explain who mugged you and broke into your place."

He insisted on escorting me up to my apartment, performing his usual security check, but for once I didn't protest.

After he left, I found myself periodically scanning the street below, peeking through the parted drapes, wondering if the killer was still out there waiting for me. I finally went to bed when I spotted a familiar Dodge, and slept better than I had in weeks.

Chapter Thirty-Six

Honolulu PD's "working theory" got leaked to the press, and by noon it had become the official story. But my inside source gave me the scoop before I'd finished my morning jog.

I spotted Koa as I rounded the lagoon. "We're closing the case," he said, his face grim as he handed me a coffee when I came to a stop.

I tried to catch my breath, taking in the news. Disheartened and angry, I swallowed the bitter drink as we walked in silence.

"You free for a little while?" Koa asked." I have to go into the station, but there's something I want to give you."

"A present? You shouldn't have. It's not even my birthday."

"You're not gonna like this."

He was right.

"Pepper spray? Seriously, Koa," I said ten minutes later. "What do I want pepper spray for?"

"In case you run into trouble."

He'd waited until we were back at my apartment before handing me a small, black canister on a quick-release keyring. It had a blue top and fit in the palm of my hand. I skimmed through the packaging highlights. The number one brand used by police not only had UV marking dye, it also came with a "be prepared" safety video. There was a second pepper spray still in the plastic packaging, this one minus the blue stripe.

"It has a range of about ten to fifteen feet. Hold it in your fist with your thumb on the trigger, ya? You'll have a stronger grip that way. There's a safety trigger, so practice using it." Koa demonstrated how to hold the pepper spray, flicking the safety switch to the side with his thumb.

He handed it back to me. "Okay, go ahead. Let me see you try it."

"You mean here? I don't want to use it all up—"

"See the blue cap? It's the practice one—it's only filled with water."

Koa insisted on practicing on the lanai, showing me how to release the safety and aim for the eyes, using a back and forth motion. After ten minutes, he seemed slightly mollified.

"Get familiar with using it. And don't throw it in your purse. I've seen that huge bag of yours. Keep it clipped to something, so it's always accessible," he said.

"Like what? My purse strap?"

He shook his head. "Try your belt loop, ya? When you're running, clip it to the drawstring on your shorts. Keep it on your person at all times. You always forget where you leave your bag."

I sighed in resignation and dropped the pepper spray on the counter next to my keys. "I'll figure something out. Anything else?"

He tried to sound casual, but I could read the subtext. "Lani says you're thinking of sticking around."

"Um, yeah. It was . . . nice hanging out with everyone at the party. But I was just thinking out loud. Why?"

His expression gave nothing away, which of course meant the news didn't please him.

"You could use some self-defense classes. I know someone. She's good. Trains all the rookies."

"I'll think about it."

"Yeah, right. I know what that means. At least let me show you a few tricks."

"Tricks?"

He took my right hand and bent it back gently, pressing on the fleshy heel. "Hit with your dominant hand and aim for the nose or throat. If you have them, use your keys and go for the eyes. Trust your instincts. If something seems hinky, you're probably right. Just like the other night in the alley."

"That could've been nothing—"

"Doesn't matter. Better safe than sorry," Koa said. "Don't forget a hard knee to the groin to take a perp down."

"Hand, eyes, balls. Got it. Anything else?" I said.

"Call me if anything happens—not 911. It's faster than going through dispatch. Doesn't matter what time. I don't care what it is—you have a hunch or get spooked. Promise you'll call me."

I knew he'd never let it go, so I promised. Koa grasped my arm, turning me to face him. "I can't watch you twenty-four/seven—"

"Not for lack of trying."

"This is serious, Maya. I can buy a couple of days to wrap things up, but if I catch another case . . . I'd never forgive myself if something happened to you."

"Nothing's going to happen to me," I said with more bravado than I felt. "I'll be fine. Quit worrying so much."

He sighed and shook his head in frustration. "I had a bad feeling the second I heard your voice on that 911 call—I knew you'd be trouble."

* * *

Koa was wrong about Adam Hale, but not about me.

Playing a hunch, I waited until the coast was clear and hit the road to Hale'iwa. The anonymous tipster from the café had been dodging my calls and texts. It was time to meet face to face.

Lucky for me, people are creatures of habit. I found her at the café sitting in the same spot in the corner at Adam's favorite table.

Snatching the adoptees' flyer from the bulletin board, I sat opposite her and slid it across the table.

"You bonded over more than a mutual love for numbers, didn't you?" I said, tapping the flyer. "Tell me about Adam Hale."

Her red-rimmed eyes told me she knew he was dead. She sniffed and nodded. "He saw me putting up flyers and asked about our group. Not that he ever came to a meeting, but we started talking. I felt sorry for him, you know? I have a large, adopted family, there's too many of us really. Both his parents were dead, no grandparents, aunties, or uncles. He was totally alone in the world. Can you imagine what that was like?"

Tears fell, and she swiped them away, her lips forming a small smile. "You should've seen him when he got his DNA test back. It was like he'd won the lottery or something."

His ex-girlfriend had told Koa about registering his DNA with one of the genealogy sites.

"I thought there weren't any matches," I said.

"No relatives were listed, but he found out he was half Japanese . . . *and* he had ancestors from Great Britain. His whole life he never knew what he was." She paused, tears falling again. "Now we'll never know *who* he was."

"Did he have any clues? Birth certificate, adoption papers, anything to go on?"

"Just some old photos of him as a baby."

With so much information online these days, it seemed odd he hadn't been able to find out anything about himself.

"It was unusual," she said. "We used to joke he was related to royalty or something."

Half the day was gone by the time I left the café. Determined not to hide in my apartment again, I took my laptop onto the lanai to get some work done. Pushing all thoughts of Koa and his self-defense lessons out of my head, I was finally making progress when my phone buzzed. I glanced at the caller ID.

"Ms. Wong . . . male . . . you."

I stood and went inside to hear better. "Sorry, Mr. Lopez. I didn't catch that. There's a man downstairs to see me?"

"You have certified mail. Can you come down and sign for it?"

"Oh, sure. I'll be right there."

A few minutes later, after a brief chat with the building manager, I was back in the elevator heading up to the twelfth floor. I glanced at the envelope I'd been expecting from my editor at the women's magazine. Deidre was surprisingly old school for someone so keen to cover the latest trends. Not only did she use snail mail to send my contract for the dating app story, she'd paid extra to make sure I received it. I stared down at the green remnants of the label still clinging to the envelope.

A memory niggled in the back of my brain. Something I'd overheard Koa telling Reyes about the address on Adam's driver's license . . . but what had he actually said? I mentally rewound twelve hours, struggling to remember Koa's exact words. Something about a male and wallet. I flashed on an image of him trying to read something on bits of green and white paper in the glaring light of the police station.

I looked down at the envelope still in my hand.

Reyes said mail, not male.

Suddenly, it all clicked.

In one of his last acts on earth, Adam Whittaker had sent a letter or package important enough to use certified mail to someone he trusted to keep it safe.

And I knew who it was.

Chapter Thirty-Seven

A bell on the door jangled, signaling my arrival at the empty bookshop. At first, nothing seemed amiss, until I ventured deeper inside and a flutter of papers drew my attention to the mess at the back of the store.

Bookmarks, postcards, and promotional flyers were strewn across the long, wooden counter. The gaping cash drawer was empty, and dangling computer cords told me someone had also taken a laptop and tablet.

I called Monica's name, my apprehension growing when there was no response. I was reaching for my phone when she appeared from behind a closed curtain.

"Can you believe this?" she asked, gesturing to what was left of the checkout area. "They got the back room too."

"How much did they take?"

"Nothing was in the till, but it'll cost plenty to replace the POS system, and I can't afford the extra expense."

"You know whoever did this was after the envelope Adam sent, ya?"

Monica froze and averted her eyes. "I don't—"

"Stop bullshitting. Adam sent you something through certified mail. I saw the envelope at the bookshop. The cops found the receipt in his wallet. It's only a matter of time before they figure out who he sent it to and—"

"They found Adam? Did they arrest him?"

Shit.

Monica didn't know Adam was dead.

I glanced through the window at people passing by on the street. "You should close the shop. We need to talk. In private."

Warily, she agreed, and locked up the store before ushering me behind the curtain.

Her back office bore the brunt of the destruction. File cabinets were overturned, papers scattered across the floor, desk drawers haphazardly dumped in a search for something Monica was still hiding.

"I've been dealing with my insurance and the cops all morning. I haven't had the energy to start cleaning," she said, straightening a couple of chairs.

"Any idea how the person got in?"

"He broke the lock on the back door. I haven't had the money to install a security system. It wasn't a big priority. I mean, who robs a bookstore? Not exactly a cash cow business."

She made tea and we settled at her desk, a plate of senbei between us. As gently as I could, I told Monica about finding her friend's body. Blocking out the images still fresh in my head, I was careful to leave out grisly details.

"The police believe he fell on the rocks while running away from the Hamilton estate," I said. I wasn't revealing anything that hadn't already been on the news.

"They're sure it's Adam?" Her face was slack with shock, and her tanned, sun-roughened skin had paled. She looked to me for a glimmer of hope.

Not for the first time, I wished I hadn't been the one to break the news. "It's not official, but yeah. They're sure."

She slumped in her chair. "I don't even know who to call—"

"Monica, you need to talk to the police."

She stiffened. "They're saying he killed Hamilton, aren't they? No way I'm going to help them."

I knew Monica was no fan of HPD, but it hadn't occurred to me she'd withhold evidence now that Adam was dead. I thought about hitting her with the legal consequences of not going to the police, but I knew Detective Reyes's approach hadn't scored any points. Koa would be furious, but I took a deep breath and crossed the line anyway.

"Tell me, then. What did Adam send you?"

Monica looked at me sharply, her eyes narrowed as she studied me. "Why? You gonna blab to that cop friend of yours?"

I met her stare straight on. "Not if you don't want me to. But Koa is the most honorable person I know. He'd never stand by and let an innocent person take the blame for a crime he didn't commit. Just ask Luke, ya?"

Monica's pinched scowl eased a fraction. "Honorable, huh? Adam was too." She sighed and stood, reaching for her keychain with the little wooden book. "I'll think about it."

She pulled back the curtain, her message clear. I had no choice but to leave her to grieve alone. A few hours later, Monica changed her mind, but it had nothing to do with my powers of persuasion.

"The fucker was in my home." Her barely contained fury came through loud and clear even over the phone. "I'm on my way to your place. I'll text when I get there."

I hurried out the door, grabbing my phone and keys. Monica was in the lobby, peering through the glass doors by the time I got downstairs. Her hands played with the miniature book dangling from a now empty keyring.

I called her name, and she straightened, glancing outside once more, before meeting me halfway. She held out the keychain, the book prized between her thumb and forefinger. I reached for it, confused until she gave it a squeeze and a USB drive popped out.

"What's on it?" I asked.

"Spreadsheets and financial records of some kind. Not my thing, which is why I paid Adam to take care of that stuff for me. But these aren't my finances—way too many zeroes."

"Is that it? No letter, or any documents explaining what he'd found?"

She shook her head, reaching into her bag for a small, manila envelope with the shop's address handwritten on the front in a messy scrawl. Green and white remnants of a certified mail label still stuck to it.

"Just the flash drive. It came the day after the murder." She handed me the envelope. "I thought it was a gift. But then he disappeared, and weird shit started happening."

"Like what?" I asked, already anticipating her answer.

"A woman came into the shop looking for a book. The only other customer was a man, who looked like he was just a browser. When it came time to pay, she couldn't find her credit card, and she left without completing the sale."

"So what happened?"

"A little while later, I went to the back office and saw some asshole had rifled through my desk. Stole my purse and laptop."

"You think the woman was a diversion."

Monica nodded. "Right after that, someone started following me. A few nights later, I was home taking out the trash when I heard a Tesla. You know that funny hum it makes backing up? When I turned around, I saw one of the cheaper Model 3s. You see a lot of them here, so I didn't think anything of it. But then I saw the same one a few days later, parked behind Lani's shop."

"How do you know it was the same one?" I asked.

"It had a sticker for a local gym on the bumper." She glanced outside again, and for once the street was clear. "After that detective came to see me, I took another look at the keychain and realized what it was."

"Did you get a look at who was driving the Tesla?"

"A woman. Long, brown hair."

I was already scrolling through the photos on my phone, stopping when I came to ones I'd taken at Kawaiaha'o Church the day of Charles's funeral. I showed her the woman in the teal dress. "This her?"

She squinted at the screen and nodded slowly. "Yeah. Who the hell is she?"

"Someone up to no good," I said. I didn't know what it all meant, but I suspected Parker and this mystery woman were involved in something shady. The proof was likely on the flash drive.

"What happened today?" I asked.

"Someone must've broken in while I was at the shop. I got home and the back door was busted just like the store. Whoever it was took a camera and some jewelry, but—" Her shoulders lifting in a shrug. "Anyway, I'm getting out of town. My friend's letting me stay with her on Kaua'i for a few days. Do whatever you want with the flash drive. Tell your friend I'll talk. He's already got my number."

A chime sounded, and she reached into her pocket for her phone. "My rideshare is here," she said, tapping the screen. "Be careful."

Monica pushed open the door and stepped into the black sedan that pulled up in front of the building, and with that she was gone.

Still holding the envelope and flash drive, I grimaced, realizing we'd both handled evidence in a murder investigation. Hastily, I slipped the keyring onto my pinky and carefully grasped the envelope along the edges. Upstairs in my apartment, I dropped both items into a Ziploc bag and hurried back out again.

Chapter Thirty-Eight

The civilian clerk behind the bulletproof window recognized me, and a few minutes later the security door opened. Detective Reyes came out, nodding at the receptionist before turning to me. "What can I help you with?"

I held up the Ziploc bag. One look and her already dour face darkened. She knocked on the glass. "We're gonna need the conference room. Tell Koa to meet us there, ya?"

Reyes escorted me through security, then briskly led me down several hallways before unlocking one of the rooms. Holding the door open, she stood to the side and let me in.

"Wait here," she said, and disappeared, leaving me alone in the interrogation room.

With just enough space for a table and three chairs, the walls were covered with white soundproof tiles with the exception of a mirrored window at the far end of the room. My apprehension grew when I saw the bar attached to one of the end of the table, no doubt for restraining suspects. I sat in one of the chairs and tried to push back away from the table, but it was bolted to the floor.

Too late, I wondered if I'd made a terrible mistake.

I avoided looking at the two-way mirror, convinced Koa and Reyes were on the other side, biding their time and watching while my anxiety and temper festered. Twenty minutes later, they finally sauntered in, silent and stoic. Maybe I was imagining things, but the air between them seemed tense.

Detective Reyes took the lead. “You mind telling us where you got the flash drive?” she asked. Koa’s jaw clenched.

“From Monica, the bookshop owner. She’s a friend of Adam Whittaker’s.”

“Why’d she give it to you and not us?” Reyes asked.

“‘She doesn’t like the police. Can’t imagine why.”

“Maya—” Koa began.

I ignored him. “You watch the news lately? She thinks you guys have already tried and convicted him, and she doesn’t want anything to do with helping you.”

“Just tell us what happened, ya?” Koa said.

With a shrug, I explained how Monica had befriended Adam and why she hadn’t been entirely forthcoming with Reyes or me until someone had broken into her store and home.

“So she called you?” Koa asked.

Slowly, I shook my head. “Not exactly.”

Reyes narrowed her eyes at me. “Then why exactly did you go there?”

I told them how I’d noticed them examining the remnants of the certified mail receipt. “I put two and two together,” I said, glossing over the bit about their overheard conversation. “I had a hunch. I went to her shop this morning and caught her when she was mad.”

Koa’s face darkened, and I averted my eyes, telling myself I would’ve remembered seeing the envelope at Monica’s bookshop even if I hadn’t overheard his conversation with Reyes.

“What’s on the drive?” Reyes asked.

“I didn’t open it, but she says they’re financial records of some kind. We’re talking big money. Hamilton kind of money. Maybe

Adam thought he could find something that would stop the Kaimukī project."

"Did you handle the evidence?" she said.

The detective's lips pursed when I nodded, and she turned to look at Koa, whose jaw had become permanently clenched.

"We need your prints for elimination purposes. Monica's too," Reyes said, her voice tight.

"She's gone. Left for Kaua'i, but she said you can call her."

Koa stood and walked to the door. Pushing it open, he whispered a command to an officer standing at the door and sent her hurrying to obey. Alarm bells went off in my head. They'd never stationed a patrol officer outside the other times I'd been interviewed by Koa and Reyes.

He came back, taking a stance against the two-way mirror, arms folded across his chest. Then Reyes went in for the kill.

Looming above me, arms akimbo, she rested one hip on the table and studied me. "You're always in the middle of a shitstorm. Everywhere we turn in this investigation, there you are. Do you realize we can charge you with interfering with a homicide investigation, not to mention withholding evidence?" She leaned in close, her voice low. "Koa told us all about you. Why you left the islands, how all you cared about was going to the mainland and being a big-shot reporter. Not much of a career left now, huh?"

Heat spread across my chest, crawling up my neck until my face burned. I'd been sucker punched.

"You know what I think?" Reyes continued, unchecked by Koa. "I think you're trying to get back in the news game, angling for one big, juicy exclusive, ya?"

Koa said nothing, his silence telling me all I needed to know. Too furious and hurt to even look at him, I faced down Reyes instead.

"I'm not writing about any of this. I'll probably get fired for the things I told Detective Yamada. I did it because I don't want some asshole getting away with murder." I stood, glaring at her. "Do you?"

I turned and left, throwing open the door and letting it slam behind me.

* * *

I stalked out of police headquarters, blindly heading toward Waikīkī on foot, although I'd driven downtown. My phone started buzzing by the time I hit the city park a block away, but I ignored it. Breathless and overheated, I paused under the shade of a banyan tree.

I couldn't stop replaying the scene in my head, my humiliation growing each time. Reyes had said "us." Who else did Koa blab my life story to? What other personal, intimate details had he spilled?

I'd been an idiot. Against my better judgment, I'd let my guard down out of sentiment and misplaced loyalty. He'd had me so suspicious of Mark, when all along it was Koa I should've been wary of. I wondered how much legal trouble I'd gotten myself into.

I took out my phone to call Luke, but before I had a chance to dial, it vibrated in my hand. I hit the answer button, without registering the caller ID.

"What?" My angry bark was loud enough to turn heads.

"Uh, hi. It's Mark—are you okay?"

I flushed, turning away from the curious stares. "Sorry, I thought you were someone else. I'm . . . not fine."

"I heard about what happened yesterday. God, Maya. I'm so sorry."

It seemed like a lifetime ago.

Before I could answer, he continued. "I know things have been weird because of this murder investigation, but I wanted to make sure you were all right. I canceled the rest of my week and got back early. If you're comfortable coming over, I could make you dinner?" Mark paused. "Not to brag, but I make a mean risotto primavera."

I shook off the voice in my head warning me to be careful. Mark and Stephen had both been cleared by the cops. The case was closed as far as they were concerned.

"I'll be there in fifteen minutes." I hung up and shut down my phone.

Who needs Uber when you can go old school?

Stepping onto the busy downtown street, I raised my arm and hailed a cab.

Chapter Thirty-Nine

I strode through the beige-toned lobby of the sleek, modern glass building rising above Kewalo Harbor where Mark lived. The doorman was expecting me, and after being waved through to the elevators, I found myself riding up forty-one floors.

Mark threw open the door, hitting me with the smell of simmering chicken broth, wine, and basil.

"Hi," he said, giving me a hug meant to be comforting. "You hungry?"

"Starving." My return smile was half-hearted. I needed to shake off all thoughts of Koa and murder. "But I'd kill for a glass of wine."

He led me through the open living area with its floor-to-ceiling windows and breathtaking view into a gleaming, state-of-the-art gourmet kitchen, where we sat at the large granite island. He'd put together a charcuterie board of cured meats, olives, cheese, and crackers. A bottle of my favorite Sterling Vineyard pinot grigio sat breathing on the counter. He poured a generous amount into a tall wineglass teetering on a delicate stem.

The drinkware in the dishwasher back at my place was stemless and plastic.

I took a long sip, letting the warmth from the alcohol seep through me.

"It must've been horrific. I can't imagine what you've gone through," he said.

It took a moment for me to realize he was talking about finding Adam Whittaker's body on the beach and not the fiasco at the police station. I nodded and lifted my glass again.

"Do you want to talk about it?" he asked, spooning broth from one pot into another.

I hesitated, unsure what I should and shouldn't say about yesterday's events, and I didn't have the energy to pick through the minefield. I was furious with Koa, but talking about him and his case could land me in more trouble.

"Do you know any good defense attorneys?" I asked. "Preferably cheap."

Mark's spoon stopped mid-scoop. "Why do you need a lawyer? You're not going to confess to killing Charlie, are you?" he said.

"No, but the police are probably going to charge me with interference, withholding evidence, and some other bullshit."

Mark wiped his hands on a kitchen towel. "I doubt Detective Yamada would go that far. It's probably just empty threats to make sure you cooperate. I know someone who owes me a favor. I'll call him in the morning."

He reached for a nearby bottle of wine and refilled my glass.

"Looks like we have the same taste in wine. Must be kismet." My gaze landed on a half-full glass of red. "Or maybe not?"

"You always order the Sterling, so I may have bought a bottle for you," he said, a slight flush in his cheeks. "Not that I was expecting—I mean . . ."

My mouth turned in a genuine smile for the first time that day, and he grinned back, sheepish.

"Smooth, huh?"

"That's okay. I don't trust smooth men."

"I get the impression you don't trust men much at all. I never quite know what's going on with you. Luckily, I'm told I have a thing for mysterious women," he said.

"You may want to rethink that." I spread goat cheese on a cracker, topped it with prosciutto before popping it in my mouth.

He smiled again and resumed stirring the risotto as I took another sip of wine. Beginning to relax, I surveyed the counter, which was bare except for the drinks, charcuterie, and neatly arranged vegetables.

I selected an Asian-style chef knife with a steel blade and wooden handle and after locating a cutting board started cutting mushrooms. He drizzled olive oil into a hot pan, the vegetables sizzling as they hit the surface. I helped myself to some olives and watched him cook.

"What exactly have you been doing on the Big Island? Is your client in real estate like Stephen?" I asked.

"Yeah, something like that. There's a big investor who has a place in Waikoloa Village. He'd rather stay there when he's in the Islands, and since he's got the big bucks, I go to him."

"What's he investing in?"

Mark hesitated. "I can't really say much at this point."

Talk about secretive. Then again, if I had money to invest in a big-time real estate project in Hawai'i, I'd probably be cagey until all the i's were dotted too.

Another glass of wine and several crackers later, Mark dished risotto into two white porcelain soup plates, finishing them with grated Parmesan and a few twists of the pepper grinder.

We moved to the dining room where we had an unobstructed view of the ocean and the harbor lights twinkling below.

"Can I pour you a glass of prosecco? It pairs well with the risotto," Mark said.

"Sure." I squelched the urge to ask for a scoop of mango sorbet with the sparkling Italian wine. It would probably ruin his careful pairing. I took a bite of risotto instead. It was delicious and perfectly balanced—the wine cut into the creamy richness. Mark was also right about the prosecco.

"My compliments to the chef," I said, and he rewarded me with a smile. "I have to admit, this definitely beats my place."

"Steve found it for me. You know the Hamiltons were the developers for the whole area. You should see his place—top floor corner unit. He kind of goes back and forth between here and the beach house. I'm pretty sure his grandfather left it to him in the will."

Poor little rich boy.

"They read the will already?"

Mark chuckled. "Always the reporter, huh? From what I heard, it was pretty standard. Parker was named head of the company and got the bulk of the fortune, minus a very nice trust fund for Stephen. There were also a few bequests to charitable organizations."

He shaved more Parmesan onto his plate and offered the grater to me. I shook my head.

"No surprises, then?" I asked.

Mark shrugged. "Nothing big. But there was some interesting language in the will, something Charlie added a few months before his death."

At my questioning look, he went on. "Language that opens the potential for any biological progeny to inherit."

My ears perked at this. "Is that typical?"

"Not at all. Usually people in the Hamiltons' tax bracket want to avoid the possibility of other beneficiaries. But it was included in some additional gifts to nonprofit groups, so it could've been an oversight."

"You'd think people in their tax bracket would have a better attorney."

He avoided responding by sipping his wine. "I think the old man did it on purpose—to piss off Parker."

Arching my brows, I looked at him skeptically. "Why?"

"Because the Hamiltons are just like my family—it's all about power and money." He stood, taking my plate. "Why don't you relax, check out the balcony. I'll bring dessert out."

Curiosity got the better of me. Instead of going outside, I lingered behind, checking out the minimalist decor and examining the few personal photos making the space Mark's home. I recognized one of him with Stephen astride a horse at the family ranch on the Big Island, judging from the brand on the animal's flank.

A memory niggled in the back of my mind, but I couldn't quite get there.

I'd already surpassed my usual alcohol consumption by at least one glass. Combined with the tumultuous past few days, I wasn't firing on all cylinders. When the espresso machine hissed in the kitchen, I gave up trying to pry loose what was bothering me and made my way onto the lanai.

By then the Pacific had turned an inky black aside from a few cresting waves. Honolulu city lights twinkled below, marking the shoreline along Ala Moana Beach as far as Waikīkī. The trade winds were warm and sweet.

Mark joined me moments later carrying a store-bought fruit tart.

"This really is a spectacular view," I said.

"One I don't get to enjoy very often. I'm hardly ever here."

He put down his plate and turned to face me. "Can I ask you a personal question? Are you seeing anyone else? Besides me?"

I shook my head. "No. I'm not."

Mark searched my face, his eyes serious. "Not even that detective guy?"

"Especially not that detective guy," I said, meeting his gaze. "Are you?"

"Me? No," he said with a chuckle. "I believe in equal pay, marriage equality, and a woman's right to choose, but I'm not quite modern enough to juggle dating more than one woman at a time."

"That speaks more to your inability to multitask than having a progressive attitude."

Mark chuckled, the freckles across his face dancing.

"Can I ask you something?" I said, alcohol loosening my tongue. "It's been bugging me for weeks now. Why didn't you say anything about knowing the Hamiltons when I told you about my job?"

He winced, an embarrassed flush spreading across his cheeks. "Because I didn't hear you. The lady on the other side of me was so excited about the auction, the only thing I caught was something about researching a book. I didn't want you to think I wasn't listening, so I bluffed my way through our date. I didn't realize who you were until I met with Stephen the day Charlie died."

A laugh escaped. Once it started, I couldn't stop, and Mark joined in. Eventually, he took my plate, letting it clatter to one of the wooden patio tables. Cupping my face in his hands, he kissed me. I wrapped my arms around his neck and drew him closer.

* * *

I woke to sunlight and soft chimes. I reached out blindly for the nightstand before I remembered I wasn't in my own bed. My eyes popped open, and I lay perfectly still, straining my ears as I tried to assess the morning-after situation.

All was silent. I was alone.

I breathed a sigh of relief, suppressing a slight uneasy twinge. Last night had been lovely, a pleasant encounter with a man I'd grown to care about. But I couldn't quite shake the feeling I'd slept with Mark for all the wrong reasons.

Clutching the blanket to my chest, I sat up and looked around, spotting a note propped against an iPad on the nightstand.

I had an early morning meeting and didn't want to wake you.
Help yourself to breakfast, coffee, or anything else. I'll see you tonight.

XOXO Mark

A bell chimed again. Mark's iPad, apparently synced with his phone, lit up with the first few lines of a message from Stephen about "The Ranch." I guessed he was referring to the cattle ranch on the Big Island.

I located my clothes, dressing quickly, before going in search of my bag. It was sitting on the dove gray leather couch, where I'd dropped it shortly after arriving at Mark's apartment. Digging out my phone, I turned it on, and it lit up with a dozen missed calls and texts from Lani and Koa.

I swore. This never happened back in California.

Switching my phone to silent mode, I headed for the kitchen, desperate for coffee, when my gaze landed on the photo of Mark and Stephen in cowboy hats.

For two preppy Ivy Leaguers, they looked a lot like paniolos about to wrangle cattle. I squinted, peering closer at the brand on the horse's flank—a series of squiggles and lines that looked like an ancient Hawaiian petroglyph.

I'd seen it before, and this time I knew where.

I grabbed my bag and slipped silently out of the apartment.

Chapter Forty

I made a beeline for my laptop as soon as I got in the door. Googling the name of a colleague I'd worked with at a small weekly paper in Northern California, I hunted for a written record confirming my hunch.

I was out of luck. Too much time had passed, and I couldn't remember enough details to find the article I was looking for.

Checking the time, I called my friend, hoping she'd remember more about the developer who'd pulled a bait and switch on what was supposed to be a walkable, mixed-use retail project.

She didn't answer, so I hung up and tapped out a long text, asking her to send me whatever information she had on the controversial project. I had to be sure I was right before I broke the news to Lani.

My phone chirped. It was a text from Parker, asking me to meet him at the estate in an hour. Depending what my friend told me, I knew it could be my last meeting with Parker Hamilton.

* * *

Dressed in a white linen top and khaki shorts, I slipped on white sneakers and hurried to the door.

As I reached for my keys on the foyer table, my gaze fell on the pepper spray. Cursing the voice in my head, I grabbed the canister and tucked it into the pocket of my shorts.

Twenty minutes later, I drove through the gates at the Hamilton estate and parked under the porte cochere.

Parker was running late as usual. "He probably had a last-minute meeting. I'm sure he'll be back soon. Was he expecting you?" The events of the past few days seemed to be taking a toll on the normally efficient Mrs. Goto, who looked at me, distracted, through puffy eyes.

"You can wait for him on the lanai. I'll bring coffee and snacks," she added.

I descended the porch stairs and made my way to the lanai just as I had a few weeks earlier. It seemed like a lifetime ago. My phone beeped as I neared the pool, and I saw I had a new email message from my friend. My resolve steeled as I skimmed scanned copies of her stories. Validation was bittersweet. I had no choice. I knew what I had to do, and it meant I'd be out of work by the end of the day. But I'd been half-expecting it.

This job had been a mistake from the start.

I sank into a plush patio chair, tapping rapidly on my phone as I drafted a letter of resignation. An alert popped up, letting me know I had another message. I started to swipe it away, until I saw it was from Koa's audio expert. I opened the email. He'd finished cleaning up the recording of my first interview with Parker and had attached a digital file. I plugged in my wireless earbuds before hitting play. Seconds later, I heard myself ask Parker what he wanted to accomplish with his biography.

"Legacy. My family made Hawai'i. I want you to write our story. It will be our gift to the people."

I cringed inwardly as I had then but continued listening until a maid arrived to clear away the food. Clanking dishes made it hard to hear the audio, so I stood and walked away. Unconsciously, I steered clear of the beach, still listening as I followed the path until I found myself back at the Japanese garden.

Drawn by the koi, I watched their golden bodies shimmy through the water, Parker's voice still in my ear. He was talking about the manuscript he'd written when Mrs. Goto interrupted to let him know about the call from the mayor.

I started to fast-forward, but stopped when I heard a rustling sound followed by a series of muffled voices I couldn't make out. I hit rewind and bumped up the volume, but it was still too garbled to hear clearly. I gave the volume a couple more taps and hit play.

This time I heard footsteps on the lanai, followed by something hard hitting the glass tabletop. More rustling and clinking ice cubes.

Then the voice of a dead man came through the airwaves faint and barely intelligible.

". . . It's done. I've given it to someone I trust, so save your breath . . . What . . . stuff in my drink?"

". . . sweetener."

". . . don't like sweet tea."

I turned the volume as high as it would go, straining to hear the other voice, but got nothing.

Sighing in frustration, I lowered the volume again and hit play.

Moments later in the recording, Parker and Elizabeth had arrived. Parker mumbled something, and then came the crash of glass.

I frowned, rewinding a few seconds. Once again, I upped the volume and pressed play.

"Elizabeth, wha—"

A slap of skin, then glass shattering on flagstone.

"Oh, Parker, you're such a klutz—"

I held my breath, looking up slowly as the last pieces fell into place.

Clicking heels on stone pavement. Swirling ice cubes in a glass of iced tea. The broken glass that wasn't an accident.

I knew who the killer was.

Chapter Forty-One

My phone vibrated, and for once I was relieved to see Koa's name flash on the screen. I hit answer.

"Maya?" His voice was urgent, almost scared.

Before I could say anything, I heard the crunch of pebbles somewhere close by.

My eyes darted up and down the path, but I couldn't tell which way the footsteps were coming from. Trapped, with nowhere to hide, I dropped the phone back into my bag.

I slipped my hand in my pocket, closing my fingers around the canister of pepper spray. The scent of her rose perfume wafted by, and I turned as the footsteps came to a halt.

"You've figured it out, haven't you?" The thinly veiled venom in Elizabeth Hamilton's voice chilled me.

Desperate to stall for time, I played dumb. Furrowing my brow in mock confusion, I flashed a quick smile. "Figured what out?"

She laughed mirthlessly. "Don't be coy, Maya. It's beneath you."

Sunlight glinted off chrome, as she aimed a gun directly at me. My heart stopped. Swallowing hard, I dropped all pretense and glared at the woman. My only hope was to stall.

"I've worked out some of it. Like how Charles was planning to change his will to include Mrs. Goto's grandson—his grandson—forcing Parker and Stephen to share the Hamilton wealth. But you couldn't have that, could you, Elizabeth?" I paused, hoping for a distraction, anything to buy me time.

"You planned to make Charles's death look like natural causes. If poisoning him with his own medicine had actually worked, I'm guessing you would've been a widow before the year was out."

Elizabeth's mouth twisted into an evil smirk as she kept the gun trained on my chest. "I look good in black. I wasted my life on Parker, but Stephen's capable of achieving everything his father never could. I won't let anything get in his way."

"You knew all along who Adam Whittaker was," I said. My voice was unnaturally loud, and I prayed Koa could hear me.

Elizabeth didn't seem to notice.

"Charles tried to pass him off as a day laborer Mrs. Goto hired. But I knew he was Parker's bastard the moment I laid eyes on him. I should've guessed the old man would keep tabs on him. He always was overly sentimental. I mean, that girl was the nanny, for god's sake."

Spittle rained tiny droplets on pristine pink silk.

"Is that why you lured him here? To kill him?"

"With Charles out of the way, I didn't need to kill that tramp's kid. But everything went wrong that day, starting with Charles waking up late. By the time I fixed his drink, the estate was crawling with people."

Elizabeth's knuckles whitened around the gun. "He saw me crushing up pills for the old man's shake. I could've made some excuse to pass it off, but there was something in his eyes . . . He knew."

I let her ramble on, glancing behind her in the hopes of spotting Mrs. Goto or one of the other household staff.

"Don't bother. There's no one left but Mrs. Goto, and I sent her off on an errand. No one's coming to your rescue."

Fighting back panic, I gripped the pepper spray, my fingers crawling up the cannister until I felt the plastic trigger.

"How'd you get Parker to stay quiet? He must've figured out it was you—"

Sharp laughter, bordering on hysterics, cut me off. "My husband is an idiot. He doesn't have a fucking clue. Besides, Parker only cares about Parker. He doesn't give a rat's ass who killed Charles or his brat. Distracting him was child's play. I got him to chase after the will and financial records, and when this is all over, he's going to look like the guilty party."

I thought of Parker's last-minute summons, realizing too late that she'd sent the text using his phone.

"How'd you know about the records Adam had?" I asked.

"He told me. A fruitless attempt to save his life, I suppose." Elizabeth's low chuckle made my skin crawl. "His mistake was running to the water. I cut him off at the tidal pools by the beach house, where I knew we kept an old set of golf clubs. I have a killer swing."

An image of Adam's body, caught on the rocks and battered by the surf, flashed in my head.

"You *bitch*," I spat.

Antagonizing the woman with the gun wasn't the smartest idea, but I was beyond caring. I tightened my grip on the pepper spray. Using my thumb, I flicked the safety to the side. I eyeballed the distance between us, trying to calculate the odds of me hitting her without getting shot, when I heard rustling.

A branch cracked.

Elizabeth swung her head toward the sound, and I took my shot. Raising my arm, I stepped forward and aimed for her eyes. I squeezed my thumb down on the dispenser, sweeping in an ear-to-ear arc, painting her face with the orangey red toxin.

A direct hit.

Her eyes snapped shut, and she recoiled, screaming. But instead of dropping the gun, she fired unseeing, bullets hitting the stone wall, rock shards ricocheting in all directions.

Another shot rang out, and I felt a sting on my arm.

I turned and fled.

I thought I heard someone shouting my name, but I wasn't going to stick around to find out. Elizabeth stood between me and the driveway where my car was parked. I headed across the lawn toward the ocean. If I could reach the beach house, I could get help from one of the neighbors.

His mistake was running to the water.

Even though Elizabeth must've been firing blindly, my escape route was too exposed, a fact punctuated by the shot echoing through the garden. A bullet whizzed past my head. I swallowed a scream, turning sharply to dive behind a banyan tree, where I found myself back at the entrance to the hidden path.

I took off down the rugged trail, running blindly through overgrown brush. Branches tore at my clothes. Sharp-edged bamboo leaves slashed my bare skin, slick with sweat. Something warm dripped down my injured arm.

Every rustle and twig snap convinced me Elizabeth was hot on my heels. I ran faster, the ground beneath me a blur. I was terrified I'd stumble on a rock or log, but even more afraid of the murderer pursuing me.

I didn't dare look back.

I could already smell the briny ocean air and knew I was close. Moments later, I reached the garden gate. Only then did I allow myself a quick glance back.

Nothing.

I pushed open the gate, crashing into a warm, solid, and very familiar chest.

I nearly collapsed with relief.

"Maya—" Koa's voice was choked. Grasping my arm, he propelled me behind the shelter of the house. He backed me against the wall and peered around the corner, keeping watch.

"Are you hurt?"

I shook my head. I could barely breathe, let alone speak. "It was her—"

"I know."

I shivered, and he pulled me into his arms, holding me so tight I could feel his pounding heart. Tears leaked from my eyes, and I let out a shaky breath.

"You scared the shit outta me." Koa drew back to examine me and paled. Letting out an oath, he stared at his hand, the fingers stained red. "You're bleeding. Were you hit?"

Gingerly, I touched my stinging arm and shook my head. "I think I got sprayed by rocks. I'm fine."

He didn't seem to hear me, not satisfied until he'd given me a once-over. "Where is she?"

"I don't know—I'm not sure if she followed me." I paused.

Koa peered around the corner of the building again, and for the first time I noticed he was holding a gun. Gripping my arm again, he pushed me toward the driveway.

"How'd you know to come to the beach house?" I asked.

"Lani."

I remembered our synced phones, suddenly grateful for technology and my best friend.

"I knew you were in trouble because you actually picked up," Koa said.

"She confessed. Elizabeth killed Adam and Charles—"

"I heard," he said through gritted teeth. "When this is over, we're going to have a serious discussion about diffusing tense situations."

Still holding my arm, he led me to the carport where a patrol car was just skidding to a halt, lights flashing, its siren silent. It stopped behind the Jeep Cherokee parked haphazardly in the curved driveway with the driver's door still gaping open.

Koa steered me to the black-and-white, opening the back passenger side door, gently but firmly pushing me inside. "Watch her," he barked at the officer and shut the door.

"Wait, Koa. Where are you going?"

"Stay here. You'll be safe with Chang."

He turned and disappeared back around the beach house. Minutes passed. Chang murmured assurances and called for backup that I knew would arrive too late.

The crack of a gunshot echoed through the neighborhood, confirming my worst fears.

Yanking on the handle, I threw open the door and leapt out, ignoring Chang's shouts. Legs churning, I sprinted back through the foliage, retracing my earlier flight. It seemed like forever before I finally caught up with Koa at the end of the path.

We were back at the garden where it all began.

Elizabeth Hamilton lay sprawled on the ground half submerged in the koi pond, her unseeing eyes still red from the pepper spray, a gaping hole in her chest.

Mrs. Goto stood a few feet away, a rifle dangling from her lowered arm.

"Drop the gun. Now," Koa commanded in a voice I barely recognized, his own weapon raised.

Straightening, she let the rifle fall to the ground. With lightning speed, Koa kicked it away and handcuffed her behind her back while simultaneously reciting her rights.

Mrs. Goto turned to look at Koa, angry tears in her eyes. "She killed my grandson. So I killed her."

Chapter Forty-Two

Chang whisked me away to police headquarters, leaving Koa behind to deal with Elizabeth Hamilton's death. I sat huddled in an interview room, swathed in Koa's sweatshirt again and feeling like a caged animal behind a two-way mirror before the door finally opened hours later.

I looked up and tried to cover my disappointment.

"Detective Reyes. Where's Koa?" I asked.

"He's taking Mrs. Goto's statement."

She placed a Zippy's takeout bag on the table and took out containers of chili and a couple of Spam musubis. Sliding a Coke can toward me, she said, "Call me Amy."

I took the drink, looking at her skeptically. "Are you supposed to be the good cop now?"

The corners of her mouth turned up ever so slightly. "I think we got off on the wrong foot." She sank into the chair across from me, opened a soda, and spoke in a low voice. "I was just trying to protect my partner. He was . . . too close to this case."

I paused, then reached for a musubi, unraveling the cling-film wrapper in silence. She pried open a takeout bowl and dug in with a plastic spoon, unearthing a scoop of chili and rice.

"How'd you figure out it was Elizabeth Hamilton?" she asked after she'd finished eating.

I told her about the cleaned-up audio recording of my first interview with Parker, digital proof Elizabeth had poisoned Charles's tea, served it to him, and then knocked the glass out of his hand to destroy evidence.

"She was there when I turned off the recording app on my phone. She must've been afraid of what was on it because she sent someone to go after it not twenty-four hours later," I said. "The guy in the baseball hat, I'm guessing."

Amy gave a shake of her head. "Koa's instincts were right on the money. He insisted those muggings weren't random, but I thought his judgment was clouded."

I hadn't believed him either. "Where's my phone? I can forward the file to you." Chang had taken my phone and pepper spray as evidence.

"It's being processed. We can have our IT guys download it."

I nodded. "Koa was already on his way to the estate when he called me. He said something about going there to arrest Parker. What for?"

Amy stopped writing long enough to give me a resigned look. "We spent all night going through the flash drive you and the bookstore owner turned over. Took us a while to work it all out, but it seems Parker had his hand in the till of Hamilton, Inc. Weird considering it's his family's company."

"Charles controlled it. Not Parker," I said.

Amy nodded. "The records on the drive are proof Parker was embezzling millions from the firm, and even taking money that was supposed to go to the running of the estate to bribe city officials to get his projects approved. The problem was, his plans never made enough money to put back what he stole."

I remembered Parker's last-minute meetings and the furtive phone conversation with the woman in the teal dress.

"He's probably involved with a woman in the planning department. Her photo's on my phone," I said. "How did Adam get ahold of those files?" The words were no sooner out of my mouth before I realized the answer. "His ex said he took a big job here. It was with Charles Hamilton, wasn't it?"

Amy pursed her lips. "Off the record, ya?"

I nodded.

She sighed. "He hired Whittaker to audit the company's books. There were emails between them on the drive too."

Charles Hamilton used his own grandson to get dirt on Parker. Had he been sizing up whether Adam was worthy of being a Hamilton?

"How did he even know who Adam was?" I asked, suddenly feeling sick.

Amy shook her head slowly. "We may never know. Not all cases get tied up in neat bows. Parker's not talking, but we'll find the woman and flip her." She reached for a tablet and tapped it a few times before handing it to me. I scanned the image of a handwritten document, taking in snatches of phrases like "sound mind and body" and "biological descendants."

"It's a holographic will Charles wrote up about a week before his death, leaving everything to Stephen and Adam Whittaker. Looks like he followed through on his threat this time, ya?" Amy said.

"Check Mrs. Goto's pockets. She showed me his baby photos once. She keeps them in her dress pocket," I said. "Did Adam know who he was?"

Amy hesitated before opening a folder and taking out an evidence bag. Sliding it across the table, she said, "We found it tucked in a book Monica took from Whittaker's place."

The fading image of Mrs. Goto's daughter and Stephen Hamilton as a toddler was almost identical to the one stolen from my apartment. Except for a name scrawled across the bottom—Cat.

Exhausted and heartsick, I swiped away a tear. "He was the real reason Mrs. Goto worked for the Hamiltons all those years. She wanted to be there in case he ever came looking for her." I stood, reaching for my bag. "Is that all? Can I go now?"

Amy closed her notebook. "I'll have an officer take you home."

"My car's at the estate."

"We'll take care of it. We'll need you to come by in the next day or so and sign your formal statement."

I turned to leave when Amy stopped me. "One last thing. Koa couldn't get hold of you last night. Where were you?"

"Is it important?"

She shrugged. "Just tying up loose ends."

I knew Koa was probably on the other side of the glass, observing Amy's interview even if he couldn't question me himself. "I was with Mark Nichols."

The detective's eyes widened slightly, and I answered her unspoken question.

"All night."

I slipped off Koa's hoodie and draped it over the chair before walking out.

* * *

The sun was setting over Waikīkī by the time I got home, and although it was still early I fell into bed and didn't wake until it had already risen again.

I spent the morning fielding calls from my worried parents, Kiyo, Lani, Mark, and even the building manager, who informed me "the nice officer" had parked my car outside the Ainahau and left my key at the front desk.

But no calls from Koa.

After lunch, I drove to a downtown bar near Mark's office. He was waiting for me, sitting at a table for two sipping from his drink. Standing, he smiled warmly, but his eyes were red with fatigue.

He leaned over to kiss me. I evaded him by sitting instead, ignoring his puzzled look.

"How's Stephen?" I asked.

"He's a mess. He adored his mom. And Mrs. Goto for that matter. We're all baffled."

I said nothing. The truth would come out eventually, and it wasn't my place to tell their story.

"Are you okay? It must've been harrowing for you."

"I know about the Kaimukī project you and Stephen have been working on," I said, dismissing his concern. "You're NHR, LLC. Nichols Hamilton Ranch, right?"

Mark stilled, looking away as he rubbed his brow. "I couldn't say anything about it, Maya. Stephen is my client, and he was very clear about the need for discretion."

"I understand," I said, nodding. "Just so you know, I wasn't snooping. I put two and two together after I saw the photo of you and Stephen on horseback. It took me a while to remember where I'd seen that symbol before—it's a cattle brand. Charles had it on his signet ring, and you decided to use it for your business logo. My friend Lani showed me the exciting new proposal that could save the neighborhood from the Hamiltons. Except there never was a mall project, was there?"

Mark looked at me, raising his hands in a hapless gesture.

"One of my first jobs was in a small county up in Northern California. There was a big flap over a shopping center," I said. "A friend of mine covered it. It was supposed to be one of those walkable, small town Main Street projects with leases local mom-and-pop businesses could afford. But after winning over the community and city council, it became just another big-box mall."

Mark's jaw tightened. "It was all perfectly—"

"Legal? I know. But maybe not so 'above board,' ya?" I said. "You would know. Your father was the developer. So when Stephen wanted to break away from Parker, make a name for himself with his own deal, he came to you."

"This has nothing to do with you and me. I've been working on this for well over a year, long before we met. It's business, Maya."

I nodded. "To you, maybe. But your business is screwing my friends, and I can't be a part of it. I'm sorry. I really liked you."

Mark took a long sip of amber liquid. He set the drink down and smiled wryly. "I'm not so sure you did."

We both stood, and he kissed me on the cheek. "I'm sorry things worked out this way."

"Yeah, me too."

* * *

"Coulda been worse, ya?" Lani said a few hours later.

I'd headed straight to her place after leaving Mark and spent the better part of the evening explaining the Trojan horse deal he'd concocted with Stephen. Luke took off to consult with his clients, leaving Lani and me to commiserate over wine and cupcakes.

"How exactly?"

"Mark could've been the killer."

I selected a pink cupcake and peeled off the paper lining. "He was Koa's number one suspect for a while."

"Guess it was a good thing you didn't bring him to Luke's party after all," she said, refilling my glass. "Talk about awkward, ya?"

A giggle bubbled in my throat, escaping into the night air as we laughed.

Chapter Forty-Three

The story made front page local news for weeks, as bit by bit the salacious details leaked out.

At first, the public had been shocked and horrified by the tragic killing of a community pillar, the matriarch of O'ahu's most prominent family, a woman who'd contributed millions to good causes all over the Islands.

An anonymous caller tipped the media to the truth.

The ensuing scandal involving corrupt city officials, a wealthy developer's greed, and long-buried family secrets soon made national headlines. There was no escaping videos of Parker, parading his grief in front of the cameras as he strode up courthouse steps flanked by attorneys. I would've bet good money his tears were fake—if I had any.

I'd already been fired by then. Thanks to Luke, I was able to keep what was left of my advance or I would've been destitute.

"So, what's next?" Amy asked.

I was back at police headquarters, summoned there to sign a typed formal statement. This time, I was escorted directly to a meeting room where the detective was already waiting.

I didn't see Koa. Amy had been the one to clear the way for me to visit Mrs. Goto in jail, where she was being held without bail.

"Tell me about him," she'd said, and I didn't have to ask who she meant.

I told her what I'd learned about her grandson from Monica and the woman in the café, holding my phone up to the Plexiglas that separated us so she could see the photos I'd found of him online. "He had a girlfriend. Back in California. You should try writing to her."

She swiped a hand across her eyes. "Mr. Charles kept track of him over the years. When he started to suspect Mr. Parker was stealing from the company, he brought Adam to Hawai'i as a test, to see if he could be a Hamilton. But it had to be secret. Not even Adam knew at first."

Not until it was too late.

Now turning back to Amy, I debated what to say, and then went for honesty. "No clue."

She was surprisingly sympathetic. "Well, if it makes you feel better, we found your things."

"My things?"

"Not your computer, just these. You need to sign some paperwork verifying it's yours."

She pushed a plastic evidence bag across the table toward me. I opened it and took out two smaller bags. One contained a pair of pearl stud earrings my parents had given to me when I graduated from high school. A gold Hawaiian heart with my initial in black enamel lay at the bottom of the second bag. I turned it over and checked for the inscription on the back—a tiny letter K.

"They're mine," I said. "Where'd you find them?"

"Pawn shop in Chinatown. The owner was very cooperative once we explained it was evidence in a murder investigation. He gave us an alias and physical description of the perp," Amy said.

"The guy in the baseball hat? He drives a late-model white sedan, I'm guessing. So who is he?" I asked after Amy nodded.

"A contract laborer who worked on the estate a few times," she said. "Elizabeth Hamilton recruited him herself. Hard to believe, but I guess she had us all fooled."

Amy had been right about Parker's bit on the side. She turned state's evidence after confessing to taking bribes and criminal conspiracy for hiring thugs to go after me and Monica.

"Right again. Not only did Parker's mistress hire him to steal your phone and laptop but turns out he was part of the gang behind the thefts and muggings in Waikīkī. Two big cases wrapped up nice and neat. The chief is pretty happy."

Parker's attorneys would be busy for years keeping him out of prison and fighting Charles's new will. Without his son's support. Stephen had refused to contest it, leaving it to the courts to decide whether Adam's share would go to his heirs, if he even had any.

I picked up a pen and signed the form Amy gave me.

"Thank you," I said.

She shrugged. "Wasn't me."

I hadn't heard from Koa since he'd sent me away from the crime scene in the back seat of a patrol car. Now I found myself looking for him in the homicide squad room as Amy led me out. But his cubicle was empty.

* * *

Two weeks later, I was home alone crunching numbers—something I tried never to do—and they weren't pretty. Deidre had raved about the story I'd submitted and promised the magazine would cut me a check within the month. But I had to find a regular paying gig soon or move in with my parents.

Then again, there was always my basement apartment back in California. I opened my laptop and logged onto the state's job line, which offered decent pay, normal hours, and actual health care benefits—a first for me. But my heart wasn't in it.

I stood to get myself a drink when there was a knock on the door. I checked the time, puzzled. Lani and Willa were coming over for dinner to plan our weekend getaway to Maui—one last splurge I couldn't afford to back out of. But they weren't due for another half hour, and Lani was never early.

I threw open the door, my teasing smile turning to a surprised one.

"You should use the peephole," Koa said.

"What makes you think I didn't?"

He leaned in, so close I could smell his sandalwood aftershave. "'Cause you suck at poker."

I pursed my lips to suppress a grin and let him inside. He was right, but I'd never admit it.

"Expecting someone?" he asked, as I locked the door.

"Just Lani and Willa."

He nodded, his gaze compulsively sweeping the living area, stopping at the framed picture of the gang at Luke's party. "Looks like you're settling in."

"I was about to have a glass of wine. You want anything?"

"Sure. Whatever you've got."

He leaned against the kitchenette, still surveying the room. I retrieved a beer from the fridge and handed it to him before grabbing a glass out of the dishwasher.

Koa watched me with a furrowed brow as I poured myself a drink.

"You've been cleaning," he said, when we'd settled at the clutter-free bistro table. "You sleeping okay?"

I wasn't. I'd chalked it up to money woes at first. Until the nightmares started. Sometimes Elizabeth's sightless, red-rimmed eyes haunted my dreams. Other times it was Adam's tentative smile morphing into a macabre grin that woke me hours before sunrise.

"I'm fine," I said, hoping he'd drop the issue.

"It helps to talk. If you—"

"Let me guess, you know someone? Thanks, but I'm fine."

"Like you were 'fine' after finding Whittaker?" He didn't wait for me to argue. "I was going to say, I'm here, if you ever need to talk."

I blinked, unsure what to say. "That's sweet of you, Koa. I will. If I need to." Still wondering about the purpose of his impromptu visit, I took a guess. "I've been reading about the task force busting the Waikīkī crime ring. Thanks for finding my jewelry, by the way."

He shrugged, twisting the cap on his bottle. "Just doing my job. Speaking of, I hear you don't have one anymore."

"Parker won't be publishing his autobiography after all. Weird, ya?"

His fingers played with the label on the bottle. "Does this mean you're going back to the mainland? I thought since Nichols took that transfer . . . Same time zone, ya?" His voice was carefully neutral.

Mark had called shortly after the real story became public. The Kaimukī project was officially dead. The scandal had scared off investors, and now Stephen was focused on restoring Hamilton, Inc., to its former glory.

"Without Parker, I take it?" I'd asked him.

"Steve's washed his hands of him. Good riddance. I knew he was a crappy father, but it was just the tip of the iceberg, apparently. He'll get his just deserts. From what I hear, odds are good he'll go down for his sins."

Mark, it turned out, had news of his own. He'd made junior partner at his law firm and was moving to the L.A. office. I'd wished him well, knowing I probably wouldn't hear from him again.

"That's over," I said to Koa. "But I was looking at state jobs in Sacramento."

Koa studied me with his serious, dark eyes. "Lani said a publisher offered you a deal to write some tell-all."

I stiffened. So that's why he'd shown up unannounced after weeks of silence.

It was tempting. A Big Five publisher dangled an advance that would've set me up for at least a year, not to mention haul my career out of the toilet. I had a few more days to decide, but there'd never been any question.

This mochi story was not mine to tell.

I stood and went to the cupboard in search of snacks. Pouring rice crackers into a bowl, I checked the time on the microwave clock. Lani and Willa were due any minute.

"Relax," I said. "I'm not taking it. I told you and Amy I wasn't writing about your case. Everything was off the record. No need to worry, ya?"

"I wasn't worried."

I turned back to Koa. "Then why are you here?"

He hesitated, tapping his finger on the tabletop. "What if it was all on the record?" he said finally. "Would you take the deal? Or do you want to go back to California?"

It was a question I hadn't been able to ask myself, let alone answer. "Did Lani put you up to this? You've been trying to get me on a plane back to the mainland since day one."

"I wanted you outta my case, not my life. No matter what I did, you kept putting yourself in harm's way, and you nearly got yourself killed." He stopped and let out a breath. "Lani wasn't the only one who missed you all these years."

I swallowed the sudden lump in my throat, unable to speak.

"I cleared it with Amy and HPD. You'll have full access, if you want it."

"How did you manage that?" I asked, finally regaining my voice.

He shrugged. "I convinced them someone was going to write about it—might as well be someone we know and trust."

"Koa—"

The moment was broken by a rap on the door. Laughter from the hallway identified my visitors, and not even Koa objected when I let them in without checking the peephole.

Lani and Willa's smiles turned to barely contained smirks when they saw I wasn't alone. Koa greeted them with hugs and pecks on the cheek but declined their invitation to join us for dinner.

"I wouldn't want to crash ladies' night out. Luke says they're brutal," he said, earning a round of laughter.

My friends had the decency to retreat to the lanai. I followed him out, standing in the hallway. Before I could find the words to thank him, he turned back to me.

"Stay, Maya," he said. "Take the deal, if that's what you want."

He pressed warm lips to my brow and turned to leave. Any lingering doubts faded as I watched his retreating back.

I was home.

Author's Notes

To be clear, I am not kama'aina.

My family moved around a lot when I was growing up, and for several years we lived on Oa'hu. It was the first time I lived in a place where I looked like everybody else, where people ate the same kind of food I ate and had last names like mine. It's where I learned how to be proud of being half Chinese, half Japanese. Even years after we moved to California, my years in Hawai'i continued to shape the rest of my life, what I studied in college, and what I chose to write about.

I still feel most at home in Hawai'i, especially sitting in a booth with my family at Kim Chee II.

Unlike Maya Wong, I wasn't born or raised in Hawai'i. I was just lucky enough to live there for a little while. I hope readers see that Hawai'i is more than breathtaking scenery. It's the people and culture that make it special.

A note about local phrases: "Chicken skin" is the Hawai'i way of saying "goosebumps." And when friends or family hang out together to catch up, they "talk story."

"Slippers" in Hawai'i means flip-flops, not fuzzy bedroom slippers, and it's pronounced "slippahs." But this confused my beta readers, so I compromised by using "slippers" in dialogue, and "flip-flops" in the narrative.

A note about the Hawai'ian language: I have used the spelling and punctuation commonly used in Hawai'i, including the 'okina, or glottal stop, and the kahakō, or macron. The exception is the name of the building Maya lives in, because in my fictional world a developer in the 1970s wouldn't have used them.

I am by no means an expert, and any mistakes are entirely mine.

Acknowledgments

It took two decades and a global pandemic for me to write GHOSTS OF WAIKĪKĪ. It's the craziest thing I've ever done, the biggest risk I've ever taken, and it wouldn't have happened without the love and support of a lot of people.

First and foremost, I'm grateful to my loving husband, Brandon. For listening patiently as I prattled on about characters, setting, and plot ideas. For handling morning drop-offs when I had to Zoom with my agent. And for making the girls Spam musubi on their first day of school because I was at my first Bouchercon. He also lets me have the last piece of hamachi. That's love.

Thank you to my beautiful, amazing daughters, Emi and Miya, for helping me make TikTok reels and choosing songs to go with them. I can even appreciate their gentle prods like "What's taking you so long to finish your book?" But most of all, thank you for making me a mom. I hope you will follow your dreams no matter how crazy they may seem.

Thank you to my parents, Aki and Susan Morita. They knew early on I was never going to be one of those Good at Math Asians and let me pursue my love of writing.

And to my beloved Pau Pau, Gong Gong, and Gong Gong Foo, who taught me that food is love.

Much aloha to my API friends in Hawai'i and on the mainland for loaning me their names and whose voices I hear in my head as I write.

I also owe a huge thanks to the wonderful, generous writing community for helping me get my book out into the world. Organizations like Sisters in Crime and Crime Writers of Color helped me find my people while the world was still sheltering in place.

Thank you to Capitol Crimes for giving me a home base to learn and grow. (Especially Penny Manson, for not taking no for an answer.) My fabulous Accountability Group—Sarah Bresniker, Jessica Arden Cline, Chris Dreith, and Karen A. Phillips—for keeping me on task and celebrating all the wins.

Thanks to Laura Jensen Walker and my former editor, the late Linda Meilink, for reading my early drafts.

I'm grateful to Kathy VerEecke, who liked my hook and reminded me I used to be good at this writing thing.

My deepest gratitude to my agent and favorite foodie, Lori Galvin, for her patience and guidance, and for believing in me and my messy manuscript.

And to my editor, Sara J. Henry, who pushed me to dig deeper and lifted my book higher.